www.united-pc.eu

Jennifer Harris

Enmity

Volume One

Germany 2039   Chapter 1

There was a chill in the air that day; it seeped through the skin in to your very bones. It wasn't a bitter chill, but cold enough to raise the hairs on your arms as its icy fingers touched you. The day in question was a typical spring day and there wasn't the slightest hint in the air that anything strange would happen. But then as things always have a habit of turning out the events that were to take place would be very different from what they appeared. No one involved in the incident that would occur on the day in question had the slightest idea of the evils that were already beginning to stir, ready to strike. A very old fear was starting to gain power once again and this time it was more ruthless and determined than ever, it would complete what it had begun but was never able to finish. It had learnt from its mistakes and this time nothing could possibly go wrong, it would make sure of that.

Sarah Murray sat quietly fiddling with her seat belt and staring blankly at the relentless tarmac, as her father's car travelled at a steady speed along the Autobahn. There was a thick blanket of clouds hovering over the landscape. There was a definite threat of rain in the air.

She could sense that her parents weren't speaking again. Her mother, who was incredibly beautiful, with long blonde hair and eyes of the darkest chestnut brown, sat in the front passenger seat of the car, quietly gazing out of the cars windscreen. Sarah's father was about ten years older than Sarah's mother and someone that Sarah already feared even though she was still too young to understand what such emotions were. He wasn't very tall, only five foot two and at thirty-five he was going almost entirely grey. He had the coldest blue eyes and massive hands that when used to defend himself could do immense damage to anyone on the receiving end.

On this particular day Sarah's mother decided that she would take Sarah on an outing to a wooded area called Prince Augustus wood. It was said that in the Eighteenth century a distant relation of the Scottish Royal family went to live for a short period of time with a relative in Germany. They had lived next to this very wood, which was originally called the Devils cove. The locals said it had the distinct shape of a Devils head and that it was cursed. The story goes that he fell in love with a local peasant girl. But back then members of the Royal family were only allowed to marry people chosen for them. The Prince had no feelings for his particular suitor, a distant member of the British Royal family. Eventually out of desperation, in the dead of night he was said to have gone into the wood. In the centre of the wood he shot himself in the head with a pistol. After this event had taken place the locals claimed that anyone who dared to enter that particular area of the wood would die a terrible death. Many people had entered that part of the wood and never come out again. Not even a trace of their existence was ever found.

"So what are you doing at work today, sweetheart?" Sarah's mother, April, asked Sarah's father, Marques quietly. She was trying desperately to lighten the sombre atmosphere. But Marques just shrugged his wide, powerful shoulders; he didn't say a single word. He merely continued to look straight ahead at the road.

Marques was an officer in the German army and for some strange and inexplicable reason he also played an important role within the German Government. Holding such important positions would have surely made anyone happy, but not Marques. He had never possessed the most easy going nature, but he was now acting as if he was concealing some terrible secret.

Suddenly a Jaguar roared past them, almost scraping the side of their own much older vehicle.

"Fucking bastard!" Marques swore out loudly. Sarah couldn't help looking at him in shock. The sound of his voice had alarmed her.

"Marques, please don't swear in front of Sarah" April said angrily, looking at him furiously.

"I'll swear in front of whoever I bloody well feel like and no ones going to tell me other wise!" Marques suddenly shouted out at her.

"Don't shout at me and what makes you think you have the right to swear in front of your own daughter?" April asked in a calm voice; that was now shaking with suppressed emotions.

"Because she's my property and I'll do what I fucking well like in front of her. Now stop giving me hassle; you bitch. I've got enough problems without you fucking nagging me as well" Marques said, looking at April with bitter resentment.

"Is that what you think I'm doing, nagging you?" April asked.

Marques made no response. He just turned right of the Autobahn onto a small dirt track overgrown with weeds. He suddenly slammed on the brakes, causing Sarah to slide of her seat and April to grab the front dashboard to stop herself from nearly smashing through the windscreen.

"Right, we're here now, so you can fucking well get out, get your stuff and go. I'll pick you up at three at this exact spot. If your not here by then I'm going without you" he said coldly, staring straight ahead.

11

He gave them just enough time to get out of the car and get what they needed, and then he put the vehicle in reverse, turned around and sped of up the dirt track, leaving a trail of dust in his wake.

"Yeah, goodbye to you too, Marques" April muttered after the receding car; she sounded like she was on the verge of tears. Then she looked down at Sarah and gave her a feeble smile.

"Come on sweetheart, let's go and pick some pretty flowers," she said, trying desperately to steady her quivering voice.

They made their way of the dirt track and entered the welcome smells of the wood. Even though there were no leaves on the trees yet, the pine trees still had a beautiful green sheen to them that seemed to brighten up the whole place. The suns rays seeped through the gaps in the trees and gave the whole place a kind of a mysterious affect, it looked like pictures out of the bible when the sun shone down on Jesus and his apostles.

April proceeded to walk over to some flowers and beckoned Sarah over. Sarah wondered over to where April stood and watched her as she leant down in the thick vegetation. Sarah heard a rustle coming from a holly bush close by. She turned towards the sound and was positive she saw some one hiding in the bushes. The bush moved ever so slightly, but it couldn't have been a breeze, there wasn't a breath of wind that day.

"Darling" April said quietly. Sarah looked at her. "You see this flower?" Sarah nodded. "This is called a buttercup. Do you know why they call it a buttercup?" she asked. Sarah shook her head. "Because you put it under your chin and if your chin turns yellow it means that you like butter" April explained. Then she placed the flower under Sarah's chin.

There was a faint glimmer of yellow that showed against Sarah's skin. "Yay, you like butter!" April said, throwing out her arms for Sarah to give her a hug. When Sarah didn't she grabbed her by the waist and swung her tiny body around in the air.

But Sarah barely reacted at all; she was such a sullen and quiet little thing and hardly responded to any form of affection. Sarah saw more than April would ever know and this was affecting her more than April cared to admit.

April shook her head sadly at such a lack of response. "Come on you" she said sadly.

They walked quietly through the wood for a little while, occasionally stopping to pick a flower. It all seemed so peaceful, maybe too so. Then Sarah heard a bush rustle again. She quickly turned towards the source of the noise.

"Love, what's the matter?" April asked, placing a concerned hand on Sarah's shoulder.

"Nothing, mummy" Sarah told her, looking up at her and smiling reassuringly.

They suddenly stumbled upon a part of the wood that appeared utterly dead. The trees had no growing buds, ready for the summer leaves. There were no needles on the pine trees. The areas surrounding the trees were completely clear of vegetation and there was no obvious evidence of any falling needles from the pine trees in the last couple of years at least. It was as if the vegetation had all died away and never grown back. The whole place gave of this illusion that some evil curse had taken control of that part of the wood and killed every living creature in it. There was certainly something there. It was quite dark and a crisp, chilly wind whistled noisily through the trees and ruffled Sarah's vivid red hair.

"Come on darling, lets get out of here. I don't like this place" April said, grabbing Sarah by the hand. She picked her up and carried her along the path that lead them away from that part of the wood. A large stump loomed up from the middle of the path, like some ominous dark mass. April sat

Sarah on the stump and dropped the bags beside her. She ruffled Sarah's hair and smiled at her.

"I'll be back darling, I won't be a second," She said. She turned around and disappeared into the bushes.

Sarah sat there, waiting patiently for April to return again, she was good at being patient as she had been taught how by Marques. She didn't like it here, there was something about this woodland that sent a cold shiver running up the spine.

The wind shifted direction and grey clouds scattered across the sky, eventually blotting the sun out completely. Dark shadows appeared more vivid and looked exactly like the forms of human beings. Sarah drew her winter's coat more tightly around her as the wind chilled her skinny frame.

Something seemed to scurry along the path directly behind her. As she swung around to see what it was, a large fast moving object ran behind the cover of a tree. She knew instantly it wasn't a bird, they weren't that big. Sarah didn't like this at all and wished that April would hurry up.

A sudden high-pitched scream rent the air; it came from close by. It sounded like April and Sarah slid of the stump to go and find her. She landed lightly on the ground and dusted herself down. She left the bags unguarded and went in the direction April had gone in.

The vegetation was high, thick and densely grown in that part of the wood. In some places it was up to a metre high. The vegetation consisted mostly of bramble bushes and stinging nettles. As

Sarah walked through the thick bushes the thorns grabbed at her clothes and tore small holes in them.

"Mummy, mummy, where are you, mummy?" Sarah called out desperately, as she stumbled through the thick foliage.

Sarah couldn't hear the response she was looking for. She was so positive she couldn't be that far away from her mother. But she was wrong, she was nowhere near her mother. In fact she couldn't find her anywhere. She ran through the wood and towards the dirt track where Marques was supposed to pick them up at three. When she finally reached the dirt track she saw a trail of chocking dust as a massive green Land Rover sped down the dirt track towards the Autobahn.

Sarah stood there for a little while, watching the

receding Land Rover disappear. Then she swivelled on her heels and ran back into the wood again. She ran straight for the eye of the cove. She came to a stop when she reached the eye and stood there on the spot looking slowly around her. Then she began to call for April, but there was never any reply. In desperation she started to cry, sobbing out for her mother.

She ran back through the wood again. It started to rain heavily, coming down in heavy sheets. Sarah's hair stuck to the nape of her neck and the rain dripped of the end of her nose. The dusty path she was running along had suddenly turned into sleek, slippery mud. She started to slide uncontrollably on the path as she ran to the stump to get her waterproof jacket. She quickly slipped this over her winter's coat and then continued along the path in search of her mother.

As Sarah ran past a large bush she upset a flock of wood pigeons that scattered into the air making her scream in terror. She came to a sudden stop, exhausted from her frantic run. She stood there panting heavily as the rain hissed down in long streaks around her.

"Mummy, mummy where are you? Mummy, mummy!"

Chapter 2 Eleven years later, Essex, England

Sarah sat at her desk; quietly fiddling with her pen and watching the world go by outside the classroom window. Her best friend, Nicole, sat next to her, drawing on her pencil case and humming

21

quietly to herself.

It was early morning and the class was having the register taken before their first lesson began.

"So what about our army being moved to the Polish border to stop the Nazis from invading Russia, isn't it exciting?" Nicole asked quietly. Like almost everyone else Nicole wasn't taking the current conflict with the Nazis seriously. They all thought that now there was a war on it would liven up an otherwise boring existence. No one even considered the Nazis might turn around and attempt to invade France; they simply didn't seem powerful enough. If Germany succeeded in doing so though then the possibility that they might try to cross the channel and attack Britain would become far more realistic.

"I dunno" Sarah mumbled quietly.

"Your foster fathers a sergeant in the armed forces, isn't he? Won't he be going to Russia with the rest of the army as well?" Nicole asked, looking at Sarah.

"What do you mean going? He's already gone. He left ages ago, Nicole. I thought you already knew," Sarah said, looking back at her. She gave her friend a questioning look.

"Gone, when did he go?" Nicole asked. Just like everyone else she failed to realize how serious the war had become, or notice the large volume of troops that were already leaving the country.

"Three months ago" Sarah said.

"Really? I didn't even know that he'd gone" Nicole told her, looking surprised.

Sarah just smiled at her and then looked at the teacher, who had now stopped taking the register and was talking to the class.

"At this precise moment in time the Germans are on the border between Russia and Poland. Now what the Germans are believed to be doing is preparing their troops for a series of attacks on the Russian border, when and where these attacks will occur is as yet unknown," the teacher explained.

"Does she even know what she's talking about?" Nicole asked Sarah.

"Yes unfortunately she does, but its not only Russia their attacking. Russia is just important because of its location and its landmass" Sarah whispered to her.

"But Russia can't be that important, can it?"

Nicole said.

"That's what the Nazis want us to think, but Stephen says if the Nazis successfully invade Russia it will give them unlimited access to an enormous army and also to Russia's nuclear weapons" Sarah explained.

"Sarah Murray, if you've got something that is so interesting you have to tell Nicole right now, maybe you'd like to share it with the rest of the class?" the teacher asked, looking furiously at Sarah.

"Oh no, miss, please continue" Sarah said

"No, come on, tell us what you were saying to Nicole" the teacher insisted.

"Well I was just agreeing with what you were saying, miss. I was just telling Nicole that if the

Nazis successfully invaded Russia they would be able to get their hands on their nuclear weapons " Sarah explained.

The class looked from Sarah to their teacher. They were waiting for the moment when the teacher would explode into a rage and send Sarah to the exclusion room. But that moment never actually materialised.

"And how exactly have you come by this information, Sarah?" the teacher asked quietly. She didn't sound angry, just curious.

"My dads an officer in the army, miss" Sarah said. "He told me before he left for Poland."

"Why haven't you told me any of this before, Sarah?" the teacher asked. She was a new teacher and knew relative little about her pupil's backgrounds, especially Sarah's; who was always so quiet and not very co-operative. She seemed such a private thing, like she had some deadly secret that she was keeping safe.

"I assumed that you already knew this information, miss" Sarah explained.

"Hmm, interesting" the teacher murmured. Then dismissing the subject she turned her attention to the white board.

"Right everybody get your English books out. Today we are going to plan out a 1000 word essay to be given in by the end of the week," the teacher announced. The class let out a grown and proceeded to open their bags.

After school as Sarah walked home from school she started to wonder that if Marques was still alive, if he would be working alongside her foster father, Stephen, or if he would have already been killed by the Nazis. Even though Marques was German he was brought up in England and the Nazis would have surely destroyed him by now. Stephen had denied ever knowing a Marques Murray. But that was understandable; Marques had left Britain a long time ago. But there had been rumours for a while that a certain Marques Murray had simply vanished and had never been found. The German army couldn't trace him anywhere. Eventually a body had been discovered twenty miles from where Marques had been stationed. But it had been so badly burnt that it been impossible to identify it. Both arms and legs had been deliberately removed and the face had been so badly smashed in that it was impossible to identify the facial features. They couldn't even identify the body by dental records; the teeth had been removed.

But that had all taken place eleven years ago, a great deal had taken place since then and this strange death had been all but forgotten.

Sarah turned on to the street towards the house she had been living in for almost eleven years, ever since Stephen had carried her in with a blanket wrapped around her when she had been but four years old, but this hadn't ever felt like her true home. Truth be told she didn't know where she really belonged anymore, she had always felt out of place with everyone else and these feelings had only grown stronger as she had gotten older and closer to adolescence.

As Sarah entered the house her younger foster sister, Janet emerged from the dinning room. Her face lit up when she saw Sarah, such a reaction from her younger foster sister was never a good sign.

"Hey, Sarah do you know what fifty divided by eighteen is?" she asked.

"I haven't got a clue and do your own bloody homework" Sarah answered.

"Bitch" Janet muttered resentfully.

Sarah chose not to respond.

"Oh, a fax came today. It's from Stephen" Kira said, as Sarah walked into the kitchen.

"Oh, I didn't know they had such advanced technology at his base" Sarah commented sarcastically, as she sat down at the kitchen table and took the fax from Kira.

The fax was short and simple, but straight to the point.

Dear all

I'm fine. Base adequate, food sufficient. Tomorrow we head for the Polish border, liven things up a bit.

P.S. The commanding officer here is actually English.

Love Stephen. xxx

"I wonder what he means by liven things up a bit?" Sarah asked.

"What I think he means is things are a bit boring where they are. So when they reach the border things will get more exciting," Kira explained.

"But what if something happens to Stephen?" Sarah asked, just as Janet walked in to the kitchen.

"What's happened to daddy, mom?" Janet asked sounding alarmed.

"Nothing sweetheart" Kira told her. Then she turned her attention back to Sarah again.

"Don't be bloody stupid, Sarah. Stephen will be fine. They wouldn't have chosen him for promotion if they thought he wasn't capable of doing the job" Kira snapped, giving Sarah a warning look.

"Don't worry darling, nothings happened to daddy. Sarah just has a big mouth, that's all. Don't you, Sarah?" Kira said nastily.

"Yes, Kira" Sarah agreed, staring down at her hands, which were trembling slightly with anger.

She also couldn't believe Janet still called Stephen her 'daddy.' Janet was still so immature and this wasn't helped by the fact that Kira still insisted on treating her like a child.

"See darling? There's absolutely nothing to be worried about. Your fathers going to be just fine" Kira said. "Alright of you go and finish your homework" Kira said and Janet left the kitchen.

Sarah went upstairs to the safe refuge of her own bedroom. She dumped her bag on her ancient relic of a chair and sat down on her bed.

It was a very simple room in desperate need of a coat of paint. Most of the furniture in here had at some time belonged to Janet. Her chair was tucked in neatly beside her desk and next to that was a chest of drawers, which were too small for the amount of clothing crammed into them. On the other side of her room were some shelves that were about to collapse under the weight of too many books and a cupboard with a door hanging loose, because one of the hinges was broken.

She glanced over at her bedside cabinet. On top of this were the usual array of objects, along with a picture frame containing an old Polaroid picture of Marques and April. Janet had chipped many of the ornaments adorning the cabinet when she was in one of her moods and was prone to throwing things, especially anything that belonged to Sarah.

Sarah picked up the picture frame and stared at it before turning the frame over. Sarah unhooked the back and the picture fell onto the bedcovers. She picked it up of the covers and gazed down at it.

Memories came flooding back. She could remember the day when she had taken that picture as clearly as if it were yesterday. It was a beautiful sunny day in June. The previous day there had been severe storms and the ground was slippery and insecure underfoot.

Marques made her take a picture of him and April sitting on a bench. Just after she took the picture the ground under her feet gave way and she fell over onto her back. Marques just laughed and walked back into the house, leaving April to pick her up.

"Hey, I said what are you doing?" Janet snapped angrily from the door, causing Sarah to jump slightly in surprise, she hadn't even been aware of Janet's presence.

"Nothing, now bugger of you nosy bitch" she said.

"Well what's that in your hand then?" Janet demanded. She walked across the room and before Sarah could stop her she snatched the photo out of her hands. Janet looked at the picture with a very nasty grin on her face

"Ah, is this a picture of mummy and daddy? Ah, never mind. Your dad was a bastard and your mum was a whore." With a crawl laugh Janet started to tear the picture into small pieces and let them scatter across the floor.

Sarah watched her in horror, trying not to cry. She didn't want to give Janet the satisfaction of seeing how much she had upset her.

Janet dropped the last pieces of photo and left

the room, laughing hysterically.

Sarah slid of her bed and knelt down by the torn pieces of photograph. She didn't cry though, she was far too angry for that. Janet was always wrecking things of importance to her. Now she had destroyed something of sentimental value to Sarah. It was the only picture she had left of Marques and April.

Memories flashed through Sarah's mind again. She could see herself running through the Devils cove with a look of absolute terror on her face. She had been getting nightmares of that day ever since she had moved into the foster home back in Germany. She was running through the wood towards some unknown place, yelling for someone, but never knowing whom. The strange thing was she wasn't a little girl in this dream. She was almost exactly the same age as she was now, maybe a little older. She would be wearing either camouflage clothing like that Stephen wore as his regulation uniform, or black jeans and a black jumper. Sarah always seemed to be running away from something, a seemingly perfect being with immense power and strength. However much she tried to get away from it, it always seemed to gain on her very quickly. Then everything would go quiet and still, she couldn't even hear birds singing. Sarah would stop; turn around to face the way she had come and she would see absolutely nothing. There would come a low growling noise behind her. She would turn around slowly. Her eyes would widen in horror and then she would let out a terrified scream. But her nightmares would never go any further than that. She would often wake up screaming in terror with Stephen shaking her, trying desperately to wake her up.

She had never fully understood what the dream was supposed to mean. But as she had gotten older the dreams became less frequent and were now almost non-existent. With a sigh Sarah stood up and put the torn fragments of photo on the bedside cabinet. When she got the opportunity she would try to go down to the living room and attempt to tape the photo together again.

Sarah walked over to her desk and got her homework out of her bag. She sat down at her desk and read through the assignment they had to complete. Write a 1000-word essay on bad experiences that she had endured during her life.

"I could write a whole fucking novel on bad experiences I've gone through," Sarah muttered. She didn't have a clue what to write. She had never told anyone what had really happened to her when she was young, or what she had seen and she wasn't going to start now.

In the end she wrote a poor essay on how she had been fostered at a young age and she described her four months at the German foster home she had stayed at after the incident in the wood, this was a place where she had suffered terrible abuse from the other foster children, and the people who were supposed to be taking care of her had been brutal to her and had constantly beaten her. Most of it was true, but not written quite so graphically or brutally as Sarah could remember so vividly.

It wasn't a perfect essay by far, but it was adequate enough. Normally she got decent enough grades that the teacher was happy with, but as Sarah was only too aware no one expected great things of her when she left school. By the time Kira called her down for dinner, she had finished her essay.

Chapter 3

At about midnight that very same evening the Nazis started their campaign of bombing on London. Which was bad news indeed for Sarah's hometown, because to reach the capital the Nazis had to pass directly over them.

Sarah was startled awake by a loud explosion in the far distance. She peered through the gap in her heavy black curtains to see what was going on; just over the peak of the hill she could see bright orange flashes as bomb after bomb struck the ground. The glows were getting closer.

"Sarah, hurry up. We're taking shelter in the cupboard" Kira hissed urgently through the door.

Sarah got out of bed, dragging her duvet with her. They hurried quickly downstairs to the cupboard where they kept all the coats, which had now been turned into a temporary air raid shelter. It wasn't big enough really, but it would do.

Janet made sure she and Kira took up the entire mattress crammed into the cupboard, so that Sarah was forced to make do with the floor. She lay down, curled up into a tight ball and tried to shut out all the noises.

She heard Kira saying to Janet, "don't worry sweetheart, this is only temporary. Tomorrow Dan and Alex will be putting up the air raid shelter."

The bombing continued through the night and it seemed relentless. But by the morning it had stopped and everything went quiet again.

As Kira left the safety of the cupboard to make some breakfast; Sarah left right behind her and went into the garden. At the back of their house lay endless farmland stretching for miles before her, so Sarah couldn't tell how much damage the town had sustained from the nights bombing yet. But it was so still; she couldn't hear a single thing, not even the sound of birds singing. Sarah didn't like it and she hastily went back inside the house. The lack of noise was telling her that something bad had happened.

They ate a breakfast of stale bread and weak tea, rationing had now become so bad that they had to share teabags. Even the basics like butter and bread had become terribly short and many people had resorted to growing food like potatoes and vegetables in their back gardens, otherwise they simply wouldn't have enough food to survive the winter.

Sarah got ready for school and left the house before Janet had the chance to catch up with her, taking her ruined photo with her.

Walking down the street she finally saw the extent of the damage on the town. The next-door neighbour had been badly hit; the whole of one side of the house was completely destroyed. Across the road two more houses were totally gutted. But Sarah was to soon learn that her road had gotten of lightly.

Sarah turned the corner and stopped dead, her face was filled with horror. The entire main street was utterly destroyed; not one building was left standing. The bustling street had been full of shops and flats for the students who went to the local College, but now that was all gone. People were running up and down the road, screaming in agony and calling for loved ones, who would probably never answer. One man ran past Sarah, his arms waving frantically in the air, Screaming in agony. His face was utterly destroyed. Where his eyes should have been were large bloody holes and there was nothing left of his nose. As he passed her he stood on a metal object. Then it exploded, tearing his fragile body apart.

Sarah stood there, staring at the destroyed body numbly. Then when she came to her senses she quickly ran for the nearest alleyway, realizing if she didn't get of that road she was putting her own life at risk. But when she reached a safe alleyway a terrible sight greeted her there.

There were dead bodies propped up on the walls of the alley, there was nowhere else to put them. Sarah couldn't bear to see all these dead people, with their huge eyes, forever locked into a petrified stare. She ran back onto the road and threw up violently into a drain.

"Hey, are you alright?" Alex asked her, as he pushed his bike up to her. Alex was the local paperboy and a good friend to Nicole and her.

"No, not really" Sarah said truthfully. "You wouldn't either if you had just witnessed what I just did."

She started to walk in the general direction of the school, feeling very unstable on her feet. Alex followed her quietly, not really knowing what to say.

Nicole was waiting at the gates for them. As they entered the school, Sarah and Alex realized there was hardly anyone else there yet.

"What's the time, Alex?" Nicole asked.

"Just gone eight o'clock" Alex answered, looking at his watch.

"So, now what do we do?" Sarah asked, as they crossed the playground and sat on the wall surrounding it.

"I don't know" Nicole said. "By the way, Sarah, are you okay?" she asked, as she finally noticed the pale expression on Sarah's face and somewhat horrified look in her eyes.

"Who me, I'm fine" Sarah lied in what she hoped was an of hand manner.

"No, she's not. I came across her throwing up in a drain," Alex said, ignoring Sarah as she gave him a furious look.

"Really, why?" Nicole asked.

"Well you would too if you saw someone been blown to bits right in front of your fucking eyes!" Sarah said furiously, giving them both looks that prevented them from asking any further questions.

"So, did you do that homework our teacher set

us for English?" Nicole asked, hastily changing the subject.

Not long after that they said goodbye to Alex and headed for their classroom. But when they got there they realised they were the only one's there, the door was open so they went in anyway.

"Oh, did I tell you we're getting the Anderson shelter put up tonight. It's going to be brilliant. We're going to get a power pack for the electricity so we don't have to use candles. There's going to be bunk beds. I'll have top bunk, of course," Nicole explained, as they settled themselves down at their desks.

"Sounds pretty good. It sounds better than ours. Janet wanted a single bed to herself, as Stephen isn't here. But Kira said that if by some miracle he's granted any leave he'll need somewhere to sleep, so we have two sets of bunk beds. Janet wasn't impressed," Sarah grumbled.

"Good" Nicole commented angrily.

"Oh, yeah and yesterday look what she did to my picture of my aunt and uncle" Sarah said taking the torn photo of Marques and April out of her bag. The reason for her lying to Nicole about Marques and Aprils true identities was because she couldn't bring herself to tell Nicole the truth about a past she didn't even understand herself.

"Oh my god!" Nicole cried out, gently taking the pieces of torn photo away from Sarah. She went over to the teacher's desk and took a role of sellotape of the top of the desk. She went back to her desk and sat on her chair so she could try and tape it back together again.

"Do you know why she did this?" she asked, as she began this pain-staking job.

"Out of spite I guess. She hates my guts, don't forget" Sarah said.

Nicole just mumbled a response as a piece of photo fell out of her hand and she bent down to pick it up.

"Oh yeah, do you want to se the gas mask Stephen just sent me?" Sarah asked.

"Yeah, go on then" Nicole said, not taking her eyes of the pieces of photo in her hands.

Sarah removed the box containing her gas mask from around her neck and she proceeded to take the gas mask out of it. Nicole whistled in admiration. It wasn't any plain old gas mask distributed by the Government; it was specially designed for the army. It was camouflaged over the top, but underneath was a strong acid proof material that would withstand every form of acid and gas known to man. There was a silver ring around the 'snout' that stopped any kind of liquid from seeping its way through, the strap on the back was even adjustable. Every part of this gas mask had been designed down to the smallest detail for the soldiers to use these masks with ease in the most treacherous of conditions.

"God your lucky, I've only got a horrible issued one. It looks like someone sneezed in it" Nicole commented. Sarah burst out laughing

Sarah jumped down on to her seat and Nicole hid the sellotape as their form tutor entered the classroom. The teacher glanced around the room and Sarah realized that no one had even been behind the teacher; they were the only pupils present.

"Oh, well today looks like it's going to be a lot of fun, doesn't it?" the teacher commented.

Nicole and Sarah didn't even respond.

"Have neither of you had your houses bombed yet?" the teacher asked.

They both shook their heads.

"Well your lucky. Almost everyone has had their houses damaged in some way last night" the teacher commented, not even seeing their horror struck faces as she shuffled through some papers.

"Well seeing as no one else is here you might as well go," the teacher said.

"Ah, thanks miss, you're the best," Nicole said, as they grabbed their bags and ran out of the classroom before the teacher could change her mind.

Chapter four

Nazi headquarters, Berlin, Germany.

The British Prime Minister, Stan Newman walked grimly down the long, cold corridors of the Nazis brand new Government building, situated in the very heart of Berlin and built only a couple of years ago, in honour of the Nazis great victory. It seemed everywhere they turned the Prime Minister came face to face with images of Adolf Hitler.

Newman had just been on the longest aeroplane journey he had ever experienced. Well it felt like that anyway. It was less than a couple of hours from London to Berlin, but it felt a lot longer. Now he was feeling stiff, tired and bad tempered. What's more he was now going to have to put up with the company of the person he loathed most in the world and he would have to be polite to him.

"Are you sure this is going to work, Prime Minister? Hitler is unpredictable and capable of almost anything. Are you positive he will sign the peace treaty? I mean what if he refuses to sign it altogether?" Robert Ford asked in an urgent voice, struggling to keep up with him, Newman was a good head higher than he was and had a much longer stride. Ford was a stubborn, miserable little bastard and the Prime Minister couldn't stand him.

"We will just have to see. If Hitler and I can come to some sort of agreement, then we're getting somewhere, aren't we?" the Prime Minister said. The Prime Minister was in his early forties, which was young for a man in his position. He was of average height, about five foot six and always calm and ready for anything. He was good at concealing his emotions and could take any form of criticism that the opposition parties might throw at him.

"But what if he refuses, Prime Minister?" Ford mumbled quietly, so that the Nazi soldiers surrounding them couldn't over hear their conversation.

"We shall think about that problem if such a situation arises and that is the end of this matter," the Prime Minister answered shortly, making it quite clear to Ford that the discussion was closed.

A German officer wearing the traditional black

uniform of the SS, with swastikas clearly visible on each arm opened the door to the Chancellors' private office. Another German officer walked in front of them as they entered a large, spacious room. There were German guards placed in precise positions around the room and three young secretaries sat at a desk in the far corner. There were pictures of famous German chancellors placed carefully over the extravagant red and gold wallpaper, including a large-scale picture of Adolf Hitler himself. In the very centre of the room was a massive antique oak table with enough chairs to hold over a dozen people. Standing by the large window with his hands cupped behind his back in a presidential like manner, looking out over the breath taking view of Berlin before him stood none other than Chancellor Gavrian Hitler.

They now found themselves standing in the same room as the most hated person in Europe and most unfortunately for them he also happened to be one of the most powerful men, with massive armies at his disposal that would obey his command with just a single word. This man spread terror wherever he went and the mere mention of his name would send entire armies fleeing from the battlefield. Not that this man had ever stepped foot onto a battlefield, he may have been using his distant relatives name to get what he desired, but he couldn't change the past and truth be told he was never going to live up to Hitler's idea of what he had considered perfection.

As the Prime Minister, deputy Prime Minister,

foreign secretary and a number of other assorted ministers entered the room, Gavrian turned to face them, smiling unpleasantly. Stan couldn't help thinking that Gavrian had the most hideous looking face he had ever had the misfortune of seeing. It was a face only his mother could love. He had an ugly personality to match. He wore a black wig that was meant to give him the appearance of his distant relative and a matching moustache that was shaped in the same style that was now so permanently imprinted in so many people's minds, this gave him a strange and untidy appearance. Gavrian had a large wide mouth that when he smiled revealed stained yellow teeth, which looked like they had never seen a toothbrush. He had eyes just like that of his distant relative, Adolf Hitler. They were small and cold, dark brown almost black. These eyes gave him an evil appearance that put the fear of god into every one he met. The Nazis had only gained power through sheer brutality and force. No one would even dare to speak out against the Nazis because the consequences were far too life threatening to even consider.

"Guten tag" the Chancellor said in a voice dripping with sarcasm. "I am so glad you could come. My country has been looking forward to your visit for a long time" he said to them. The look in his eyes told them otherwise. He made his German accent even more pronounced than ever.

The German soldier saluted him. "Prime Minister Stan Newman, Deputy Prime minister Robert Ford and Foreign secretary Liam

Woodworth, Mien Fuhrer." He saluted again and marched quickly back to his post.

"Ah, now how was your flight, Prime Minister?" Gavrian asked, as he shook each ministers hand briskly. "I hope it wasn't too rough. I know the air turbulence over the Alps can be very strong."

"Oh the journey was fine, thank you" the Prime Minister commented, finding this chat all too friendly and cosy.

"Well, that is good. Please be seated. The maid will be along in a minute with drinks and light refreshments," the Chancellor said, gesturing to the table.

They all sat down at the table. Gavrian sat at one end, while Stan took his place at the other. Gavrian clasped his hands together and smiled around the table at each of them, it was done in such a way though that gave the impression that he was gloating more than anything else.

"So, Prime Minister, how are your wife and children? You have three children I believe, they are well, are they not?" Gavrian asked.

"Their fine, thank you" Stan answered curtly, showing only too clearly his discomfort at this conversation. He didn't want his family put in danger, especially at the hands of Gavrian Hitler.

A young maid in her early twenties entered the room, pushing a tea trolley in front of her. She was dressed in a knee length black dress with a white pinafore and a white headdress. Her blonde hair was coiled neatly under it and a few small strands had escaped the hair band to hang loosely around her face.

She began to serve the crockery, which was strangely Royal Dolton. There was a choice of tea or coffee, accompanied by crumpets and fruit scones. Followed by a choice of cream cakes or fruitcake. 'This bastard has got to be taking the piss,' Stan thought, as he unfolded his napkin. 'This is like fucking afternoon tea.'

As the young maid was pouring Gavrian his tea he suddenly cried out in anger, pointing to his cup. The maid mumbled something apologetically. The Prime Minister didn't have a clue what they were saying, because he didn't understand German and they were speaking too fast, although this didn't sound like any German he had ever heard. But as the maid leaned forward to retrieve the offensive cup Gavrian bent towards her and with incredible force slapped her across the face, uttering a German curse. The girl did no more than flinch at such a violent outburst and immediately left the room with his teacup.

This horrified the Prime Minister. He couldn't see what the young maid had possibly done wrong that warranted striking her so brutally. But obviously Gavrian had thought otherwise.

"What the bloody hell was that all about?" he asked the foreign secretary, who was sitting next to him.

"The tea was discoloured, sir. The Chancellor is very particular about the colour of his tea. It was how he put it, like piss water. The Chancellor said it was a disgrace especially in front of his guests and if she didn't sort it out he would punish her for her reckless carelessness" Liam Woodworth explained to him with a look of complete disgust on his face. Liam Woodworth could speak six different languages, which included German and Russian. But even Woodworth had a slightly puzzled expression upon his face as he tried to listen to what was being said. There was a slight variation to this German that he didn't recognise.

"Now lets get down to business," Gavrian said as he buttered his scone. "Now you have come to discuss the matter of this peace treaty." As he said 'peace treaty' he said it with a disgusted hiss and look of utter hatred. It was becoming all too clear to Newman what course this meeting was going to take. Alarm bells were going of in his head already. They were following an all too familiar pattern and he knew he should have seen this coming. But he in his foolish stupidity had thought that Gavrian could be reasoned with. He saw now what a stupid idea that had been. A man like Gavrian could never be persuaded, he was far beyond that now. Newman should have never forgotten the events of so long ago, but he had come too far now and knew that all he could do was persevere.

"That is correct" Stan answered. "Hopefully we can come to some sort of agreement over this dispute."

"What kind of agreement do you propose to make?" Gavrian asked, looking at him.

"That you retrieve all your troops from every

country you have invaded, including Austria and Poland," the Prime Minister answered simply.

"I think you are overlooking my countries needs here, Prime Minister. What's in this for my country?" Gavrian asked, looking from the Prime Minister to Robert Ford.

"We will give your country its freedom back. Allow you to have military weapons with a fully sized, workable army with which you will be allowed to command. You will also be allowed a Navy again, with a full fleet of battle ships," the Prime Minister explained, chewing slowly on his crumpet.

Gavrian sat there pondering over what had been proposed. He seemed to be thinking about it; which could be a good sign, but with Gavrian Hitler you could never be entirely certain. Every one waited quietly for his reaction, dreading the worst. The Prime Minister looked at the foreign secretary for his reaction, but he gave him none. 'Why the bloody hell is he taking so long?' Stan thought angrily in frustration.

"I would just like to ask your foreign secretary a question" Gavrian announced, breaking the silence.

"If you keep your side of the bargain does that mean we are entitled to over a thousand troops?" Gavrian asked, as he turned his attention upon the foreign secretary.

"Yes it does, chancellor" Liam answered. "You will be permitted 500,000 soldiers, 20,000 Marine soldiers and a hundred battle ships."

"What air craft and tanks will we be issued? Battle ships alone are no good to me, secretary" Gavrian said.

"You will be issued with fifty fighter planes and fifty tanks. No more and no less" Liam explained.

"Only fifty?" the Chancellor asked, raising his eyebrows. "That is not good enough, secretary. This is a big country and it needs a large amount of battle equipment with which to protect its borders," he said, sounding frustrated now.

"Planes and tanks are not cheap, Chancellor. We can afford no more than that. Take it or leave it," the foreign secretary said.

"Hum and what about the United States?" Gavrian said, as he started to eat a rather large slice of fruitcake.

"The Americans, Chancellor? They wish to be kept out of this complicated disagreement. They say it's a purely European matter and they don't want to become involved, Chancellor." Liam explained, his face showing signs of impatience.

"And what may I ask are the hidden issues behind all this generosity?" Gavrian asked, wiping his mouth with a impeccably clean handkerchief.

"Hidden issues, Chancellor?" the Prime Minister asked, now confused and very worried. He glanced at Robert, who looked at him and just raised his eyebrows in question. The Prime Minister wasn't the only one who was now feeling very anxious.

"Hidden issues yes, Prime Minister. All the important deals have hidden issues. I mean would you not give me all this expensive equipment without some sort of purpose to it?" Gavrian explained insistently.

"Well, we also request you discontinue your bombing raids on England. In particular the capital and surrounding areas" the Prime Minister said, leaning back in his chair.

He glanced over at Liam who nodded slightly in encouragement, telling him to continue what they had discussed earlier on the flight over.

A heavy silence filled the room now, everybody watched Gavrian anxiously waiting to hear what he had to say on the subject. He certainly seemed to be in no hurry, he was chewing quite calmly on his food and seeming to consider carefully the propositions put towards him. But Newman knew this was a clever ploy to simply unnerve his very apprehensive guests.

"What about Switzerland and the Czech. Republic?" Gavrian asked, putting his handkerchief on his plate.

"You must retrieve your soldiers from those countries. We also request you keep your troops away from the Russian border," the Prime Minister said.

"And what will happen if I don't?" Gavrian asked.

"The peace treaty will be broken and the conflict with your country will continue" Stan explained. But he knew that Gavrian already suspected he would say this.

"Well it's been a pleasure talking with you,

Mr. Prime Minister. But I do have other business to attend to" Gavrian explained. Then to everyone's surprise he stood up, they could only follow suit. He shook hands with each of them, thanking them for coming. As Gavrian shook Stan's hand, the Prime Minister saw in his eyes a look that alarmed him.

As they turned to leave Gavrian walked back to his seat and picked up the piece of paper he had to sign in order for the peace treaty to be complete.

"Oh, Mr. Prime Minister" he called out in a mocking voice. Every one in the room suddenly froze. Then the Prime Minister turned slowly around to face Gavrian. The look on Gavrian's face absolutely terrified him. Gavrian was smiling again, that cold, unfriendly and calculated smile.

But there was something about his face that froze the Prime Ministers very blood. There was a look in those ugly brown eyes that showed pure evil, capable of destroying the world.

"I just wanted to say something before you left," Gavrian said, walking back around the table again. "I know we haven't always seen eye to eye, but I have considered your offer carefully. I suppose you didn't realize that when I invaded Switzerland and the Czech. Republic I also seized all their military weapons. We now have aircraft and tanks far beyond anything that you are offering. I suppose you had no knowledge of this information, did you? I have also ordered all men under the age of fifty and over the age of sixteen to join my army. We now have a larger army than the whole of

France and Great Britain combined. So I'm afraid there will be no peace treaty as I refuse to sign it." Gavrian placed the paper before him and tore it clean in half.

As he continuously tore the paper into small pieces, everyone could only watch him. Then he dramatically threw his arms out, scattering the pieces on the floor. He raised his eyebrows mockingly and grinned showing his rotting teeth in all their glory.

The Prime Minister ground his teeth together and turned around. He walked out of the room hastily, trying to hide his frustration. Everyone followed him, leaving Gavrian Hitler to gloat in his own triumph.

"I warned you. I told you the bastard wouldn't

do it. We should have seen what was about to happen, he is playing out the Second World War almost exactly, it is so obvious what he is doing now. Why didn't we realise that when they invaded Switzerland that they would seize their military equipment?" Robert Ford grunted angrily.

"There's nothing we can do about it now. He is completely controlled by his own insanity and his ideas are totally influenced by that of a dead man. People like that can't be reasoned with," the Prime Minister mumbled softly to him, so that the Nazi officer marching beside them couldn't overhear their conversation.

"He is quick thinking though and clever with it. A dangerous combination, Prime Minister. I think we would be foolish to underestimate him," Liam admitted quietly and then he glanced at the Prime Minister.

"So what will this mean, Prime Minister?" Robert asked. He looked at the Prime Minister with an unsure look of dread in his eyes.

"I really don't know. But I do know one thing, this means we are yet again at war with Germany" the Prime Minister said, slowly shaking his head sadly at the consequences of today's meeting. What happened now he had no idea.

Chapter 5   Two days later

The class sat patiently watching the clock by the white board. They were waiting for the school bell to ring twice, the signal for a gas raid. The rules were that they had to wait for the bell to ring, and then they had to put their gas masks on and got out of the building as fast as possible. They had to proceed to the gas shelters situated under the P.E hall by the teachers.

"Five-four-three-two-one" the teacher counted out loudly, looking at her watch. Almost instantly the bell gave out two very loud rings that echoed through the corridors.

There came loud scraping noises, as the pupils dragged their gas masks of the table and pulled the straps over their heads.

Then everybody got up and walked to the door. Outside the classroom the corridors were packed.

Sarah found it difficult to see in her gas mask. The eye sockets kept steaming up. The mask was incredibly hot and making her sweat.

"Are you okay?" Nicole asked, her voice sounded muffled. She stepped in line beside Sarah. Sarah was started to sway and feel dizzy. These gas masks may have been better designed than the one's her fellow classmates were wearing, but they were made of a much thicker material that didn't allow the skin to breath and she was now suffering accordingly.

They passed through the main entrance to the school. But the cool air outside offered no relief to everyone's hot and sweaty faces.

To get to the gas shelters they had to cross the playground at the front of the school, go down a flight of stairs to a short underground passage. Then they had to proceed through some metal double doors with no windows. They entered a large airy room that had once been used as a sports hall, but had long since fallen into disrepair. Now it was used as the air raid shelters for the school and nearby residents.

The form tutors took the register while the pupils waited impatiently fiddling with their masks, they were all itching to remove them. They were supposed to be going home now and it was well past four o'clock.

"Well done everybody, that was a brilliantly co-ordinated gas drill," the head teacher said loudly, standing on his chair so they could all see him properly. He was proudly surveying the room full of school children like an uncle surveying his favourite nephew.

"If you're this good when a real gas attack

happens then you should all be perfectly safe. But remember leave the classrooms quietly and walk, don't run" he said.

"You are all dismissed" the headmaster shouted. There were murmurs and snapping noises as pupils started to remove their gas masks in relief. Everybody had red faces as though they had been badly sunburnt.

The pupils left the room in a less organized manner than they had entered it. The teachers followed them, carrying the chairs they'd been using to sit on as they were taking the register.

On the way home Nicole talked almost non-stop about her mums new job. Like all the other women who hadn't been sent to war because she had children, Nicole's mum had joined the civil service. She now had a job erecting bombs that were to be distributed to the main battlefields. This job was nothing special; thousands of women were doing it. What made it different for Nicole's mum was that she was always concerned with her own appearance. Sarah doubted she would last two days in a factory.

"Sarah, what's the matter? You've hardly said a single word since we left the school gates" Nicole finally asked, sounding worried.

"Who me? I'm fine. Its just Stephen I'm worried about. I don't think I should tell you though. You might think I'm being stupid or something," Sarah told her, staring down at her feet.

"Try me" Nicole said, looking straight at Sarah.

"Hum... okay, well you know his based in

Russia somewhere, I don't know where, right?"
Nicole just nodded. "Well yesterday he had a small
accident on the battlefield...it involved a Nazi and
some kind of weird new weapon that they are
apparently using. They had some slight
disagreement, which escalated into a fight. The
Nazi tore Stephen's leg open with this weapon.
Stephen managed to get away with what remained
of his regiment, however the rest weren't so lucky.
They lost over five hundred men out of that unit
and only fifteen survived" Sarah explained quietly,
as she explained this incident it was as if all the
colour was draining out of her face, she now looked
as white as a sheet.

"Fucking hell!" Nicole exclaimed in horror.
This made her suddenly realize that no one had

heard from her dad in over two weeks. He was a private who was based in France. Anything could have happened to him. He could be lying dead in the bottom of a ditch somewhere for all she knew.

"So is he okay now then?" she asked.

"Yeah, he's fine now. He has fifty or so stitches running down the side of his leg though. He's been allowed some time to recover in hospital, and then he has to report back for duty. What their going to do with him I don't know, as he doesn't have a regiment to lead at the moment. But so many soldiers are dying that new regiments are being created all the time, so he won't be bored for long, he'll be ok" Sarah said, she smiled on the last couple of words, knowing full well he wasn't fine. Not as long as he stayed where he was. They turned a corner and walked slowly up the street heading towards Sarah's house.

"Have you got any homework tonight?" Nicole asked, trying to change the subject.

"No, not tonight. No one turned up again today, so there's no point anyway. Their all far too scared of what might happen to them. The Nazis could attack at any time," Sarah said.

They stood on Sarah's driveway for a little while chatting, because Sarah was reluctant to go in and face the onslaught of one of Kira's mood swings. She eventually had to when Kira was tapping on the kitchen window and then pointing to the kitchen table, indicating that tea was ready.

After tea another fax came from Stephen. This time it was surprisingly long for Stephen. It read like this.

Dear all,

At this precise moment in time I am leaning against a canvassed wall staring at needles and other unimaginable hospital instruments. Hospitals are such depressing places. I can't wait to return to duty. Anything is better than this. The food is tasteless; all they give you is broth.

Apparently there is no lasting damage from my injury. The bloody Nazi only slashed a clean cut through my muscles and the doctor said that there is no permanent damage to my leg. It still absolutely kills me though. In a couple of weeks they will remove the stitches and I shall report back for duty hopefully within the week."

Give my love to the girls and tell Janet I'm fine. Lots of love Stephen. Xxx

"Do you reckon he's really okay, Kira?" Sarah asked, noticing the look on Kira's face. She now looked seriously ill and grief stricken. Her face was pail white: she looked like she had already received the worst telegram a soldier's wife can ever receive.

"I'm not sure, I'm really not sure, Sarah. But there must be something that he's trying to hide from us; it isn't like him to go on about how awful the hospital food is, I mean we know that it won't be good. He normally keeps everything short and to the point, he hates to drag things out. Oh shit, what is it he isn't telling us?" Kira swore angrily, pacing the kitchen in her agitation.

"Do you think it could be something serious, mum?" Janet asked curiously, not thinking of the consequences of such words. Sarah looked at her in horror, but it was already too late.

Kira let out a sob of anguish and ran out of the room. Janet realizing what she had said ran after her mother yelling, "I'm sorry, mummy!"

Five minutes later they came back into the kitchen. Kira had her arm around Janet, comforting her.

Kira walked over to Sarah and picked up the shopping list.

"Okay, Sarah, lets go get the groceries" she announced.

Then Kira walked out of the kitchen to get the

keys to the car, Sarah close at her heels.

Little had happened since the beginning of the new Millennium. Well that's what Kira's mum had told Sarah before she had died two years ago, two years after war was originally declared on Germany. The only noticeable changes had been the energy resources. Kira's mum said before the Millennium the main source of energy had been crude oils. But at the end of the 20th century fossil fuels were fast running out, so an alternative had to be found. Some scientist, Sarah could never remember his name, came up with the idea of using animal waste as an alternative to fuel. This was by far one of the best ideas for replacing crude oil, because there would always be an endless supply of animal waste and it was much more reliable than battery power. Electricity had gone through dramatic changes as well. Earth materials now ran everything. Right behind Sarah's house were four huge wind turbines. The older people in the town detested them, saying that they were a blot on the landscape. But Sarah liked them. Being a teenager her ideas were a lot more modern in thinking, she thought they looked quite majestic.

As they drove past one of many bombed out houses, Sarah saw some of the local boys rummaging through the burnt out remains of the once proud house.

None of the boys were wearing what could be called fashionable clothes. The attitude towards clothes had completely changed and it no longer mattered what they looked like, as long as they fit.

The Nazis had been attacking the English ports for some time, and now most of the ports were damaged beyond repair and it was virtually impossible to import or export anything.

In fact Britain was in the worst state it had been in for years when it came to food and house hold products. Although that did have its advantages, crime was at an all time low, now literally non-existent. But apart from that the advantages were minimal. People were starving, as there just wasn't enough food to go around. But the important thing was everybody got their equal share of food. Poorer people got healthier food they couldn't afford before the war and the richer people got a taste of what it was like to be poor. People were helping others when times got hard, like if a loved one died in an air raid or a soldier died on the battlefield. Even if you ran out of trivial things, like food coupons people would lend you theirs until you could repay them. Everything had changed beyond recognition since war broke out.

Kira pulled the car into the car park of the tiny, local supermarket. She swung into a parking space and accidentally pressed her foot on the brake too hard. The car jerked violently causing them to lurch forward. Sarah hit the dashboard sharply with her head. For one terrifying moment she was back in the car with April and Marques. She could hear their distant voices, Aprils calm but fearful and Marques' loud and angry. But she didn't remember either of them sounding like that in the car as Marques was dropping them of on that fateful day.

There had certainly been some disagreement, but nothing like what she was hearing now. They sounded like they were having a proper row and she could hear her name mentioned several times. Then she heard April scream, over and over again.

She sat perfectly still, staring out of the front windscreen. Her face was frozen into a look of horror, her mouth hung open and her eyes were open so wide that Kira could clearly see the whites.

"Sarah, are you okay? Sarah, speak to me darling. Sarah are you alright?" Kira asked in panic, shaking her arm quite roughly to get her attention. Sarah suddenly jumped, coming back to full awareness of where she was and she stared at Kira in alarm.

Then she slowly nodded.

"Right, lets go then. Before they run out of everything" Kira said, stepping out of the car. Sarah got out and let the door slam behind her. Kira locked the doors and they walked across the car park to the supermarket.

Since the beginning of the war the common supermarket had changed dramatically. Because of the shortage of food most was either stored away so that it could last as long as possible, or sold the very day it was delivered. The traditional isles had been removed to be replaced by large counters.

One of Stephens's old army colleagues, who had been fortunate enough to retire just before war broke out; stood at a counter and smiled happily in greeting as they approached him.

"Hello Nigel, what are you doing working? I

thought you'd retired?" kira asked.

"I did, Kira. But everything's too bleeding expensive these days, what with the price of bloody fuel going up and food is now sky high I have to work to be able to make ends meet, bloody typical isn't it?" Nigel grumbled, sounding rather too cheerful and happy about it. The expression on his face said otherwise though.

"What's the matter, the army not giving you a big enough pension?" Kira asked.

"Oh I bloody wish. My daughter and her husband just had their first baby and their finding it hard to afford everything. So my good lady wife said they could stay with us until they get themselves sorted out. Now he's been sent to the front line and my daughter can't look after a newborn baby on her own. So my wife is helping her to look after it. The problem with that is I only get enough pension to look after the wife and myself. So here I am."

"Well it's all in a good cause, isn't it? Anyway I need three large potatoes," Kira said, changing the subject abruptly.

Nigel gestured to a large barrel by the counter. Kira looked at the barrel and sighed in exasperation. Handing her bag to Sarah she walked towards it, rolling up her sleeves.

"Nigel" Sarah said.

"Hum?" he muttered, looking at her.

"I was just wondering if you knew anything about the attack on Stephen the other day?" she asked

"Yes I do, why?"

"Well I was just wondering what would have happened if he had been caught by the Nazis?"

"What do you mean?" Nigel asked confused.

"I mean would they have tried to get certain information out of him. Or would they have just killed him straight away?" Sarah asked.

Nigel seemed to falter, taken back by this question. The problem was he was still in close contact with Stephen and he knew a lot more about what had really happened to Stephen than either Kira or Sarah were ever likely to know. The thing was he had sworn an oath to Stephen that he would never tell them anything about that particular event.

"I don't know, Sarah. They would have killed him probably. But if they had taken him hostage I hear the Nazis have a really nasty method of getting the information that they desire out of their hostages" Nigel said.

"Oh yeah, what sort of methods?" Sarah asked eagerly.

"I can't tell you, Sarah. No one knows what the Nazis do to their hostages. A lot of the time the surviving hostages either commit suicide, or are so traumatised by their experiences that they can't talk about it" Nigel explained.

"What are you saying to my Sarah, Nigel?" Kira asked, walking over to them and looking suspiciously at them both.

"Nothing, she just asked me a question and I gave her the answer." He gave Sarah a reassuring wink and she smiled at him.

As Kira headed for the bread counter Sarah quickly turned to face Nigel.

"How's Stephen really? Now give me a straight answer because even though Kira thinks I don't have a clue, I know a lot more than she realizes" Sarah told him.

"He's fine really, there's nothing wrong with him. I swear on my life he's perfectly safe," Nigel said, trying to keep an honest face. But Sarah was good at reading people's expressions and she could tell that Nigel was lying about Stephen.

"Are you sure?"

"I'm positive. Now go to Kira, she's waiting for you" Nigel said, with an impatient jerk of his head and Sarah knew when she was beaten.

"Okay" Sarah said. Then she turned around

and walked over to the bread counter, where Kira was now waiting impatiently for her at the back of the very long queue that was always there.

As they left the supermarket it was just starting to get dark, so Kira would have to drive really carefully as use of car lights was strictly prohibited. Sarah noticed as they walked across the car park everything had grown deathly silent.

On the way back in the car, Sarah heard the low hum of a plane. She glanced up at the sky, but couldn't see anything.

As they reached the end of their journey the humming sound grew even louder and Kira looked up at the sky with a worried expression.

Sarah heard the drone of the engine as Kira picked up speed. They were already five miles over the speed limit and going faster with every second. Kira was starting to panic.

Kira turned the car sharply around the corner. Sarah could feel the car start to skid and Kira gripped onto the wheel for dear life trying to regain control. As they reached the driveway the car skidded to a stop and Kira turned the engine of. As they got out Sarah glanced at the driveway and noticed the fresh marks that were clearly visible.

Kira was already entering the house and Sarah quickly ran in after her.

Janet ran furiously out of the living room, her face was pale with terror and wet with tears.

"How could you leave me like that, I hate you, I hate you!" She screamed indignantly, hitting Kira with all her strength. But Sarah knew she wasn't hurting Kira, Janet had hit her enough times for Sarah to know that she had no strength in her arms. But Kira did look alarmed at her daughter's outburst all the same, grabbing hold of Janet's wrists as a means of trying to calm her down.

"Its alright, darling, I'm here now. I promise no ones going to hurt you. Your safe" Kira told her gently, hugging her until she calmed down and stopped trying to hit her.

Sarah moved past them into the kitchen and dumped the shopping bag on the table. The German bombers were now flying directly overhead and were clearly visible in the darkening sky.

As Kira and Janet walked into the kitchen the sirens suddenly went of, scaring them all half to death.

Everybody went very quiet, waiting for something to happen. Then it did. A very loud explosion could be heard near by. The whole house shook with the force of the explosion and bits of flying debris struck the kitchen window, causing it to smash into tiny pieces. Everybody in the kitchen screamed out loud in terror and covered their faces with their arms to try and protect themselves from the flying glass.

Sarah could hear Janet screaming continuously, but all she could see were the German bombers flying closer to them through the shattered window. There was a whistling sound followed by a flash of blinding light, and then the loud explosion as the bomb was detonated making contact with the ground.

Objects started falling down all around them and smashing on the floor, hitting them with a barrage of broken glass and crockery.

With all her strength Kira picked Janet up and dashed for the back door. She kicked the door open and ran into the back garden, towards the safety of the Anderson shelter. Sarah ran after them, terrified and feeling a trickle of blood going down her cheek. All around her she could see the flashes of light from the exploding bombs.

They ran down some concrete steps and entered the protection of the Anderson shelter. Sarah ran in after them and Kira securely locked and bolted the door after her.

Sarah walked over to one of the bunks and was about to sit down on it, but Janet barged past her and lay with a happy sigh on the one Sarah was about to sit on. Sarah just hefted herself up onto the bunk above Janet and watched as Kira lit a lamp.

"Oh I wish Stephen were here" Kira commented, lying down on the bunk opposite the girls. "Everything seems so much safer and more secure when he's at home."

"I miss Daddy too, mum. I wish he would come home; this war is so silly and pointless." Janet said.

Kira glanced over at Sarah and they gave each other significant looks, knowing that the situation was far more complicated than that.

As Sarah looked at Kira she could see the fear in her eyes. The fear of not knowing what will happen. The fear of knowing that they could loose Stephen and might never see him again.

The bombs continued to bombard the capital throughout the night, attacking the surrounding countryside as they went. Several times the bombs hit close by and every time Sarah thought dear god, don't let that be our house.

She lay awake all night listening to the planes flying overhead and to the explosions as the bombs went of. But all she could think of was how much better it would be if they lived somewhere else. Some place they would be safe in the knowledge that a bomb or a gun wouldn't kill them. A place far away from the troubles of the world that she knew could only get worse with time.

Next Morning <u>*Chapter six.*</u>

They woke up to the peaceful sound of birds singing. It was a completely different atmosphere from the destruction of last night. Everything appeared so calm and tranquil that it didn't seem possible that last nights events could have actually taken place. But happen they did and soon Sarah's family was to find out how bad the situation was slowly getting and they were to get an idea of how bad it was to become.

But they were to discover even sooner why everything was so quiet when they left the safety of the Anderson shelter. Their house appeared to be the only place that hadn't been completely destroyed by last night's air raid. Dead bodies were burning in the streets and unexploded bombs lay scattered in the middle of the roads. The place was a complete disaster zone, not even their house was left untouched. All the windows were smashed in from the force of the blasts and the roof had sustained serious damaged.

As Sarah left the house and walked down the street towards school, Nicole came running towards her, a frantic look of shock, anger and pain on her face. Tears were running down her face, but she didn't even seem aware of them.

"Sarah, I'm so glad I found you. The bomb raid last night, I was really praying we wouldn't get hit again. But it shows you how wrong a person can be. Now they did it, Sarah, the fucking bastards did it, now we don't have anything" Nicole cried out in a rush of anger and pain. Everything came out so fast though that it was nothing more than a jumble of words that Sarah couldn't comprehend.

"Didn't catch a word of that, Nicole. What did

they do to you?" Sarah asked.

"They blew up my fucking house!" Nicole cried out in frustration. Then she burst into tears and Sarah grabbed hold of her, hugging her tightly to her. She could feel Nicole's whole body shaking with emotion.

Sarah glanced over at Nicole's house and saw a smoking pile of bricks and rubble. Nothing had survived the blast. All the hard work Nicole's dad had gone through to get that house had all been in vain; he spent every penny he had trying to pay the mortgage for that house; only to have it totally destroyed by the Nazis.

"Mum says its no longer safe for us to stay here any more. So as soon as possible we're leaving for America, it's the only place where we will truly be safe. The only good news is that they found my dad, he is alive and returning back to England even as we speak" Nicole said.

Sarah let go of her and stared at her in shock. Nicole angrily wiped away her tears.

"What you're actually going to leave England and move to America, permanently?" Sarah asked in bewilderment.

Nicole nodded slowly. She obviously hated the idea as much as Sarah. But she had no choice in the matter, she had to go. She had lived her entire life in England and had never been further than a holiday to Greece. The family would be safe and that was more important than anything. Well to Nicole's dad it was anyway; he had seen enough of this war to know just how deadly the enemy was.

"Come on, we'd better go, otherwise we'll be late for school" Sarah said quietly. She slipped her arm through Nicole's and literally dragged her down the road. Janet ran frantically after them, not wanting to be left behind.

They walked through the streets, seeing for themselves the extent of the destruction the Nazis had inflicted on their innocent town. A family stood on the corner of a pavement by the smoking remains of their house. The mother was holding on tightly to the father, wailing hysterically with grief. The father was just staring helplessly at the sky. Next to them was their young daughter, clutching tightly onto her teddy bear. When Sarah and Nicole walked past the family the little girl gazed up at them. Her eyes showed no fear; it was a look of pure innocence. It was a really horrible sight that would haunt Sarah for a long time afterwards.

As she stared at Sarah and Nicole, Janet walked past and the little girl focused her attention on Janet instead.

"What the fuck are you staring at?" Janet asked rudely, looking at this innocent little girl spitefully.

"Janet, stop being a bitch" Sarah called to her.

"I'll tell mum you called me a bitch," Janet warned her.

"Yes, well I'll tell her you were rude to an distraught little girl then. That little girl doesn't have a home now and she didn't need you to be nasty to her like that, Janet," Sarah answered back.

Janet chose not to respond.

Sarah glanced up at one of the street lamps; she

didn't know why she had looked at that particular one. Then she noticed that it was still lit, it hadn't been blacked out. No wonder the town had been so badly hit by bombs. The Nazis had seen the light and attacked.

Sarah picked up a piece of brick and with careful aim she threw it at the lamp. The brick smashed through the glass, shattering it. The bulb burst into a shower of sparks and flickered out.

"Fucking lamp!" Nicole screamed out furiously, making everyone jump. Then she started to cry again

They continued along the road, which sloped steeply up. Their feet crunched on broken glass and rubble. The dust from the concrete of the destroyed buildings became unsettled by the wind and started to blow in a chocking cloud around them.

The three girls reached the summit of the hill, which gave a view of the entire town. They all looked around in utter disbelief, no one could say anything; even Janet was silenced by what she was seeing.

The number of houses destroyed seemed to follow a strange pattern; they hadn't been blown up at random. The houses that had been targeted were set in straight lines, almost as if there had been a specific pattern of homes the Nazis had been ordered to bomb.

"How could anyone do this?" Nicole muttered quietly.

No one else could find anything appropriate to say, so they all just stared down at the horrific scene that lay before them in utter silence. Janet was the first to move, turning her back on what they all knew would soon become an all too common sight.

The others followed Janet down towards their high school. They had just left one of the highest vantage points in the town, but what the vantage point didn't show them was the school. It was situated in a valley out of view from the hill.

Sarah noticed as they approached the school that instead of heading towards it everyone was walking away from it. Some people were crying; but most just had solemn expressions on their faces.

"Here, what's going on?" she asked, stopping a girl that she knew, who was walking past with her boyfriend.

"I think you'd better take a look for yourself," her boyfriend told Sarah bluntly. Then he took his girlfriends hand and walked on past her.

Sarah looked at him in confusion; she glanced back at Nicole.

"What was he talking about, Sarah?" Nicole asked.

"Well there's only one-way to find out, isn't there" Sarah said. "Come on."

She grabbed Nicole's arm and they ran the rest of the way to the school, where Janet and a few of Sarah's friends were standing. They weren't actually doing anything; they were simply staring at the school.

As Sarah and Nicole approached the group of girls they all turned around and looked at them.

One girl suddenly burst into tears. Another girl called Lucy, who was a friend of theirs, ran over to them and threw her arms around Nicole, sobbing heavily. Nicole looked at Sarah with a bemused expression on her face as she patted Lucy awkwardly on the back.

"What's going on?" Sarah demanded angrily. She wished someone would give her an answer instead of just bloody crying.

Lucy however didn't answer; she instead took hold of Sarah's arm and pulled her towards the edge of the valley where the school was.

"I don't understand. What's everyone so upset about?" Sarah asked in bewilderment. Nicole gently tapped her on the shoulder and she looked at Nicole.

"Look at the school, Sarah" she said quietly.

"But why, what's wrong with the-oh fuck!"

She had finally turned to face the school. It was now just the crumpled, burnt out remains of what was once a prosperous establishment. There was a burnt hole in the concrete where the bomb had struck. Even the bike sheds, which were in the furthest corner of the school grounds had been damaged, the metal was all twisted and bent into strange angles. Power lines, which were still alive, set of electric sparks. Papers were scattered across the immediate area. But the thing that was shocking everyone was a human arm sticking out of the wreckage.

"Oh god, the poor bastard. Surely he heard the sirens though?" Sarah said in shock.

"Probably not. Sid was almost completely deaf," Lucy told her.

The hand in question belonged to Sid the school caretaker. He must have been locking up at the time, because some of the teachers often stayed late. Obviously he didn't get out in time before the bombs fell. The poor idiot had been seventy-eight and even though he was supposed to have been retired he still worked for the school and the war effort. Everyone had liked him, because he let the children get away with murder. It was just such a tragic way to die, being on your own in a big school. Sarah would hate to die in such an undignified manner.

Behind her, Nicole who had been so bravely trying to control her emotions couldn't take any more. She stood there sobbing and wailing, while everyone looked at her with expressions of concern and discomfort, they didn't know what to do.

Sarah felt tears come to her eyes, wondering how people could do such crawl things to an innocent old man.

Nicole finally had enough. She turned away from the others and ran as fast as she could up the road towards her house.

"Nicole, where are you going?" Sarah yelled after her.

"Anywhere better than this fucking place!" Nicole yelled in answer, as she disappeared amongst the rubble.

"I-I'm going home. There's no point staying here, I'll see you lot later. Are you coming, Janet?"

Sarah said. Her voice sounded really weird now, as she was trying her hardest not to break down and cry. She sounded like she had a terrible cold or something.

"Yeah, I'm coming" Janet answered, for once not even trying to be difficult. She followed Sarah up the hill, leaving the others to grieve.

It was at this point Sarah understood her life was about to change forever and would never be the same again. Nicole, her best friend was leaving for America. There were also a number of her other friends leaving for safer grounds. Her whole life was falling apart around her and there was nothing she could do to stop it. It was like a mad roller coaster that had no end to it, just endless loops and turns. Sarah could still remember the Prime

Minister announcing the beginning of the war like it had happened yesterday. It just suddenly came on the TV without any warning. Janet had been furious with the whole announcement, because it had been halfway through her favourite soap. Stephen had just laughed and said, "I wouldn't worry about it. It's nothing more than a load of political nonsense thought up by a madman. This conflict will probably be over in a couple of months." Sarah had actually believed what he had said, now she realized what a fool she had been to believe that. That had been two years ago now. Now Stephen was in a hospital somewhere in Russia and the rest of the world was literally falling apart all around her. There seemed to be no end to this conflict and nobody seemed to have a clue what they were doing anymore. The future had never looked bleaker than it did right now.

CHAPTER 7

As Sarah walked up the driveway of her house she spotted a lone German plane flying overhead. She looked at it in fury, never thinking that she could ever hate anything so much. She hoped that it would get spotted by the enemy and would get blown out of the sky.

Kira gave her a surprised look as she walked into the kitchen and dumped her bag on the kitchen table.

"Your home a bit early, aren't you?" she commented, as Sarah sat down on one of the chairs.

"There's a very good reason," Sarah explained.

"Well tell me then" Kira told her impatiently.

"The Nazis blew up the school. Its all-just rubble now. They even killed Sid the caretaker," Sarah cried out angrily.

"Sid? Oh, how could they" Kira commented angrily.

"It was the only decent school we had as well. The only other half decent one is in the general direction of Norfolk. Now it's all gone, it's all bloody gone." Sarah started to cry, the tears rolling slowly down her cheeks.

"I wouldn't worry, love. They'll come up with some kind of a solution," Kira said, offering her no comfort. Not that Sarah had actually expected her to mind.

"What? With a school my size?" Sarah asked.

Her school was a large school and it would be almost impossible to find so many places for the huge number of pupils.

"No, I see what you mean" Kira said. She stood there for a while. "Anyway I'm sure they'll find some kind of alternative," She said finally, dumping the knife she was holding in the kitchen sink and walking out through the back door on to the patio.

Sarah watched Kira's retreating back with a mixture of hatred and loneliness. Kira had shown this same uncaring attitude towards her ever since she had given birth to Janet. Stephen was the only one who had ever shown her any kind of affection, but he wasn't there now, which made her feel even more isolated. The cause of all this loneliness was

Janet. Janet always had to be the centre of attention and would do anything to get it. She wasn't going to let anything stand in her way, especially not Sarah. There was just no getting away from the fact that Janet was the favourite and always would be, especially in Kira's eyes. To her Janet was her baby, her special girl. Sarah was nothing more than an inconvenience, a nuisance that simply got in everyone's way and would soon be gone.

She stared down at the kitchen table and saw a newspaper lying there; it was by the date at the top printed yesterday. Sarah picked the paper up and read the headline on the front. The main headlines read "the day Europe came to a stand still." The main picture was of a young Romanian woman clutching her child tightly. She was covered in dust and her tears left streaks of pail skin on her face. The infant was clinging to its mother for dear life. It was in such a state you couldn't tell whether it was a boy or girl. In the background was a main street that was now just a pile of rubble. Hundreds of bodies were lying in the street, some of them just tiny babies. These scenes were becoming all too common in the newspapers. But what was most concerning was what the story revealed. The Nazis were gaining even more control over Europe with every passing day, crushing any armies that stood in their way. They had become ruthless in their attack methods and no amount of reasoning would stop them. They had taken control of all the countries that surrounded them and they were now getting dangerously close to France; as well as invading land around Russia. The newspapers were describing scenes of torture, especially towards the Jews; the Jews were suffering the most. The number of dead had now run into it's millions and was still rising. No one was quite sure how many had died and the true estimate might never be known. No body was quite sure what they were going to do next; they could launch a surprise attack on Britain. Everyone was just holding their breaths and waiting. The danger of them taking control of the UK was the fact they had control of the Atlantic and could therefore easily launch an attack on the US. But the USA showed how ignorant they were by refusing to believe the Nazis would be so foolish. So everyone was waiting and praying. Sarah wondered onto the patio where Kira sat with a glass of water in her hand and an old battered library book sitting open in her lap. Sarah sat down in one of the deck chairs and continued to read the paper. They sat there for a couple of minutes not saying anything, deep in their own thoughts.

"So if Russia's been invaded by the Nazis, where's Stephen then?" Sarah asked, finally breaking the silence.

"Oh don't you worry about that, his safe and sound in Sweden now" Kira told her, not looking up from her book.

"But won't the Nazis try to invade Sweden though?" Sarah asked.

"Oh god no, it would take too long" Kira said to Sarah, and then she took another sip of water.

"So is Stephen okay now then?" Sarah asked, not giving up that easily.

"Yes Sarah, his fine. Apparently his already up and about and his fighting fit. Well that's what he said anyway. He said his leg has fully healed and the bandage is being removed tomorrow," Kira said. With that she turned her attention back to her book again.

Sarah looked at her, and then she folded up the paper and stood up from her deckchair.

"I'm just going over to Nicole's," she announced quietly. With that she walked back into the kitchen.

She made her way through the kitchen, dumping the paper on the table. She walked out through the front door, slamming the door with all her force.

Dust fell over her like snow. She shook the dust out of her hair as she walked down the driveway.

Chapter eight

That night they slept in the Anderson shelter as Kira felt it was no longer safe to sleep in the house, there was no knowing when the bombers would strike. Her caution paid of. At precisely ten o'clock the sirens went of. But the bombs didn't start hitting until somewhere around half past eleven. There was definitely more of them and they seemed to be striking harder and more frequently than last night, if that was at all possible.

There was one particular bomb that seemed to explode directly over head. The Anderson shelter rattled on its foundations as it took the back draft of the explosion and covered them all in a shower of dust; it was a miracle the bloody thing hadn't collapsed under the pressure of the explosion. Janet screamed in pure terror and hid under the blankets, still screaming. Her screaming sounded fucking louder than the actual bombs did.

By the next morning the bombing had stopped. But low-lying cloud seemed to cover England for the entire day. It rained continuously, but the rain felt very acidic. Some people suspected it was because of radiation from the bombs.

With great caution Kira left the safety of the shelter to see if the house had been hit. But she gave Sarah and Janet strict instructions to stay in the shelter. They sat on their bunks waiting patiently for Kira to return. They heard a high-pitched scream coming from just above them. It bounced back of the walls and seemed to go straight through them. Janet jumped of her bunk and totally ignoring Sarah's pleas to stay where she was she ran out of the shelter. There was no other choice but for Sarah to go after her. She followed Janet, jumping the three small steps and ran over to where Kira was standing. As they approached her Sarah knew instantly something was very wrong. Kira didn't even look at them as they approached her. She just stared straight ahead, her bottom lip shaking and the whites of her eyes showing, as if hypnotised by something.

"Kira, what's wrong, what is it?" Sarah asked, walking up beside her.

"L-l-look at the house. Oh Jesus Christ, look what they've done to our home!" Kira said in barely a whisper, pointing shakily in the direction of the house.

Sarah hadn't even thought about looking at the house, worrying about Kira. But she now looked over to where Kira was pointing. She gave a loud gasp that turned in to a sob.

There was nothing left of the house, it was completely demolished. All that remained was a pile of rubble; everything they owned had been destroyed. It was like a scene from the front pages of the papers that had grown so frequent of late, only it was happening right now and to them.

It took her a while to become fully aware that Janet was standing next to her. Janet started to cry; Kira who was crying herself walked over to Janet and hugged her tightly as they both surrendered themselves to their grief.

Sarah started to walk slowly backwards, away from Kira and Janet. Then she turned around and fled as fast as she could down the back garden, running over the burnt remains of their house. She ran towards the bridle paths that lay to the back of their house. Tears were streaming down her face and stinging her eyes so that she couldn't see properly, but she ignored this discomfort and simply kept on running.

The bridle path slopped up into a hill that over looked the town. Then it led to nearby farmland where a fallow field lay in wait for the next season.

Sarah was still running, but it was starting to burn with pain when she breathed. She began to stagger. Her legs had gone numb, but she was oblivious to the pain.

All she wanted to do was get away from everything, the town, the bombs, the dead and wounded people, the destroyed houses and school. She just wanted to escape from all of it.

Finally when she reached the fallow field she slowed down to a walk and dragged her exhausted body over to the fence surrounding the field. Careful not to slip on the wet wood of the fence she climbed over it and jumped lightly into the springy grass that covered the field like a thick blanket. Looking around to se if there was anybody in the field she walked slowly away from the fence. Her whole body seemed to slump with exhaustion and she fell to the ground in a heavy heap. She lay there oblivious to the wetness from the grass that was soaking through her top. She stared numbly up at the sky, her breath coming out in short and painful gasps. A fine misty rain slowly fell from the clouds, wetting her hot, sweaty face and bringing her some cooling relief.

She slowly fell into a sleepy daze and everything went vague. She had no idea how long she had lain there, but when she woke up it had stopped raining, however the clouds stubbornly refused to break up and clear.

Sarah just lay there for a while. She then realized she was soaking wet. Her hair hung loosely in rat's tails and her clothes were sticking to her skin. She began to shiver uncontrollably and decided to get back to what remained of the house and dry of before she caught pneumonia. Sarah slowly heaved her wet and exhausted body up of the grass and walked back up the field. Her shoes squelched loudly as she walked.

When she got back to the house Janet and Kira were going through the rubble of their once proud home to find anything that might have miraculously survived the blast. They didn't even glance up as Sarah approached them, they just continued with what they were doing. Little had survived the bomb and what had was black with dust and of little use.

"Stephen just got in touch through the fax in the shelter. He heard what happened. How he found out I will never know. Anyway he says it's far too dangerous for us to stay in England anymore and wants us to join him in Sweden" Kira told them, walking over to them with a piece of fax paper in her hand.

"Sweden, why does he want us to join him in Sweden? They're just as vulnerable as the English. Why can't we go somewhere else, like America? That's the safest place to live at the moment" Sarah cried out in dismay.

"You only want to go to America because Nicole's moving there" Janet sneered mockingly.

Sarah ignored her and looked at Kira with a pleading look.

"No it's out of the question, it's too far away. It's on the other side of the world, Sarah" Kira said. "If we stay with Stephen in Sweden we've got a massive army to protect us. In America we'd be on our own, it's far too risky. Especially if the

Japanese attack and they could very well do so, if they continue to support Germany like they are. We're going to Sweden and that's the end of it." With that Kira turned away from her.

"Oh couldn't Sarah get her own way, ah, never mind. Don't forget, bitch, you will never have it your own way. Because I always win, don't you forget that. Especially now Nicole's going, you'll be all on your own. That's the story of your life, isn't it? You know your parents probably committed suicide, through frustration over the regret of having you" Janet sneered, standing in front of Sarah with a triumphant smile on her face.

"One day you're going to get what you deserve, you bitch. And when you do I'll be there, watching you and savouring every second" Sarah said coldly.

She brushed roughly past Janet, giving her a little shove and causing Janet to stumble.

Sarah walked down the steps to the Anderson shelter and ducked through its tiny door. She slumped down on one the bunks, in a foul mood. She was simply fed up with the whole world and everything going on all around her.

She sat there gazing ahead of her, but not really seeing anything. Her mind kept flashing back to that day in the wood back in Germany, long before all the troubles that were now taking place. The day that Sarah's life changed forever. Little did she know back then where her path would eventually lead her. What would have happened if she had been adopted by another family? Would she even be living in England? Would she be living in

Germany and cheering Gavrian on the television as he was tearing the rest of the world apart?

A small tapping on the door broke her train of thoughts.

"Janet, if that's you just fuck of and leave me alone!" Sarah yelled furiously at the door.

"Well, that's a nice way to talk to your best mate, isn't it?" Nicole called through the blackened wooden door. She sounded amused though instead of insulted.

Sarah jumped up of the bunk and ran over to the door. She flung it open and gave a surprised Nicole a hug of pure relief. It took all of Nicole's strength to wrench her back of again.

"Hey, what's the matter?" Nicole asked, concerned as Sarah burst into tears.

"Nothing, everything. The situations just gotten to me. You're leaving for America, our house getting destroyed by a bomb and Janet's not helping."

"Why, what did she say this time?" Nicole asked. She knew all too well how nasty Janet could be. That's why Janet had no friends, because everyone disliked her so much.

"The bitch said some things about my past that she has no right to be saying" Sarah told her.

"Do you want me to go and beat her up for you?" Nicole asked.

"No, no, leave her. Don't worry I can handle her" Sarah insisted, failing to hide a small smile and a gentle chuckle at Nicole's comment.

"Okay" Nicole said, sitting down on the bunk

next to her.

"So how are you? Or is that a stupid question" Nicole then asked curiously.

"No its not a stupid question and I have been better" Sarah answered wearily. "I'm coping I guess. It all just seems so pointless now," Sarah got up and began to pace the shelter.

"We're leaving by ship for America tomorrow. Please say that you'll be there to say goodbye? It would make it so much easier for me to have someone waving me of" Nicole asked, changing the subject. She looked at Sarah hopefully.

"What, you're leaving tomorrow?" Sarah asked, shocked.

Nicole nodded.

"Of course I'll be there, you don't even need to ask me. I'll be standing on the docks waving you goodbye" Sarah said.

"Oh, good, because I'm going to need all the encouragement I can get, I'm afraid of boats and this is going to be a long journey, we have to stop of at Ireland on the way," Nicole said with a grimace. Sarah could see just how nervous her best friend was.

"Hey, it might not be so bad once you get to America. You might make loads of friends and before you know it you could become really popular. With your cute English accent and all." Sarah said, trying to comfort her. She doubted she was helping though.

"Not too bad? Sarah, it's going to be like a

living hell. I've never been to America in my life. I know nothing about the people or their culture. The school system is completely different and I'm going to have to start my education all over again. To top it all of I have a very strong Norfolk accent, because of my dad. So that's another thing I'll get teased about." Nicole looked at Sarah helplessly.

"Stop being so negative. Okay things maybe tough for a little while, but it's not as if your stupid. You're clever and will soon catch up. Just give it time," Sarah told her.

"Yeah, well I still don't want to go. Why does everything have to be so complicated? Why do the Nazis have to go and blow everything up, Sarah?"

"Who knows?" Sara h said simply.

"Anyway, when I leave England I'll be leaving you."

"We can still keep in touch, Nicole. We can write to each other and send post cards and photos. Also don't forget E-mail and face book," Sarah said.

"Sarah, we can't write to each other because any planes or ships get blown up, especially one's delivering mail. Also don't forget you don't have a computer, it got destroyed with the house, remember?"

"Oh, yeah" Sarah mumbled, with a downcast expression.

"Ah, I wouldn't worry though. The war will be over in a couple of months. Once the Americans join us Hitler won't have a hope in hell" Nicole assured her.

"That's what they said two years ago. But it hasn't happened. When are people going to wake up to the fact that this is really happening and Gavrian will continue to attack until he has full control of Europe" Sarah said.

"Yeah, well they can't keep going forever. Under all that military equipment their nothing more than a bunch of cowards" Nicole said, trying and failing to sound positive.

"I'm not so sure, Gavrian seems pretty determined to me. He probably inherited it from Hitler and that can't be a good thing" Sarah said, shaking her head.

"You worry far to much" Nicole told her.

"No, I don't. I just think about things too much, that's all" Sarah said.

"But you do worry too much, come on you need to be enjoying these last precious moments with me instead" Nicole said, smiling warmly at her distressed friend.

Sarah looked at her with a smile. But Nicole could still see the worry in her eyes, the fear of not knowing what was going to happen. Nicole leant forward and gave her a hug.

"Listen, I have to go now. I have to finish packing what few belongings I have left" Nicole said jokingly, trying to lighten the mood.

Sarah nodded in answer.

"Okay, I'll see you tomorrow" Nicole said again.

"See ya later" Sarah mumbled in answer, hugging Nicole.

Nicole left the shelter. As she left Janet strode in, carrying a cardboard box.

"Are you just going to sit there all day on your fat ass and do nothing, or are you actually going to help?" Janet asked furiously, dumping the box on the floor with a loud clatter. Sarah heard the distinctive sound of something delicate smashing.

"Oh, I thought I might watch you. It being a miracle your actually doing anything" Sarah answered coldly. She had never seen Janet doing any house cleaning in her life. She was honestly surprised Janet was helping now, although the offered cleaning was unenthusiastic.

She slid of the bunk and bent down to inspect the box. Janet turned around and walked out of the shelter in a huff.

There was little in the box and most of it was burnt and blackened from the dust. She picked up a photo frame. Unsurprisingly the glass had shattered and the photo was almost unrecognisable through the dust. Sarah wiped away the dust with the sleeve of her shirt. There were a number of completely unrecognisable objects that Sarah just ignored.

Sarah left the shelter and walked over to Kira, who was rubbing her forehead tenderly.

"Kira, Nicole's leaving for America tomorrow. I was just wondering if we could go to the port and say goodbye to her and her parents?" Sarah asked hopefully.

"What time are they leaving?" kira asked.

"About midday Nicole said. But they are leaving from Dover, is it ok if we go with them? Nicole's dad said he would appreciate it if we could drive them down as well. He would be quite happy to cover the cost of the fuel" Sarah asked hopefully. She could see Kira was in one of her better moods and Sarah might just be able to pull this of.

"Okay then" Kira agreed. It was the best outcome that Sarah could have hoped for.

"Oh thanks, Kira. Thanks so much" Sarah cried out happily. She ran out of the garden to Nicole's house to tell her the news.

"Oh, thanks a lot, mum, how could you let her get away with that?" Janet cried out angrily, rounding on her mother as soon as Sarah had left.

"Look you don't have to come if you don't want to. You can stay here and look after the rubble, how does that sound?" Kira asked.

"Oh, yeah okay" Janet agreed, sounding and looking a lot happier.

Janet turned around and skipped down towards the other end of the garden.

Kira watched her for a minute. Then she gave a heavy sigh and lay back on the short, burnt and blackened grass of their once proud lawn.

CHAPTER NINE

She had no idea what time it was, but to Sarah it might as well be the middle of the night. They were at Portsmouth, waiting for Nicole and her parents to board the ship that would take them away from their friends and family to a new world they knew nothing about.

Nicole stood quietly next to Sarah, staring unhappily at the ship. Tears slowly rolled down her cheeks.

She was holding a small brown suitcase in one hand. On her shoulder she carried a rucksack containing books and objects of sentimental value. Everything else she was wearing.

Nicole's parents were standing nearby with Kira. They talked quietly and kept glancing at the girls to make sure they were okay. But they were giving them the space they needed to say a proper goodbye.

Sarah stared at the ship thinking how unfair life was. She was loosing yet another person she cared about because of the Nazis.

The ramp to the ship was finally fixed into place and people started boarding the ship enthusiastically. Sarah watched them angrily, wondering why they were so eager to leave.

Nicole turned around and looked at Sarah. Then Sarah suddenly burst into tears. Nicole grabbed hold of her and hugged her tightly.

"I'm going to miss you" Sarah cried out.

"I'm going to miss you too, Sarah" Nicole cried, her throat clogging up.

Nicole let go of Sarah and held her at arms length.

"Now promise me you'll not forget me?" She asked fiercely.

"Oh, you stupid cow. I'm not going to forget you, am I? Your my best friend" Sarah told her.

"I don't know how I'm going to cope without you, Sarah. It's going to be so hard," Nicole said.

"No, you'll be fine without me. Just make sure you remember me when you settle in and make loads of friends. Okay?"

"It's not likely I'm going to make many friends is it?" Nicole muttered, the doubt creeping back into her voice.

"Of course you will. Now stop being so negative, you're going to be absolutely fine. You'll make friends in no time, you'll see. Just be your usual crazy self and the Americans will love you.

In a couple of months or so you would have forgotten all about boring old England with its overcrowded cities and its wet, miserable weather" Sarah told her quite firmly, gazing up at the massive ship behind them. She wondered just how far it would sail before it was finally spotted by the enemy.

Nicole's father walked up to the two girls and placed a hand on Nicole's shoulder. He had been allowed two weeks leave to help them move their stuff to America and get them settled in.

"Alright dad, I'm coming" Nicole said quietly.

She turned to look at Sarah again and she started to cry once more. Sarah took hold of her and they cried in each other's arms, while the grown ups waited patiently.

Finally Nicole let go of Sarah and allowed her father to lead her away gently.

Sarah watched helplessly as her best friend was being taken away from her. They showed their passports to the people at the entrance to the ship. Then Nicole disappeared from view. She glanced once more at Sarah, giving her a wave as she disappeared from view.

Sarah stared at the ship for a while, the cold sea breeze chilling her bones. Then she started to cry, covering her face with her hands.

Kira walked over to her and put a comforting but awkward arm over her shoulders.. It was the first sign of affection she had shown Sarah in a long time and the discomfort was clear on her face, but Sarah appreciated the effort.

That was the last time Sarah ever saw Nicole. She would never see her again.

Barely a couple of days after the ship left port a terrible accident happened when the ship was barely a couple more hours from docking in its final port, New York. It had in fact been so close that the passengers could actually see the statue of liberty and they were all out on deck when the incident took place.

Kira found out from a neighbour who was a close relative of Nicole's father. She had been clearly distraught for days, almost inconsolable and when Kira finally asked her what was going on she gave her an E-mail that was sent to her by the American Government.

She took the piece of paper straight away to Sarah; it was one of the most compassionate things she had ever done to her foster daughter. Unfortunately the contents of the letter would prove to not be so kind. It contained some truly terrible news.

Sarah was lying on her front on one of the bunk beds reading a book when Kira walked in, followed by Janet. Kira had been crying heavily, her cheeks streaked with tears and her eyes were all puffy and swollen.

"What's the matter, Kira? What's happened?" She asked sitting up.

"Something really bad has happened, Sarah" Kira said, when she was finally able to pull herself together enough to actually talk.

"What?" Sarah asked wearily, she didn't like where this conversation was going.

"It's about Nicole."

"What about her?"

But Sarah had the feeling she already knew what Kira was about to say to her and she could tell from the way that Kira was crying that it wasn't going to be good news either.

"Well they were only a couple of hours away from New York, when something happened to the ship. You see the thing is the Nazis have never attempted to attack America before and everyone assumed that America was safe, but the truth of the matter was they weren't. There was a German submarine laying in wait close to the ship and when it was issued the orders it let of a rocket that hit the ship head on. The ship was completely destroyed in the initial explosion. There was nothing left, there were no survivors. I'm sorry, darling, but Nicole's dead. The only comfort is she would have suffered no pain," Kira explained.

Sarah felt like someone had punched her straight in the lunges, all the air seemed to be sucked out of her and she couldn't breath anymore. She had just lost her very best friend.

"No, this isn't fair. Why is this happening, Kira? Nicole was innocent, she wouldn't have hurt a fly, why did they have to kill her?" Sarah asked, feeling like her whole life had come crashing down around her and she was powerless to stop it.

Kira just shook her head sadly in answer. She didn't know either.

Sarah turned over onto her front and burst into tears of anger and pain. She hid her face under her blanket.

Kira got up of her bunk and went over to Sarah. She gently placed a hand on Sarah's head and ran her fingers through her hair, not really knowing what else to do.

For several days after Sarah seemed to be in a world of her own, not hearing or seeing anyone. It wasn't as bad when Nicole left for America because she knew she was safe and she may one day see her again. But now Nicole was dead, a whole life had been wasted and such hopes had been shattered.

What brought Sarah back to reality was when Kira gave her the news that they would be leaving for Sweden the next day. Then she screamed out she didn't want to go to Sweden, she wanted to stay in England where it was safe, like Nicole should have done.

But she had to go, whether she wanted to or not. Kira and Stephen were her legal guardians and where they went she had to go. She had no choice on the matter and yet again her whole world was about to turn upside down as she was once again leaving for a new country and a new life.

CHAPTER TEN

The next morning they locked the door to their Anderson shelter for the very last time and made their way over to the waiting coach. There were a large crowd of friends standing by the coach, waiting to say goodbye to them. They gave them good luck cards and food for the long journey ahead. It would be the last time Sarah would see any of these friends, she was about to leave England and travel to a country she knew nothing about.

The journey itself was long and uncomfortable, there were many stops they had to make before they reached Dover and in doing so they would have to pass very close to the Capital. It was a dangerous route to take at the moment as the roads would be fraught with dangers, from unexploded bombs to collapsing buildings. All it would take was the smallest of tremors and the coach could be crushed under an avalanche of rubble.

Around midnight the next night a loud explosion suddenly woke Sarah up. The whole of the large cruise liner that was taking them to Sweden seemed to shudder and shake. Sarah started to wonder whether the ship was sinking, she could hear a lot of screaming and shouting directly outside their cabin door.

Sarah slid out of her bed and walked quietly over to the porthole. They were getting very close to Gothenburg. It would take another hour or so to dock and reach safe land. But at the speed they were travelling at the moment they might not get there at all.

Outside the sky was completely clear and dozens of stars shone brightly into the gloomy darkness. There was a full moon that night and a sure sign of bad luck if it was ever needed.

But that wasn't what Sarah was looking at. A couple of yards North East of the ship a submarine was emerging eerily from the murky depths of the sea. The moon reflected of its smooth surface, giving the submarine its eerie appearance. Sarah was just hoping and praying it wasn't German.

Bombs were falling everywhere. Water splashed against the windows of the ship as the bombs broke its surface.

She heard a shuffle from behind her, then a hand touched her shoulder, making her jump violently. She turned to face Janet who was standing behind her. Janet looked at her in fear; she looked so small and innocent in the dark.

There was a loud knocking on the door and someone yelled through the door, telling them to put on their lifejackets and remain in their cabins.

"Mum, what's going on?" Janet asked, in a small scared voice, as Kira took their lifejackets from under their beds.

"I don't know, darling," Kira said, handing Sarah a lifejacket, which Sarah handed to Janet.

"Don't worry, we'll reach the dock very soon" Kira said, seeing the worried expression on Sarah's face.

"How long do you think it will take to get there?" Sarah asked.

"Probably half an hour or so" Kira answered her.

"Half an hour. God, Kira, we could be blown to kingdom come by then!" Sarah cried out, looking terrified.

"Oh no" Kira reassured her. "We'll be okay. They've got bigger fish to fry. This place is full of Royal Navy war ships."

Sarah gave a heavy sigh and sat down on her bunk bed.

It took a further two hours before the ship was given clearance to dock at Gothenburg.

Unlike Dover had been Gothenburg seemed deserted. A guard sat in a far corner, writing by the light of a small candle, obviously the electricity was out again.

Gothenburg port was small, crumbling and old, but in a strange way, quaint. The bricks were old and decaying, through lack of attention. The place was freezing cold, the wind howled through the enormous archways of the building like some lost animal.

As they walked through the small stream of people there was no sign of Stephen. Kira grumbled angrily to herself as she scanned the crowds for a glimpse of her husband, but she couldn't see him. He had promised her that he would be there.

As they walked through the exit of the building a Swedish soldier was waiting by an army truck. He was wearing an ordinary camouflage uniform with a Swedish flag sewn crudely onto his left arm. He had greasy looking black hair that was swept back over his head. He had an unshaven face, with a scar running down one side of it. A black revolver hung visible from his utility belt, while a belt of bullets ran across his chest from his shoulder.

Kira walked up to him to shake his hand and Sarah noticed how tiny he was. Kira wasn't very tall, only five foot six. But this soldier was even smaller. Sarah had always assumed that you needed to be a certain height to enlist in the army.

"You are Mrs. Collins, I believe?" he asked, as he shook her hand. He spoke excellent English with only the smallest hint of an accent.

"Yes, that's correct and you are?"

"My name is lieutenant Turchisi. I am what you could call your husbands right hand man. But I will be moving units soon. So you will soon see the back of me," the lieutenant explained. He chuckled at his own feeble joke. Sarah took an instant dislike to him.

"Where's my husband, lieutenant?" Kira asked impatiently.

"Your husband is conducting a training course with ground troops. He says to send his apology, but you see it's absolutely vital we get ground troops used to fighting on the battle field" the lieutenant explained.

"Right, thanks for telling me" Kira said, the lieutenant seemed to not notice this sarcasm.

"Follow me please and I will show you to your transport" the lieutenant said, gesturing to the army vehicle.

The truck was a typical army truck. The whole thing was encrusted in mud and the roof was just really a set of poles that had a camouflaged waterproof sheet thrown over them and nailed to the side of the truck.

Kira sat at the front of the truck with the lieutenant, who talked continuously to her about the battles he had been involved in with Stephen. Sarah sat in the back with Janet. They had to sit on hard benches while the truck rattled and shook continuously. It didn't absorb any of the bumps and potholes in the road. The poles holding up the sheet were badly in need of repair and Sarah kept glancing up at them, fearing that they might collapse at any moment.

Janet complained throughout the entire journey. All Sarah wanted to do was ring her neck.

The journey they were taking from Gothenburg to where Stephen was stationed would take the best part of a day. The only time they would stop was at Falkenberg to have lunch and get necessary supplies. But they wouldn't be stopping at any other time; it was far too risky.

By midday the sun was at its peak and the heat was getting unbearable. Sarah lay on her back with her knees drawn up and her arms folded over her chest. Janet leant against the cover waving a book in front of her face in a desperate attempt to cool down. Kira sat in the front seat, staring straight ahead of her, enjoying the cooling breeze that came with sitting in the front seat of the vehicle.

Chapter Eleven.

They arrived at the base in Copenhagen at six o'clock that evening, having made good progress, even with Janet's constant complaining. The base was spread out over a large field. To the left were the bunkhouses and first aid tents. On the right were the buildings where the planes and army vehicles were kept stored. In the centre of the field was a large, flat roofed concrete building. This was where it all happened; everything that was organised was planned in that building. Later on Sarah was to find out the building was also used for training and preparing young recruits for battle.

Kira followed the lieutenant through the crowds of soldiers that were standing around, smoking and talking, awaiting their next orders. They all stared at Kira, Janet and Sarah as they walked past them. They had no woman on that base, women were situated elsewhere. To the men on Stephens base women might as well be on a totally different planet.

The lieutenant spotted Stephen talking to a large group of trainee soldiers and started to walk in his direction. Stephen glanced up and saw them coming towards him. He excused himself from the group of soldiers and walked towards them.

Kira smiled happily as he walked up to her. They stood still for a couple of minutes just staring at each other. Then Janet impatiently cleared her throat and they looked down at her. Stephen stepped forward and gave Kira a hug and kiss.

Then he turned to Janet and gave her a big bear hug. He took hold of Janet's bag and led the way to the barracks.

The rooms weren't very spacious and the walls were covered with a cheap white emulsion. As Sarah ran her hand across the wall the paint flaked of onto it. The beds weren't any better, they squeaked whenever you moved and had sagging, wet mattresses because of the amount of condensation that hung in the air. The room was damp and cold, stank of sweat and was altogether uncomfortable.

The large bathroom was no better. There was just the one huge bathroom for every body, which included Sarah, Kira and Janet. It was a long, dimly lit room, and separated into specific sections. At the far end were the toilets. Then there were the shower cubicles, which had very thin waterproof boards and white, almost see-through curtains so the person using the shower could enjoy some kind of privacy. The washbasins were in an even worse condition. They were meant to be white, but had become stained with age and most of them leaked. The taps gave little more than a trickle of water and there was no hot water. Luxuries like that were far too expensive in times of war. Not even the showers had hot water, most of the time the soldiers were so dirty they didn't even care. The only way to get hot water was to boil it over a fire. Electricity was also kept down to a minimum. The only time that electricity was permitted was for lighting and computers. If anybody was caught using electricity for any other purpose they could receive a severe punishment.

Sarah glanced around the room and dropped her suitcase on the floor. She glanced over at Stephen and Janet. He was pointing things out to her, explaining what each of the planes on the runway did. Sarah felt a pang of loneliness and jealousy come over her.

But she knew he wasn't her father and one day she would leave them. She had never felt close to them. To them Janet would always come first and she accepted that. But that made her wonder why they had ever adopted her in the first place. Was it pity for a child who had just lost both her parents so tragically? Or were they forced into adopting her by someone and if they had by whom? She would rather be left in the adoption home, getting teased and abused by the other kids, than live with a family who didn't love her.

There was a loud knocking at the door and a soldier entered, walking very stiffly. He was very thin and his flesh seemed to fall away at his chin.

But as he saluted Stephen and Stephen nodded in acknowledgement it was obvious Stephen was of much higher rank.

"Sergeant, sergeant Parker requests that you report immediately to the control room, your regiment has just reached its desired destination and is even now awaiting further instructions. But orders can not be issued without your approval as you are in charge of this regiment at present, sergeant" the young private practically barked.

"Well I must admit that regiment moved swiftly, I hadn't expected them to reach the village until night fall. But I would have also thought it would have been too soon to launch an attack. But if I must then I must, because as you so eloquently put it that is my regiment" Stephen said with a rather annoyed look upon his face, underneath that annoyance Sarah could also sense a certain degree of concern.

"Well, sergeant?" the private asked, waiting for Stephen's next order.

"Yes, private, you may tell Parker that I am on my way and I am bringing some important guests, so everyone had better be on their best behaviour, do you understand me?" Stephen answered.

"Yes, sergeant." The soldier saluted him and left the room.

Stephen turned back around and walked to a long and narrow locker in the corner of his room. Everything he now owned was in that locker; all other possessions had been destroyed along with the house. He opened the locker door and started to go through his belongings.

Sarah tried to put such thoughts to the back of her mind; she found it too painful to think about it. She just wanted to forget about everything that had happened in England. Sarah was the type of person who tried to conceal her feelings. She kept them bottled up inside her; this couldn't be good though. It wasn't healthy keeping your emotions concealed like that. Especially at Sarah's age, something she could regret later on in life.

Janet sat perched on the windowsill, staring at the planes as she watched soldiers running frantically around them, preparing them for their journey. Planes were already being eased into position for take off. It was amazing how swiftly things were done on the air base.

Stephen had now changed into battle gear and was checking everything was in perfect working order.

"Right, Kira, you and Janet will follow me up to the control room. When we get up there I'll introduce you to the other sergeant" Stephen said, straightening out his uniform.

"Okay, what about Sarah?" Kira asked, pointing towards Sarah.

"She can come if she wants to" Stephen grumbled, not really caring either way. "Now get a move on, we have to hurry," he said urgently, heading towards the door.

"Right come on, Janet, let's go. You don't want to miss all the excitement do you?" Kira asked looking at Janet, who was still perched on the windowsill.

"Yeah, I'm coming" Janet muttered, getting down of the windowsill and walking over to Kira.

They started to walk across the room to the door. Then at the door Kira stopped and looked at Sarah who stood in the middle of the room, staring at them.

"Are you coming, Sarah?" she asked.

"Yeah, alright" Sarah answered, walking across the room towards them.

Kira shut the door behind them and they walked down the corridor. Stephen was waiting impatiently at the entrance for them. He opened the door for them and shut it securely behind him.

They made their way across the runway towards the control building. They could already feel the ground shake as the planes took of.

As they passed through the hundreds of frantically moving soldiers, Sarah saw not only aircraft but a vast amount of army vehicles as well, more than likely these were the types of vehicles used to move Stephen's regiment to its desired location.

"Wow, this place is amazing, Nicole would have loved to see this," Sarah murmured quietly to herself. She looked curiously at the array of equipment that was spread out into sections. The aircraft would take of first to begin the air raids on Germany. Then the army vehicles would start the journey across land, take the short journey across the sea that separated Denmark and Sweden. Travel through war torn Denmark, then finally reach Germany where the land attacks would begin.

The main building was enormous, with three floors and a massive cellar, but Sarah didn't quite know what the purpose of the cellar was. It was probably a magazine.

Kira quickly followed her husband up the stairs to the second floor. He passed through some double doors. As Janet went through them she swung the door back with all her force, hoping to hit Sarah in the face with it. But Sarah stopped the door with the palm of her hand.

But all that was forgotten when they stepped into the main control room. The first glimpse of the room left the two girls speechless. They stared around them in awe as soldiers passed them quickly to prepare for the attack. The main control room was a massive and incredibly long room with computers stretching the whole way around the room. There must have been millions of pounds worth of electrical equipment in this room alone. At the other end was a large window taking up the entire wall. It was there to give the people in the room a clear view of what was going on outside.

The place seemed to be in complete chaos as people rushed around, hastily completing their assigned tasks.

Kira followed Stephen as he walked over to a middle aged man. That was where their similarity ended though. This man was huge, well over two metres tall. He also had an air of authority about him. He stood with his chin tilted up and his back as straight as a pole. He had a bad habit of rocking backwards and forwards on his toes.

"Kira, I would like you to meet sergeant Parker, a good soldier and an even better friend" Stephen said, introducing Kira to the sergeant.

"Ah, it's a pleasure to meet you at last, Mrs. Collins. I've heard so much about you" sergeant Parker said, as he grasped her hand and shook it.

"It's a pleasure to meet you too, sergeant Parker" Kira said.

"I don't think you've met my daughter and foster daughter yet," Stephen said. "This is my daughter, Janet and my foster daughter, Sarah."

"Which one's your foster daughter?" the Sergeant asked, looking curiously at Sarah and Janet as if they were a new, undiscovered species.

"The older one with the red hair" Kira explained, pointing to Sarah.

"Yes, I thought as much. She doesn't resemble either of you at all, does she?" the sergeant commented. He looked Sarah up and down with a look of contempt on his face. Even now people treated orphans like some disease-infested creature that should be gotten rid of swiftly.

"No, she doesn't" Kira agreed, looking at Sarah, as if she wasn't really there, just a figment of the imagination.

Sarah stared at them, feeling her anger start to bubble over. Why did they treat her like this? Why did they try and act as if she was a creature with absolutely no emotions. She wanted to go up to them, smack them all in the face and yell, "stop ignoring me. I do exist you bastards. Treat me like a fucking civilised human being." But she didn't, she stood rooted to the spot, staring at them and feeling her anger build with each passing moment. She was clenching her fists so hard that she was leaving fingernail marks in the palm of her hands.

CHAPTER TWELVE

"Sergeant!" a young private suddenly called from a monitoring screen. "The first vehicles are entering Denmark's territory, sergeant."

"Ah, good, now we can get a bit of action, hey?" sergeant Parker exclaimed excitedly. He hurried over to the young soldier and peered eagerly over his shoulder at the monitor screen. The screen was illuminated by hundreds of tiny lights that Sarah would later discover represented each soldier, as there was a sensor in each backpack that gave the exact location of every soldier and more chillingly the death toll of each regiment.

"Ah, their just approaching Copenhagen" sergeant Parker muttered. He gestured for Stephen to approach him.

"You stay here and look after the kids," Stephen said to Kira. She nodded and placed a hand on Janet's shoulder.

"You two stay out of trouble, okay?" Stephen said looking at them.

"Yes, dad" Janet answered. Sarah just nodded her head.

"Lieutenant Gibbons, are you receiving me?" Stephen asked, speaking loudly into the radio.

There was a sudden crackle of static. Then they could just make out the sound of a voice.

"Yes, Roger, I'm receiving you" lieutenant Gibbons said.

"Can you state your destination?"

"Yes Roger, we are three miles North east of Copenhagen and are approaching fast."

"Is there anything going on at the moment?"

"No, Roger. Everything seems quiet at the moment. Copenhagen seems to have taken quite a hit, Roger, but apart from that everything appears to be clear."

"How badly hit is Copenhagen?"

"Very badly, Roger. No large buildings visible are standing. Civilian casualties should be high. Nothing seems to have escaped the attack, Roger," the lieutenant explained.

"Now state your destination."

"Entering Copenhagen right now, Roger. Hang on, I can see something in the distance, it's hard to tell whether it's the enemy, Roger."

"It can't be one of ours. We don't have any other units out there at present" sergeant Parker muttered to Stephen.

"State its Nationality" Stephen ordered, ignoring sergeant Parkers comment.

"Affirmative, I can't from this distance. Wait a minute ... it's getting closer. There's some sort of red symbol on the left shoulder. I can't quite make it out, they're still too far away."

"Well, try" Stephen said, angrily grinding his teeth together in his frustration.

"Roger, it's a Nazi. If there's one of them then there's bound to be more. They wouldn't send out just one of the bastards, he'd be dead in no time."

"Right, I want a full scale scan of the whole of Denmark. I want every movement the Nazis make monitored. We're not failing this time" Stephen ordered. A young private behind them saluted and ran of.

By this time everyone in the room had stopped what they were doing and were listening attentively to the conversation between Stephen and the lieutenant. Sarah and Janet glanced up at Kira, whose face was contorted with concentration. Sergeant Parker stood behind Stephen, his head tilted to one side so he could listen carefully to everything that was being said.

"Right, lieutenant, continue on your current course. I'm sending the unit behind you west so as to confuse the bastard," Stephen ordered.

All of a sudden the entire room was filled with the sound of skidding vehicles and the sound of gunfire.

"Oh, shit!" the lieutenant screamed in utter panic.

"Lieutenant, can you hear me? I repeat can you hear me?" Stephen asked in concern.

"Roger, I'm fine. The vehicle behind has been struck though. His engine is on fire. I can't be sure if there are any casualties or not."

A loud explosion echoed through the room. Then there was loud, continuous static as they lost contact through the force of the explosion.

"Lieutenant, can you hear me?" Stephen cried out, changing frequencies, as he looked frantically through the charts.

"Roger, I hear you" the lieutenant's voice came through faintly, when they were able to regain contact with him.

"What just happened there?"

"The vehicle behind me exploded, Roger."

"Can you give me the identification of the soldier driving the vehicle, lieutenant?"

"Private Matthew Adams, recruit number 623."

"Are there any more Nazis within your range, lieutenant?"

"Yes there are, Roger. They seem unaware of our presence though, Roger. Should we launch an attack on them, Roger?"

"No, leave them. I want to see what they do" Stephen said thoughtfully.

"Oh Jesus Christ almighty" Sarah muttered under her breath. She was totally mesmerised by what she was hearing, it was utterly terrifying but at the same time so exciting. She had never experienced anything like this before.

"Continue on your original course, lieutenant. Only if more Gerry turn up can you attack. Do you understand me?" Stephen ordered

"Yes, Roger, understood, Roger" the lieutenant answered.

There was silence in the room. The only noises that could be heard were the gentle hum of the vehicles engines and the rhythmic breathing of the lieutenant as he still held his portable radio transmitter close to his mouth. After a couple of minutes though his breathing started to quicken rapidly.

"Lieutenant is there a problem? I repeat is there a problem?"

"There are a large number of Nazis just entering the road ahead, Roger. There must be at least a hundred, Roger."

"Which way are they heading?"

"Straight for us, Roger."

"Are they showing any signs that they could attack you yet?"

"Not yet, Roger, but they seem to be doing something that I can't quite make out, Roger."

Stephen looked up at sergeant Parker with a worried expression. If there were a lot of Nazis then more would surely follow and Stephen's regiment was small and ill equipped. If they were attacked by a full sized Nazi regiment then they would stand no chance. It was starting to look more and more like they would have to abort the operation before it had even begun.

There was a sudden sound of gunfire. Everyone in the room jumped in fright. They all strained their ears to hear what was happening.

"Shit, Roger their shooting at us. They've seen us, what do we do, Roger?"

"Lieutenant, can you see any more Nazis?"

"There are another dozen or so behind them and they have their guns ready and loaded, they know that we're here, Roger."

"Why would they send in such a large volume of Nazis to attack one small British regiment? It seems like a foolish amount of man power is being wasted if you ask me" Parker asked baffled.

"Who knows how Hitler's mind works," Stephen muttered, glancing at the monitor screen. The Nazis seemed to be using some form of tactic, but he couldn't quite work out what it was.

"Damn, they have double the men we have" Stephen said, angrily hitting the table with his fist, causing everyone to jump in surprise.

"We may be able to pull this of. Such miracles have happened before. Give them a chance" Parker said.

Stephen straightened up from the table and started to pace around the room, growing more agitated with every step he took.

"Tell the lieutenant that the regiment will split up to try and confuse the enemy and hopefully make them a lot more vulnerable" Stephen suddenly ordered.

"Yes, sergeant" said the corporal at the main monitor screen. He turned to the men behind him and began to issue out orders to them.

Orders were given out for all the men to break up in to groups of three. For a minute or so it looked as if hope was on the horizon.

Sarah sat on one of the tables totally enthralled in what was going on. She felt the emotions of the battle wash over her like a tide over a beach.

"Ah Jesus, what the bloody hell was that?" the lieutenant cried over the radio. There was a loud explosion, the other vehicle behind the lieutenants exploded as it received a direct hit from a bomb.

"What's going on, lieutenant, I repeat, what's going on?" Stephen said in panic.

"There's even more Nazis, Roger. We can't carry on, we need to abort this operation immediately, Roger," the lieutenant cried out.

"You will abort the operation when I say, lieutenant. Now continue on your course and that's an order," Stephen said furiously.

Explosions could be heard clearly, they just kept coming and didn't seem to be easing.

Another soldier got the attention of Stephen and pointed to a monitor screen. It kept a recording of all the men who had been killed. Stephen stared at it in horror.

"Their dieing like flies. There's twenty down already," Parker observed over his shoulder.

"How many are privates?" Stephen asked the soldier, he completely ignored Brown.

"All of them, sergeant. They seem to be just attacking the privates, sir. Not one officer has been hit" the soldier informed him.

Stephen sighed in frustration and glanced at Kira. She stared straight back at him; her expression was calm. He looked back at the soldier who was patiently waiting for his next orders.

"Okay, tell them to abort the operation," he said finally, knowing that this was his only option.

There were murmurs and sighs of relief as orders were distributed for the regiment to return back to base.

"Roger, over and out" the lieutenant said thankfully, as sergeant Parker delivered the orders. He turned his radio of. But other radios hadn't been turned of and they could still clearly hear the agonising screams of soldiers as the Nazis gunned them down.

"Get them out of there!" Stephen yelled angrily, once again striking the table.

CHAPTER THIRTEEN

It wasn't the worst battle Stephen had been involved in since he arrived in Sweden, but what did make it bad was that he wasn't meant to play any part in this operation, he was still injured and was still unable to run properly on his leg, but he was a good commander and the men listened to him. He now harboured a mixture of feelings, mostly consisting of confusion and anxiety.

He wasn't used to navigating his troops in this manner, but he liked this regiment; they were almost as good as his own regiment. But this unit could never replace his men, as he had a hand in training them and knew exactly how they ticked, he could never get that sort of closeness out of any other soldiers. But until he was fit enough to fight again they would have to do.

Unfortunately the Nazis also seemed to know exactly how the mind of the British soldier worked. They somehow knew exactly the next move the British were about to make and every time the British tried to advance forwards to attack the Nazis would be there to stop them and force them to retreat yet again. The British couldn't see a way around this problem and they didn't know how the Nazis were staying one step ahead of them. It seemed that the only answer was that there was a spy amongst them.

As the orders for the retreat were issued Stephen gave a sigh of relief and for the first time since the beginning of this operation he actually sat down. He watched the screen as the little black dots turned around and headed back towards Sweden.

But as soon as the vehicle started to retreat the Nazis were in hot pursuit, continuing their attack on the now very vulnerable vehicle.

Stephen watched horrified as one of the men was actually shot out of the back of the army vehicle. Even from his position Stephen could imagine the limp body of the soldier tumbling out of the truck and rolling helplessly over the smooth tarmac of the roads.

A Nazi on a motorbike rode up behind the lieutenant.

Everyone heard him say out loud. "Don't think your getting me that easily, you bastard."

The engine of the vehicle groaned loudly as the lieutenant slammed down on the accelerator and tried to make the army vehicle go as fast as it possibly could, the whole time those present in the monitor room could hear everything that was going on.

Another noisy engine was heard going past the army vehicle and then a loud explosion followed.

"Oh, Jesus Christ!" the lieutenant screamed.

"What was that, lieutenant?" Stephen asked into the radio.

"A Nazis getting blown up, Roger," the lieutenant answered quite calmly now.

The lieutenant then focused his full concentration back on his driving. There was a German still directly behind him. He forced the vehicle to go to its maximum speed, leaving a dust cloud in his wake. Hopefully this would obscure the Germans view causing him to crash. He gave a sigh of relief as he saw the German veering of dangerously, the next moment the Nazi lost control of his bike completely and the front wheel caught on the ground and then in the blink of an eye the Nazi flew right over the handlebars of his bike, the

British vehicle leaving him staring into a cloud of dust.

"Ha ha, that's what you get for trying to attack the British, you bastard," the lieutenant cried out happily, as he eased his foot of his pedal.

"Lieutenant, is everything alright?" Stephens voice came through the radio.

"Yes, Roger, never felt better."

"Well stop messing about and get you're ass moving then."

"Yes, Roger."

"Now would you please state your destination" Stephen ordered.

"Just leaving Copenhagen. Will be approaching our own base shortly, Roger" the lieutenant said.

"Okay, look forward to hearing from you shortly then" Stephen said.

"Roger, over and out" the lieutenant said and switched of his radio.

"Right, Dougy, I want a full report of this mission on my desk in an hour. Don't leave anything out" Stephen ordered.

"Yes, sergeant" Dougy said.

Stephen turned around and left the navigation room with sergeant Parker. Kira quickly followed them with Sarah and Janet.

As soon as the planes that Sarah had seen taking of earlier started to touch down and the surviving pilots started to get out of their planes, Stephen went over to them. Janet followed closely behind him, looking very eager.

Sarah couldn't take anymore of this. She turned around and headed back towards the main control building. Just behind the building were the training fields. This was where the trainee soldiers were put through their paces.

Sarah didn't want to tell anyone, because in her own mind the idea sounded ludicrous. But she was starting to really consider enrolling in the army, this was something she had considered for a long time, but had never really pursued. But now especially after everything she had just witnessed, the subject was at the forefront of her mind. At least in the army she was part of something, because in the army she would be part of a number, she wouldn't be alone and she wouldn't be ignored. She knew the reason why Stephen and Kira ignored her though. The first time they saw Sarah instead of seeing a thin, ugly, mournful creature they saw something they could love and call their own. But two months later Kira miraculously fell pregnant with Janet. Before that happened the doctor told Kira the terrible news she was unable to conceive and therefore could never have children of her own. That's why they adopted Sarah. So when Kira fell pregnant with Janet everyone said it was a miracle. Kira had Janet who was born two months premature. She was born on the third of June at 3: 00 pm. Afterwards Sarah may as well have been invisible the way Kira and Stephen treated her. Instead they lavished all their attention on Janet. Later on Stephen confessed the reason they had acted that way towards her. When they found out

Kira was pregnant it seemed like a gift from God. They were just so happy when they had Janet that they simply forgot Sarah was there. From the moment Janet came out of the womb, the whole family treated Sarah like an outcast; after all she was just an orphan. Plus Sarah was the total opposite to Janet. Janet was clever, petite and pretty, which gave her a sweet innocence. Sarah on the other hand had suffered bad Dyslexia and her foster family had thought she was stupid, even saying so to her face. She was popular at school though, unlike Janet who was considered by everyone else to be nothing more than a spoilt brat. People had naturally warmed to Sarah's cheerful character and Janet had resented that. In Primary school, Janet had tried to make Sarah a victim of bullying. But it hadn't worked. Sarah was strong willed, never allowing the bullying get to her. So gradually the bullying had subsided until eventually it stopped altogether. But Sarah never forgot she was an outcast in her own adopted family. Now she didn't even have her friends to look to for support. She was on her own. She was good at putting up with pain though, mental and physical. So she knew she could cope with joining the army. She had the courage and the strength to do it. She felt it was her destiny. What she was born to do.

The approach of footsteps brought her back to reality. She turned abruptly around expecting Stephen or Kira to be walking towards her. Then she realised there was no chance of that happening as Dougy, Stephens latest recruit walked towards her.

"Hi, sergeant Collins sent me to find you" he said stating the obvious. "He said when I found you to tell you to return to the bunk houses."

"Typical, I knew he wouldn't come to find me himself" Sarah muttered angrily. "Why didn't he come to find me himself?" she then asked as an afterthought.

"He had other matters to deal with."

"What kind of matters?"

"He has to organise the troops. I don't know exactly what his doing" Dougy said.

"Yeah I'm sure. Was Janet with him?" Sarah retorted mournfully.

"No, his daughter wasn't with him. He won't let her go anywhere near the equipment, he says it's dangerous. She could hurt herself" Dougy said.

Sarah frowned at this explanation.

"His worried she'll start messing about with the equipment again and hurt herself badly, like she did last time," Dougy explained.

The incident he was referring to was when Stephen first took Janet to his base back in England. He was wanted by a new recruit who needed help with some equipment and turned his back of Janet for just two seconds. But that was enough time for Janet. She spotted a pocketknife lying on a bench and she picked it up. She tried to open it, moving the instrument really close to her face so she could see it better. She tried to prise it open with her fingers, to no avail. Then she spotted a tiny button on the handle of the knife. She pressed it. It suddenly sprung open, slashing Janet right across the cheek. Stephen had vowed never to take Janet to the base again. But now with war raging he had no choice but to just watch every move Janet made.

"Yeah well, Janet's very stupid at times, she has no common sense" Sarah muttered.

"You don't like Janet that much, do you?" Dougy commented, sitting down beside Sarah.

"No, not at all" Sarah said truthfully, staring at the field, where two captains were doing something with several objects that looked oddly like swords.

"Why don't you like her?" Dougy asked.

"She's a spoilt brat, always has been. She loves to show it as well. She's always so rude to everyone, especially me," Sarah said spitefully.

"Why?" Dougy asked. He didn't know why but he couldn't imagine Janet being rude to anyone. She seemed like such a nice kid when he first met her. But obviously appearances could be deceiving.

"I don't know. She gets jealous easily. I don't know why, it's bloody stupid. Stephen and Kira aren't even my real parents" Sarah said.

Dougy looked curiously at Sarah for a minute. The curiosity was taken over by sympathy as he got the distinct impression that Sarah was one of those children that nobody seemed to want and was lumbered onto the first family that wanted her.

"I didn't know you weren't his daughter," He said.

"Well that doesn't surprise me" Sarah commented sarcastically, but she didn't look at him.

"He don't like you then?" Dougy asked.

"No he doesn't, although I wouldn't quite call it loathing," Sarah said.

"That's a bit harsh, isn't it?"

"It's the truth though. Janet is the most important thing in the world to him," Sarah muttered glumly.

"That isn't the truth. You probably have other qualities that Janet doesn't possess" Dougy remarked.

"Do you think so?" Sarah asked, looking at Dougy with a curious expression on her face.

"Yeah, I do" Dougy answered.

"Do you think I could join the army then?" Sarah asked, the slightest hint of excitement rising in her voice.

"Well you seem strong enough, you have the right attitude and you seem pretty smart. Yeah I think you would make a good soldier" Dougy remarked.

"How old do you have to be to join the army?"

"You have to be sixteen" Dougy explained.

"Do you think it would be possible for someone under the age of sixteen to join the army?"

"I don't know" Dougy said, frowning slightly now, wondering where this conversation was leading.

"How old were you when you joined the army?" Sarah asked curiously.

"Me, I was nineteen when I first joined the army" Dougy told her.

"How old are you now then?" Sarah asked.

"Twenty."

"God, you haven't been in the army that long, have you?" Sarah exclaimed in surprise.

"Nah, you don't get much training. A couple of months is enough. Then you get thrown out onto the battlefield and have to learn the rest by yourself" Dougy said.

"Wow, really?"

"Well there is a war on. They need the soldiers," Dougy pointed out.

Sarah just smiled in response, she seemed deep in thought.

"So how old are you then?" Dougy, asked wanting to break the silence.

"Me, fifteen, nearly sixteen" Sarah told him.

"You act very mature for your age" Dougy commented.

"Thanks."

"No you do. You'd be good for the army."

"That's the thing. I actually want to join the army. But because of my age I don't think anybody would even allow me to do so" Sarah explained.

"You don't know until you try" Dougy said.

"That's the problem. No one will listen to me, I am after all just a child," Sarah told him.

"Give it a try."

"It still won't work" Sarah grumbled.

"I could always put in a good word for you" Dougy said.

"Alright, you've got yourself a deal there. First we have to convince Stephen though, I'm capable of doing that. Then we have to persuade those of higher authority I'm capable of coping with the army" Sarah said thoughtfully.

"Wait a minute. Where did the 'we' come from?" Dougy asked.

"Well it was your idea, so you're going to help me. I can't do this on my own and you did offer. So you talk to those in command, while I will convince Stephen" Sarah explained.

"How come you only have to persuade sergeant Collins?" Dougy demanded.

"You got the better deal. You have no idea how strict Stephen can be," Sarah explained.

"Okay, you got yourself a deal there" Dougy said. They shook hands to seal the deal.

Sarah stood up and stretched all the muscles in her body until they clicked loudly in protest. Then she followed Dougy as they made their way towards the bunkhouses.

CHAPTER FOURTEEN

Dark rain hissed down heavily, running down the windows in long streaks. Lights glittered through the rain-covered windows like little stars.

There was occasional movement as a soldier ran across the concrete square in the centre of the bunkhouses. Apart from that everything was calm and peaceful; the total opposite of what had taken place earlier that day. As Sarah stared out the window she could hardly believe it was just an hour ago she was sitting by the fields discussing her plan with Dougy.

Stephen sat on his bed, cleaning his army boots vigorously. Every minute or so he would glance at Janet, who was dozing on a bunk bed. Sarah sat on the windowsill staring out of the window. On the windowsill beside her was a small book issued to all new recruits. Dougy had leant it to her. It gave her all the basic information she needed to know. She kept glancing over at Stephen, wondering whether now was the right time to have a word with him. But then she thought against it. He wouldn't allow her to join the army anyway. He probably wouldn't even think about it. He would just say no and then forget about it.

But then she reasoned there was no harm in trying. After all he might take her completely by surprise and say yes.

"Stephen" she said cautiously, after a moments thought.

"Hum?" He mumbled grumpily.

"What would you say if I said I wanted to join the army?" she asked.

"I would say you were mad, but it would be entirely up to you," he answered, still cleaning his boots and not even looking up at her.

"So you wouldn't mind if I enlisted in the army then?" Sarah said hopefully.

"I would mind. But as I said it would be entirely up to you" Stephen said; now reloading the gun.

"So you would allow me to do so then?" Sarah asked again.

"Why are you asking me all these questions, Sarah?" Stephen asked, finally looking at her.

Sarah looked at her feet and swallowed hard. She tried to gather her thoughts together. "Because, because I want to join the army."

The whole room went totally silent. All that could be heard was the hiss of the rain outside. Stephen stared at Sarah in disbelief. Kira, who was sitting next to Stephen looked from him to Sarah.

Every one waited to see how Stephen was going to respond.

"Your serious, aren't you?" he asked, looking at her thoughtfully.

Sarah merely nodded in response.

"Okay," he said simply. That was all he said. Just like that he was letting her join the army. This left Sarah feeling confused, but at the same time relieved.

"What?" Kira cried out angrily.

"But!" Stephen said. "I hope you know what you're letting yourself in for. Being in the army isn't easy, Sarah. Especially with a war on."

"I know, Stephen. But I feel I have to do this. I want to follow in my father's footsteps. That's why I want to join the army," Sarah explained. She completely failed to notice the worried expressions that Kira and Stephen exchanged as she mentioned her father.

"I just hope you know what you're letting yourself in for," Stephen said.

"Yeah, I know" Sarah said. She felt so relieved that Stephen had agreed to allow her to join the army, but she did also wonder why he put up such little resistance; he had barely said anything that would persuade her otherwise.

"We'll meet the sergeant major in the morning to discuss this matter and persuade him to let you join the army" Stephen announced.

Sarah glanced at her watch. It was nine fifteen. She could still taste the horrible bitter flavours of the armies so called evening meal. Still apparently the British army was getting proper food, while the German army was starving to death. At the moment the Nazis were eating whatever they could lay their hands on.

Sarah stripped down to her t-shirt and climbed into her sleeping bag. She could feel the horrible soft, over used mattress underneath her. She shifted her weight so that she wasn't lying on a spring sticking into her back. But all she achieved was to lay on another spring. She gave a heavy sigh and tried to forget about how uncomfortable her mattress was and just tried to go to sleep. Things would look better in the morning; well she hoped they would anyway.

*   *   *

But by the morning Sarah was in near hysterics. All sorts of negative thoughts were going through her mind. What if the sergeant major took one look at her and refused point blank to allow her to join the army? She would end up where she started.

She had to wait until gone six before she could get a shower, then she quickly washed her hair and brushed her teeth. She glanced at her appearance in the cracked mirror in the bathroom. She decided it would have to do; she then met up with Stephen. He straightened out her collar, nodded in approval and led her towards the main building.

The base was almost deserted. The regiments were out training and wouldn't return until nightfall. All Sarah could hear were the distant sounds of shouting and gunfire.

The rains of last night had subsided, leaving large puddles of water on the surface, making it very treacherous for the foot soldiers.

Stephen led her around the back of the control building and he entered through a fire exit. He led her up some concrete stairs that were lit dimly by one single bulb. They took them up to the first floor and Stephen walked down a long, dark, narrow corridor with the occasional skylight letting in blinding sunlight. They finally reached a large metal door that could only be accessed by punching a code into a keypad. Stephen entered the code as if he did it every day.

This door then took them to a much shorter corridor and they eventually approached a small wooden door. Stephen knocked on the door and took a step back.

"Enter!" they could clearly hear a loud voice command from inside the room.

Stephen opened the door and walked in. Sarah followed after him and shut the door behind her.

The room was large and cold. It had tiny windows that were high up so that Sarah was unable to see out of them.

The only light came from two flue cent light bulbs. The only furniture in the room was a large desk, three chairs and a large filing cabinet. It all looked so formal and intimidating. Sarah felt all her fears come rushing back in one fell swoop. But she knew there was no turning back now.

"Hello, sergeant, I hope your keeping well?" sergeant major Taylor said in a calm, clear voice. As Sarah looked at him her heart sank. He had a shaved head and stubble on his chin that gave him a rough look. He looked cold and unapproachable.

"I'm well, thank you, sir" Stephen said politely.

Stephen gave Sarah a gentle push and she walked tentatively up to the sergeant major's desk. She stopped in front of the major's desk and glanced at the disorganisation. There were papers and pens everywhere and there seemed to be no order to it.

"So this is the young girl you've been telling me about, is it?" the sergeant major asked.

"Yes, sir" Stephen said.

"She looks very young, how old is she?"

"She's fifteen, sir" Stephen answered.

"Fifteen, fifteen you say. Yet she wants to join the army at such a young age? She is still far too young, sergeant. The army is far too demanding for someone of her age. She wouldn't be able to cope with it. She's still only a child, sergeant. I don't think she even knows what being a soldier entails" Taylor criticised. He leaned forward onto the desk and stared at both of them.

"Sarah is fully aware of what being a soldier entails, sir" Stephen said, as Sarah glanced at him with a worried expression.

"She is still far too vulnerable, sergeant. She wouldn't be able to look after herself. The army is completely different from anything she may have seen on the T.V" Taylor said.

"As I said, sir, Sarah is fully aware of this fact" Stephen repeated.

Sergeant major Taylor stood up and walked casually around his desk. He walked over to Sarah and stood in front of her, staring at her. He was trying to see how long she could tolerate such pressure. She just stood still and stared straight back at him.

"She's very patient, isn't she" he commented. "More patient than some of my own troops. Is she any good at handling fire arms?"

"I don't know, sir. I haven't tried her with firearms yet" Stephen said.

"She has to be good with weapons, sergeant. If she isn't good with a gun she can't be a soldier. You have to have faster reflexes than the enemy. If you don't then you are as good as dead. In a life or death situation you would be down in a matter of seconds. A soldier has to be good with a weapon, sergeant" Taylor explained.

"Yes, sir."

"Even though I must admit she does seem to be patient, there is no proof she will be a good soldier as of yet."

As he said these words Sarah glanced with trepidation at Stephen. Stephen just stared straight ahead of him. While sergeant major Taylor stood in front of Sarah, studying her as if he could tell what her capabilities were from appearances alone.

He finally turned around and walked back around his desk to sit down. Stephen and Sarah stood there waiting with mounting trepidation for what he was going to say next.

"You do realise that if she does join the army the troops aren't going to be too happy about it, she is after all still really just a child," officer Taylor said. "But I can tell she has a pretty determined streak in her and that she will join the army no matter what."

Sarah glanced at Stephen, who looked back at her. As he gazed upon her face he saw a great likeness between her and someone else he knew long ago. She had the same features as this unnamed person. Her face held the same strength and power, but Stephen didn't yet know if she would share the same amazing talents as that individual. She had the same powerful hands;

although long and thin they were still incredibly strong for her age.

"Tell me, Sarah, why do you want to join the army?" officer Taylor asked Sarah, a question he had been eager to ask her almost as soon as she had entered his office.

"Well I always wanted to, sir. I wish to follow in my father's footsteps, sir. With all due respect, sir, the army does need more recruits. I'm able and willing and as good as any man, sir" Sarah said loudly and clearly. She showed no fear or signs of nerves and looked quite composed.

Officer Taylor sat there drumming his fingers on the table, deep in thought. Stephen and Sarah waited nervously for his verdict.

"Your father sounds like he has had quite an influence on your life. May I ask who your father was?" he asked.

Stephen grimaced. He had been afraid that such a question might come up.

"My father? He was called Marques Murray, sir" Sarah said. She was confused as to why he had asked her that question. After all why would he care about who her father was? They were in armies fighting for different countries. The chances that Sergeant major Taylor knew her father were very remote.

However as he heard the name 'Marques Murray', officer Taylor felt a cold fear surging through him. He blinked a couple of times and ground his teeth together.

"So you were fostered by sergeant Collins. Am I correct, sergeant?" the officer asked, turning his attention back to Stephen.

"Yes, sir."

"So what do you think of your foster daughter wishing to join the army then, sergeant?"

"Well I think she is perfectly capable of doing it, sir. She is very quick at picking things up and will become a good soldier with time. I recon she will make a fine soldier, sir" Stephen said truthfully.

"Of course, that is a matter of opinion, sergeant" officer Taylor commented. "How well educated is she?" he asked, this was a question Sarah had been dreading.

"I'm afraid she is Dyslexic, but it isn't severe, sir. She can read and write, sir. But she does struggle a bit" Stephen explained.

"That is no problem, sergeant. You will find a certain amount of soldiers can't read and write well. No, that's not a problem. But as long as she has mastered the basics then that shouldn't be a problem" officer Taylor said. Sarah could still hear the doubt in his voice though.

Sarah found herself holding her breath. Her patience was starting to wear thin and she was getting slightly fed up with answering all these questions. All she wanted to know was whether the answer was yes or no?

Officer Taylor sat deep in thought again. He sighed heavily and looked up at Sarah. His face softened and he smiled for the first time. His face suddenly looked completely different, much younger and kinder looking. She could now see the man behind the soldier.

"It seems the decision has already been made for me. Tomorrow I will give word to higher authorities and then you may be allowed to enrol in the army," he said finally.

Sarah felt her heart lift. Suddenly her whole future looked so different. She glanced at Stephen who was smiling with pleasure. He gazed back at her and she grinned uncontrollably. She had done it; at last she was going to be a soldier.

PART TWO

CHAPTER ONE

It was three years ago exactly that war had broken out. Two years before that Gavrian Hitler had been elected chancellor of Germany. At the time of the elections Gavrian had boasted to the German people he could bring prosperity to the country like it could only dream of and make Germany the most powerful country in the world. What's more they had believed him, it seemed they had shut out the rest of the world and would only listen to Hitler. Even though the world pleaded with them to be cautious about Gavrian Hitler. Everybody but the Germans could see what Hitler was becoming. He was the exact image of his long distant relative, Adolf Hitler. He put fear into the heart of those who opposed him and gradually moved up the political ladder by using force and aggression. If anyone tried to disagree with Gavrian's political ambitions for Germany they became an instant outcast, disowned by family and friends. Even worse they would receive severe punishment, sometimes even death. Gavrian refused to accept anyone who disagreed with his ideas. He pursued his dreams with a bloodthirsty hunger. He would achieve his goal at any cost and would destroy anyone who dared stand in his way. His ideas were based entirely on his own beliefs and those of his distant relative, Adolf Hitler. Adolf Hitler had been related through Gavrian's mother's side and Gavrian worshiped him like some would worship a God. As the months led up to the election many people worshiped Gavrian in very much the same way he worshiped Hitler. The streets had been lined with posters saying 'Hail Hitler'; they had adorned them with two pictures. One was depicting Adolf Hitler and the other of Gavrian. On the day of the election the whole of Germany came to a complete stand still. They eagerly awaited the results, even though the final outcome was only too clear to all present. As the announcement came through that he was chancellor of Germany fireworks were let of everywhere in celebration. It was like the new Millennium all over again. The celebrations went on for days. There. Germany this was an extra long bank holiday and one massive celebration. But Poland were somewhat sceptical of this new German Chancellor. The previous German Chancellor had died suddenly in mysterious circumstances and they didn't trust this newly elected predecessor. They feared his beliefs in Hitler would cause him to try and invade them again. If this happened then the piece of Europe would be broken. But several years passed and nothing happened. Germany was silent. Unfortunately that period of calm tranquillity was short lived. As the next elections for Poland were approaching things suddenly took a turn for the worst. Germany suddenly launched an attack on Poland. It seemed Germany had been waiting for just the right moment to strike. When it did it attacked with it's full army and with no warning what so ever. As The Polish leader was ill and weak he wasn't able to summon orders properly. Germany gained ground with alarming speed. Poland had a small, weak army, which was unprepared for such a strong attack from such a powerful enemy. They had to literally surrender within the first twenty-four hours of the attack. Poland was forced to literally plead with other countries for help. The only country that would listen to their pleads was Great Britain. But it would take too long for their troops to reach Poland to be of any help. Poland was unprotected and quickly defeated. Even when NATO sent ground troops to help it was already too late. The Polish Government was forced into the far northwesterly part of Poland and made to surrender. Russia didn't even acknowledge what was going on in their neighbouring country. They completely refused to deploy their troops to help Poland. So Poland had to try and battle on with what army it had left to keep control of its country. But it was all to no avail. Within the twenty-four hours that the German army had started its surprise attack on Poland they had taken control of the entire country and Poland was practically begging on its knees. NATO tried every thing within its power to stop Germany and make it surrender. But Germany just had too strong a hold on Poland and there was nothing any one could do to stop it. The German army and Gavrian knew that if they had control of Poland they would have a great advantage. They could now take control of the Polish army to strengthen their own forces and launch attacks on other countries. This came only too soon, firstly on the Czech republic and then Austria. Gavrian was beginning to do what many people feared he would do, launch an attack on Europe. Meanwhile Britain were sending troops across France, through Belgium and the Netherlands to get to Denmark. From there they could easily reach Poland and attack the German army to make them surrender. But things were never quite that simple. The Germans had other ideas. Using the Polish army to back them up and strengthen their already immensely powerful forces Germany launched a mounted campaign on Austria. Even though Austria was more prepared for this attack then Poland had been, even their army wasn't powerful enough to fight Gavrian's strengthening grasp over Europe. In a matter of days they had control of Austria as well. At this point France and Spain reluctantly joined forces with the British army to try and stop the German army from invading any more countries. It was around this time that the British Prime Minister tried to get Gavrian to sign the ill-fated peace treaty. But none of this distracted Gavrian from his grand plans; he continued his invasion of Europe. The more countries the Germans took over the more hostages they seized control of. In every country they invaded they would take every man capable of fighting and that man was forced to fight for the Nazis. If they refused then they were tortured until they resisted. If they still refused to fight then they were shot to death along with the rest of their family. The German army was now so vast it was larger than the British, French and Spanish forces put together. After that it was a continuous battle to try and stop the German army progressing any further. Then the Germans suddenly turned around and with no warning started to attack the British, French and Spanish troops. They were slowly forced out of Poland because the Polish winter had begun and there was a shortage of food; the soldiers were beginning to catch Pneumonia, amongst other diseases. It affected the German army as well, but they had Polish troops, who were used to the harsh weather conditions. The war got progressively worse from there on and now the whole of Europe was involved and it had turned into the European war everybody had feared. All the other continents refused to get involved in this particular conflict. Africa was such a poor continent and had neither the resources nor the means to fight. Australia said it was too far away to get involved, because of its position it was too big a task to move the entire Australian army all the way over to Europe. America didn't want to get involved in another major war and it was also in recession and didn't have the funding to support the army. Germany started to bombard Britain's Capital and tried to invade Russia. The Russian army had been all the way on the other side of Russia and by the time they had reached the German army on the Westerly side of Russia, Germany had already gained too much ground. Britain knew that if Germany had control of Russia they could then launch an attack on Asia. But far from being scared Asia seemed to be supporting Germany and Japan actually helped Germany with it's attack on Russia. Then as if things just couldn't get much worse, they did. Gavrian ordered all of his army to turn around and launch an attack on France. He was trying to reach British soil. He saw Britain as the reason why Germany had lost the other two wars and he was wreaking his revenge. With the threat that Germany would do exactly that Britain and France retreated back onto French soil. They were trying to stop Germany from gaining power over France, as they would then be in a perfect position to attack England. After that it was a continuous battle between Germany and the rest of Europe, with neither side gaining nor loosing control of anything. The Germans refused to retreat from France and the British refused to stop their attacks on the German army. No one seemed to be winning and none were loosing. It was a continuous battle to the end and nobody was going to give in.

These thoughts were imprinted on the minds of every soldier as they marched neatly in lines along the dirt tracks near Braintree. Many old bases such as this had been reopened to cope with the large volume of troops that had to be trained for the war effort. The tracks had been turned into watery silt by over night rain, making the paths treacherous to even walk along. Sarah Murray could think of a number of other different places she would rather have been than this. But her old life had been completely eradicated. Their old house and the rest of the town where she had grown up had been utterly destroyed by the Nazis. Now Sarah was back on English soil, with no friends or family, feeling more isolated than ever.

She marched solemnly alone the slick and slippery path, trying to keep in perfect formation with the rest of the company. She was the youngest person in the company and the only girl. This meant every one despised her and treated her as such. When the sergeant, who was the only one who gave her the slightest hint of respect, wasn't present the other soldiers made her do their chores for them, often bullying her into doing so.

But Sarah just put up with it. She knew she would soon be moving regiments back to Sweden and among people she knew. But for the moment she was stuck in this God damned, bloody awful excuse of a regiment, where every one hated her for who she was.

The sergeant suddenly barked out an order and the regiment came to a stop. The sergeant walked slowly down the line, doing an inspection of every uniform. He pointed out every crease, loose button and any other fault he could find. As he came to Sarah he looked her up and down and then made a face. He could never find anything wrong with her uniform; it was always immaculate, with every button straight and every crease in its proper place.

"Attention!" he bellowed, as he returned to the front of the line. "Company march on."

They continued their march up the track, coming into view of the base. With its old bunkhouses and tiny, freezing cold buildings this training base was quite possibly the worst in England.

"Come on you, lazy bastards, the war won't wait for you. Just think in another month we'll be in France and showing those good for nothings bastards what we're really made of!" the sergeant screamed out happily at them. He smiled smugly, an ugly smile that showed up every wrinkle and scar on his face. He had a shabby appearance that was unshaven and dirty. He was in a worse state than his soldiers. Definitely not the face anyone would expect to be that of a sergeant.

The regiment marched sombrely through the main gates to the base and the privates that stood guard at the gates clicked their heels together and saluted the passing regiment. The sergeant nodded his approval.

When the entire regiment had entered the main square and marched into the centre of it the sergeant barked out the orders to halt.

"Stand at ease" he ordered. The regiment followed these orders and stood calmly waiting for their next orders.

"Your all improving, lads. But none are as yet good enough in combat. That is why the colonel has decided to send you pretty boys on a nice holiday to Denmark" the sergeant explained. "So we are going to teach you as much as possible in what little time we have. So as you fucking lazy bastards can be totally prepared for the unexpected. Which could prove impossible as most of you can hardly look after yourselves, let alone anybody else. I warn you though, if one single one of you puts a foot wrong on the battle field I shall take great pleasure in inflicting the punishment on you myself."

"Okay that's all I have to say for the time being. Attention!" The regiment rigidly snapped their legs together. "Dismissed!" the sergeant screamed loudly and the whole regiment broke up. Sarah as usual wondered of by herself, away from the others.

"Private Murray, I would like a word with you in my office, now!" the sergeant called out to her, before she headed of towards her bunker.

"Yes, sergeant" she said. She turned around and headed toward the sergeant.

She followed him obediently as he marched straight to his office. A tiny bunker that was always cold, even in the middle of summer, when most soldiers were suffering through heat exhaustion because of their heavy and suffocating uniforms.

Sarah closed the door behind her and stood to attention in front of the sergeant's desk, waiting for what he had to say.

"Now you have been in the army for what? Five or six months. Yet you seem to be progressing more rapidly than any other soldier I've ever trained. You show great potential for some one so young. One day you may even make it to the top, if the army doesn't throw you out at the end of the war that is" the sergeant observed, he leaned back heavily in his chair, causing the ancient relic to squeak loudly in protest.

Sarah stood patiently, eagerly anticipating his next words, wondering where all this was leading and what it meant for her.

"It seems to me, the major and indeed everyone else agree that your skills are wasted in England and should be put to use where they are needed. So sergeant Collins has pacifically requested that you be sent back to Sweden to complete your training there" the sergeant explained, for some reason not sounding at all happy about the situation.

"Permission to speak, sergeant" Sarah said.

"Permission granted, private."

"When will I be sent back to Sweden, sergeant?" she asked.

"Tomorrow private. You must be packed and ready by 06:00 hours tomorrow morning, private. The safest time to fly. Sergeant Collins will pick you up on the main runway and take you back by silent copter," the sergeant explained.

"Permission to speak, sergeant" Sarah said again.

"Permission granted."

"Am I really ready to go through my final stages of training, sergeant?" she asked.

"After careful consideration and from what we have seen of your skills we have agreed that yes, you are ready. So everybody is in agreement that you should be sent back to Sweden," the sergeant said.

"Is that all, sergeant?" Sarah asked.

"Yes, private, that is all. Dismissed" the sergeant said.

Sarah saluted sharply and turned to face the door. She marched to the door stiff backed and marching straight, determined to leave in style. She closed the door silently behind her and marched down the concrete stairs. When she was out of earshot of the sergeant she leapt into the air and gave a small shout of joy.

She walked rapidly back to her bunkhouse, passing a grieving soldier on the way. He had just learnt that his wife and his baby girl had been killed in an air raid. Now he had no family to greet him at the end of the war when he would return home, scared and permanently damaged from the memories of the conflict.

Sarah took the rucksack issued to her by the army from under her bunk bed and started to neatly pack her belongings into it. As she was a private she owned very little and most was army uniform. She had just her uniforms, a changing of clothes and a few bare essentials. Apart from that she owned little else. Anything else she had owned had been destroyed when the bomb had struck her old house. The only other thing that was really hers was a beautiful silver cross. In the centre was a tiny diamond that seemed to glitter like a star, even in the darkness of night. It had been given to Sarah for a christening present by a distant cousin on April's side of the family. Sarah didn't know of any other family and didn't really want to. April's parents had died in a car accident when April was eighteen.

Which caused her out of desperation to marry Marques, who was her partner at the time. Marques was only too willing to offer her a shoulder to cry on. Within four months they were married, in a tiny ceremony with two other people they had never even met who served as witnesses. Ten months after that Sarah was born. That was when everything started to go wrong. Marques' parents had immigrated to America and had not been in touch with their son, furious that he had married someone so much younger than him. There was no one else to help support them, every one else had passed away or had immigrated to other countries like Marques' parents. At that point Marques was moved up in the ranks to lieutenant and that was when he started to slowly turn into the bastard

Sarah remembered so well, before he and April passed away in such mysterious circumstances.

"Attention!" the sergeant's voice echoed through the bunkhouse. It was 09:30 at night and it was the last inspection before the lights went out. Everyone scrambled into their positions by their bunks and stood to attention. The sergeant walked slowly around the room inspecting every man carefully.

As he came up to the soldier next to Sarah the sergeant glanced at his bed. The soldier had a look of absolute terror on his face as the sergeant walked over to his bed. The sergeant ripped back his neatly tucked in sheets and there on the pillow for the whole world to see was a bottle of half drunk whisky.

"Stand to attention!" the sergeant screamed furiously, as some of the soldiers started to fidget.

He walked back around the bed and stood in front of the now absolutely petrified private. He held the glass bottle in front of the private's face.

"What is this, private?" he asked.

"It's a bottle of whisky, sergeant," the soldier almost whispered in terror.

"Say it louder. I don't think they heard you at the back" the sergeant said cruelly.

"It's a bottle of whisky, sergeant!" the soldier almost screamed out loud, his voice was shaking with terror.

"Right, it's a bottle of whisky. A bottle of alcohol; private. Now you know the rules. They clearly state that no alcohol is permitted on army property. Do you know what happens to soldiers who disobey that rule, private?"

"They get punished accordingly, sergeant" the soldier answered.

"That's right. That's exactly what I'm going to do with you. Now get on the floor and do a hundred press ups. After that do a hundred fucking laps of the circuit. Then I'm going to make you run around the entire fucking campsite, until we have drained every last drop of alcohol out of your ugly stinking, worthless little body. Now get on that floor and start doing those fucking press ups. NOW!"

The helpless soldier dropped to the floor and started doing rapid press ups as the sergeant counted the times he did them.

Then the sergeant left him to continue his inspection. As he walked past Sarah he nodded his approval. Sarah gave no response to that compliment, they weren't to be taken lightly and if she responded to the compliment she would regret it later on.

But apart from the sergeants incredibly prompt nod of goodbye no one else seemed to care that she was leaving. In fact Sarah doubted they would even notice when she was gone She didn't resent this in any way though. She even felt sort of glad about it. She knew she wouldn't miss the place. It was part of a past she would rather forget. Like England really. She never wanted to go back to England again. She thought about this with a pang of loneliness as she sat back in the comfortable seats of the silent copter that was taking them to Sweden. It had been refuelled and they were now on their way.

She stared at the lush green landscape with a disconsolate feeling of knowing she may never see England again.

"So how are Kira and Janet, then?" she asked Stephen, who was sitting next to her. She hadn't been in touch with any of them since she had left for England.

"Their both fine. They've moved of the base now and Janet's started at her new school. It's a school for the soldier's children. It's just on the outskirts of Lund and a five-minute walk away from their new house. Janet hates it though; she says they all pick on her. But I said she'll just have to put up with it. It's the only school of its kind in Sweden" Stephen said.

"What did she say to that?"

"Well she wasn't too happy about it, lets just put it that way" Stephen answered scornfully.

"How's Kira doing?"

"Oh, she's fine. A little bit het up about this war, but then everybody is" Stephen said. There was something in his voice that concerned Sarah. She didn't know quite what it was, but he sounded worried about something.

As they neared the base the place looked relatively peaceful. Everybody was out training. As Sarah looked at the main navigation building she noticed that there were a number of people waiting for her arrival. Officer Taylor, major Johnson and corporal Adams. They all stood patiently watching the helicopter as it circled once and made a rather bumpy landing.

They walked over to the helicopter and watched as Stephen unlatched and opened the door. Sarah slid out of the helicopter and quickly climbed down the tiny steps of the copter. She stood to attention as they walked over to her. She saluted them, but only corporal Adams returned the salute, the others were staring at her intently, as if figuring her out.

"Sergeant, I need a quick word with you" Johnson ordered, leaning into the copters cockpit. Stephen followed major Johnson in the direction of the training fields behind the camp. Although they were hiding it as best as they possibly could Sarah could tell something was wrong by the looks on their faces. She watched them as they disappeared behind the main navigation building. Then they were out of earshot of her.

"So, private Murray. I hear you recently completed your training. Congratulations" corporal Adams said cheerfully, trying to divert her attention away from Stephen and the major.

"Yes, corporal, thank you, corporal" Sarah said, but she didn't smile gratefully at him, her attention was focused on Stephen and major Johnson.

"Your very young, aren't you. How old are you?" he asked.

Sarah almost smiled at this question. She was asked that question so many times she had grown quite used to it now.

"Sixteen, corporal," She answered.

He smiled and nodded and they started to walk slowly towards the main training building and away from Stephen and the major.

CHAPTER TWO

The tiny regiment sat on crates in one of the main bunkers. The first signs of dawn were starting to show in the east. It was freezing cold, the wind was howling and it was pitch black outside. The issued uniforms offered very little in the way of warmth.

A dawn attack was going to take place in Hamburg. It was to try and stop the Germans from advancing into Denmark. The plan was to eventually force them back into Germany. But as dawn approached the plan looked less likely to work with every passing moment.

Sarah listened intently to the instructions given out by major Johnson. She was going to join another private who would keep an eye on her throughout the mission. This private had completed his training some months ago and Stephen thought he was now ready to have a young private join him and learn from his experience. It all seemed rather confusing to Sarah at the moment though.

Two other regiments were to join them when they reached Copenhagen and then they would all break up into two groups. Sarah's half would head east, while the other half would head west.

"Right that will be all for now. Good luck" major Johnson said, coming to the end of his little speech. He glanced around at the group of weary soldiers; his eyes rested on Sarah. "Dismissed!" he barked.

Everyone stood up from the crates with relief. They walked out of the bunker picking up any necessary equipment on the way. They all chatted amongst themselves as the private Sarah was to accompany walked up to her side.

"I didn't really understand what the major was talking about back there, what exactly was he explaining to us?" Sarah asked straight away. She wasn't going to try and hide her lack of experience; it was crucial that she knew what was going on.

"Well, it's simple really" he said. "There are two regiments. The other regiment will deploy the main attack and we shall only come into the battle if any complications occur. That's why the sergeant has placed you in my regiment. As you have little experience in battle he felt you should be in my regiment, where any risks will be minimal."

"Yeah, but what happens if we run into complications?" Sarah asked.

"Then both regiments will have to abort the mission, there will not be enough soldiers to fight the Nazis if we come under heavy attack from them" the private said, fixing his helmet onto his head. He clipped it firmly into place.

They approached the helicopters that were taking them to their appointed location. There were engineers running around the helicopters, making last minute checks on them.

Sarah climbed up the small, cramped stairs after the private and sat in the seat next to him, the other soldiers followed closely behind. Soon they were all sitting comfortably in their seats and an engineer shut the door with a loud crash that made the whole helicopter shudder from the impact. Then the helicopter began to vibrate as the silently humming engines suddenly burst into life.

Then Sarah felt the whole helicopter shudder even more violently as the helicopter took of from the helipad rather unsteadily, the winds were rather strong and unforgiving that day, but that didn't mean the operation was going to be aborted, such an important mission wasn't going to be grounded merely because of the bad weather.

Sarah looked slowly around at the other soldiers. They all looked grim faced and emotionless. They were too accustomed to these missions to allow their emotions to get the better of them; they had experienced it all before. But Sarah hadn't and she wasn't afraid to admit that she was more than a little scared; this would be her first official battle. This was no longer simply training and she was now in as much danger as every other soldier around her.

There was a breath taking view of the rising sun as the helicopter approached the Swedish coast. It was a bright orange disk, with an orange and yellow back wash.

They continued to sit in silence listening to the wind whistling loudly as it surged past the helicopter. There was the comforting hum of the helicopters engines as it travelled on towards its destination.

Then came a crackling sound as the main control building made contact with the helicopters officers.

"Corporal Adams, are you receiving me?" Stephens voice came through the speakers.

"I'm receiving you, Roger" Adams replied through his portable radio transmitter.

"Right, you must follow everything I say very carefully, this is a very dangerous operation you are about to undertake and you must obey every command. You will be reaching Hamburg in about thirty minutes. Be careful as you approach Hamburg, the Germans might be expecting you. We don't know for sure, but be alert anyway."

"Thanks for that, Roger over and out."

"Private MacDonald" the corporal said.

"Yes, corporal?" Sarah's private asked.

"When we begin our mission you must stay at the back with private Murray. Neither of you is experienced enough to fight on the front lines. Is that understood?" the corporal ordered.

"Yes, corporal, understood, corporal."

There was another crackling sound as the control room changed frequencies.

"Corporal, the French should be coming into view. Their helicopter will be close by, but they will not be joining you on your mission. I repeat the French will not be joining you on your mission."

"Yes, Roger, over and out" the corporal answered.

The French approached from the left side. Their helicopter came up alongside the British helicopter. The occupants in the British helicopter were hardly even aware of what was going on outside the helicopter; there were no windows for them to look out of.

Sarah listened as the corporal was talking with the French colonel. What exactly the French were even doing there wasn't clear to Sarah.

Everything seemed so peaceful and tranquil within the interior of the helicopter, unlike the terrain that the helicopter was flying over. It seemed every single town in Germany had been turned into unrecognisable rubble. Dozens of bodies lay scattered everywhere. Nothing had escaped the onslaught of bombs. Animals lay dead and completely disembodied among the rubble. It looked like hell on earth. But the Germans had elected someone crazy and insane and they could only blame themselves for their current situation. Everyone had warned the Germans what the consequences would be, that Gavrian was just like his distant relative, completely deranged and incapable of listening to negotiation. But the Germans had refused to listen and had sealed their own fate. They were once again left with a war torn and battered country.

In the distance the pilot could just make out some black objects that were glittering in the sun. But at the distance the British helicopters were flying at no one could make out what these objects were quite yet.

The pilot felt a shiver of fear come over him as he realised that what were at first unrecognisable objects were in fact planes.

There was a very long conversation-taking place between the British corporal and the French colonel. With corporal Adams and his strong London accent and the French colonel with his even stronger French accent, it would have all sounded very amusing had the situation not been so serious. They were trying to identify what the mysterious flying objects were. They knew they were aeroplanes; they just couldn't make out what sort of aeroplanes they actually were.

Suddenly more planes could be heard. They were just to the left of the helicopter and it was only too apparent what their intention was.

A loud roaring sound vibrated in Sarah's ears and she cringed. She spotted a glint of metal as a jet fighter flew past. It was fast, but not fast enough so she couldn't see the Swastika on its tale fin through the dusty windscreen at the front of the helicopter.

"Right helmets on and brace yourselves," corporal Adams ordered.

Sarah placed her helmet firmly on her head. She saw the private next to her grab hold of his rifle and hold on tightly to it.

"Okay, major, it's over to you now. Tell us when to fire at will, sir," the corporal requested.

"Okay, corporal. Fire at will, I repeat fire at will" the sergeant major ordered.

The co-pilot of the helicopter began to fire at the approaching Nazi aircraft. He was quite young and inexperienced though and his hands shook quite violently as he shot frantically at the Nazis planes as they flew directly at the British helicopter, the Nazi planes were so close now that he could see their faces through the planes windows and he didn't like what he saw.

Then miraculously the young co-pilot somehow managed to get a bullet through the planes front windscreen and the bullet struck the Nazis arm. This in turn caused the pilot to loose complete control of his plane and he swerved dangerously to the left, smashing straight into the plane flying alongside him. As both planes collided they exploded in a ball of flames and the burning wreckage of the planes swiftly fell to the ground below.

"Nice shot" corporal Adams complimented. Then he watched in horror as another German plane made a perfect u-turn and flew directly towards the helicopter.

Now with renewed confidence the co-pilot took a more careful aim at this German aircraft. But he swore furiously as the helicopter shuddered from the impact of German fire. The helicopter was unharmed from such a small attack; it would take far more than mere gunfire to bring this helicopter down. But the pilot was loosing control from the shock of the impact and the co-pilot had to assist him to regain control of the helicopter, because it was flying perilously close to the French aircraft.

They managed to regain control of the helicopter and avoided total chaos, but only just.

They both managed to pull the helicopter sharply back to the right. But any sense of order was now completely gone and chaos was reigning supreme. The French aircraft that was accompanying the British helicopters had now dispersed as they pursued the determined Nazis.

A plane, Sarah couldn't tell whether it was French or British exploded in front of them as it's petrol tank took a direct hit. They were all momentarily blinded as a ball of fire flashed over their windscreen. The pilot grimaced, but managed to keep control of the helicopter this time.

The sky was a total confusion of planes, fire, explosions and bullets. As British planes and Nazi planes alike chased each other across the skies.

The helicopter manoeuvred in and out of the chaos, trying desperately not to get hit by a stray bullet. Though it proved to be an almost impossible task. The Germans training was far superior to that of the French or the British.

"Sir, with all due respect" the corporal began. He gritted his teeth as he watched the planes that were all around them. "But I really think we should abort the operation. This attack is getting far too out of control, sir. We have no chance of even reaching the ground, sir."

"I agree, corporal. Will all units abort the operation. I repeat all units abort the operation. Return back to the base," the sergeant major ordered, his voice sounded so quiet against the background of gunfire and explosions.

All British and French helicopters and planes suddenly turned right and headed north back towards Sweden. Confused Germans went in pursuit, determined that this time they wouldn't get away.

"Hello, I think we've got company" private McDonald commented, noticing the Nazis on their tails.

The helicopter shuddered dangerously as the petrol tank took an almost direct hit from a bullet. Fortunately for them it narrowly missed, although they were now in great danger. If the petrol tank was struck again then the whole helicopter could blow up, taking the troops on board with it.

"Sergeant, I'm going to have to resort to battery power. Will I have enough battery power to last me until we reach the base?" the pilot asked frantically.

"I'm not sure, corporal," the sergeant major told him truthfully. "But I should presume so."

The pilot shook his head in despair. He turned of the two petrol engines and pressed the ignition button for the electric engine. Nothing happened. The pilot pressed the ignition button again, still nothing. He checked the amount of battery power left, which was fully recharged.

"Come on you bastard, start up" he muttered under his breath. He kept on frantically pressing the ignition button.

In his desperation he pushed the throttle forward. The engine seemed to cough and then by some miracle the engine burst into life. A split second later and he would have lost complete control of the helicopter and collided with the ground. He regained control of the helicopter and flew at a low level for some time before making the helicopter rise again. He gently brought the helicopter level with the other planes again.

It took him a while to realise there was a Nazi on his tale. He decided the only way to get rid of the bastard was to out ride him, or cause him to crash some how.

The corporal moved his joystick forward and the helicopter dipped down. He picked up speed and checked his radar screen.

Mean while a British plane flying alongside the helicopter was having no end of problems trying to get rid of a determined Nazi.

This private was still young and inexperienced. It was clear the Nazi behind him was far more knowledgeable than he was.

The private dipped his nose to the ground and saw with relief that the Nazi was following him, not yet realising his plan. He dipped even further down and the Nazi followed suit.

As he suspected it would the dust on the ground was disturbed by the plane and started to rise in the air behind him. It rose straight in front of the Nazi, obscuring the Nazis view. The Nazis plane started to swerve dangerously. The British pilot could see the Nazi was loosing control of his plane; it was just a matter of time before he lost control altogether.

In the blink of an eye the enemy planes left wing made contact with the ground. The whole plane literally flipped over from the impact and exploded into a ball of flames as it made contact with the ground.

"That will teach you to try and kill me, you bastard!" the private screamed out in delight.

He spotted his comrades plane and realised he was being pursued by another Nazi. He banked left and followed the other plane.

The private took hold of the guns joystick and tried to get as close to the Nazi as possible without him realising he was there.

Checking the radar constantly for any other Nazi aircraft he carefully aimed the gun at the enemy planes petrol tank. He pulled the trigger and watched as the bullet headed towards the Nazi aircraft. Within a split second the bullet had made contact with the petrol tank and the plane exploded into a ball of fire and debris. The private smiled smugly as he watched the burning debris falling to the ground.

"Thank you, private," the private's comrade said. The relief in his voice was only too clear to hear.

"Your welcome" the private answered simply. They all watched more calmly as the last enemy aircraft exploded into a thousand peaces of burning debris.

The remaining British and French planes reformed around the helicopter and limped back up the coast of Denmark, towards the Swedish coast and the safety of the base.

CHAPTER THREE

Sarah stood straight to attention. She was gazing at a target at the other end of the training field. The target was stuck on a tree and was really little more than an old sack, stuffed with straw and sewn together. There was a piece of paper stuck on the sack that was to be the target. This old sack was supposed to represent a Nazi and the idea was to shoot as accurately as possible at the centre of your assigned target.

At the other end of the field stood a long, neat line of twelve new recruits, including Sarah. She was still feeling painfully stiff from being stuck in a cramped helicopter for such a long period of time yesterday.

There was a cool but pleasant breeze and it was a beautiful warm summers day. The sun was behind a thin blanket of fluffy white clouds. This would at least prevent the sun from obscuring anyone's vision of the target.

"Okay, you lazy bastards, lets see what you're really made of," Stephen barked.

"Raise your weapons." The young recruits lifted their rifles up, the barrels facing towards the ground. They gripped the hilts of their guns, awaiting their next orders.

"Aim." They raised their weapons up to their faces, aiming the barrel carefully at the target.

"And ... Fire!" There was a chorus of loud bangs as the guns were fired at the targets. The bangs echoed around, causing Sarah's ears to ring.

There was a split second of complete silence. Sarah's ears were still ringing.

"Stand to attention!" Stephen bellowed across the field. They all stood to attention and awaited their next orders.

Major Johnson nodded his approval at the new recruits and then with Stephen at his side he walked slowly along the line of sacks, carefully inspecting each individual target.

All eleven bullets had hit the sacks, but most had not hit the actual target. Only one bullet had hit the target, it had in fact penetrated right through the very centre.

"Who's target is this?" the major asked, pointing at the target.

"Private Murray's, sir" Stephen answered.

The surprise was evident on everyone's face; they hadn't expected anyone with such little experience to shoot with such accuracy. The major looked taken back by this news, Stephen just stood there, a rather proud smile touching the corners of his mouth.

"That was a nice shot, private, well done" the major remarked praising her.

"Thank you, sir" Sarah said.

"As for the rest of you, you need to try harder. You need to be one hundred percent accurate, because on the battlefield such skills will be crucial. You will always need to be one step ahead of the enemy, or they will get you first. So you must start practicing more. By the end of this week I want to see every one of you get every bullet through the centre of the target. Understood?"

"Yes, sir, understood, sir!" they all yelled at the tops of their voices.

"Sergeant" the major then said, as he handed the field back over to Stephen's command again.

"Right, stand to attention." They all responded immediately. "Place your weapons over your right shoulder." Sarah picked up her gun and swung it onto her shoulder.

"Dismissed!" Stephen yelled.

The line broke up and the soldiers headed towards the bunkhouses for a well-earned rest and some thing to eat, before work on the training fields really began.

"Private Murray, I want a word with you, right now" the major called, as he was talking to Stephen.

"Yes, sir" she muttered under her breath.

She turned around and walked over to the major and Stephen.

"Yes, sir?" she asked curiously.

"That was a nice bit of shooting, private. If you carry on shooting that accurately you will complete your training easily. When you complete your training you will go on a very important mission to the French coast. It will certainly be a challenge but I think you can cope with it. It will take place on Le Havre beach. At the moment the beach is occupied by the Germans, but the plan is to force them to surrender it back to the French" the major explained.

"Permission to speak, sir?" Sarah asked.

"Granted, private."

"Why me, sir?" Sarah asked in confusion.

"Because you are young, very agile and I think more than capable of doing this sort of a mission" the major answered, she could se in his eyes there was something more to his answer than simply her age and confidence though.

"Permission to speak, sir?"

"Go ahead."

"Sir, don't you think I'd be too young and inexperienced to take on such a mission?" she then asked.

"No I don't, private. I think that you are perfectly capable of coping with this mission" the major insisted; now looking slightly annoyed by her questions.

Sarah really didn't know what to make of this, she had never been in a situation where someone was offering her such an opportunity, she had always found herself over looked by those who were more confident than her, who were able to cope under such pressure.

"Permission to speak, sir?"

"Granted."

"How long will this mission last, sir? "

"As long as necessary, private. No one knows how many Nazis there are occupying that particular beach. The longest it will take is approximately six days," the major explained. The way he talked about this mission made it sound like an all expenses paid holiday.

"Six days sounds like a very long time, sir" Sarah said critically.

"It does now. But once there it won't seem so long. You will find you won't even have time to think, the worst part will be getting there" the major explained.

"How come, sir?"

"Because, my impatient little private, it will be very long and tiresome."

"Really, sir?"

"Well the British channel isn't easy to cross at the moment. It is watched constantly by the Nazis, who know just how important this small strip of water is" the major explained.

"And what happens after that, sir?"

"Depending on how that mission goes you may return or you maybe deployed on another mission."

"Is that all, sir?"

"Yes, private that's all, dismissed" The major gave her a salute; she saluted back.

She headed thankfully down the field towards the bunkhouses. Dougy who had been waiting for her by the bunkhouses was deep in conversation with another private. He gave the private a cheerful goodbye and walked over to Sarah's side as she approached him.

"So what did the major want with you?" he asked.

"Don't know, something to do with a mission to France that's meant to force the Nazis away from the French coast" Sarah explained.

Dougy clicked his tongue and nodded his head, understanding . "Mission Le Havre" he said.

"What?" Sarah asked.

"That's the name of that mission," Dougy explained to her.

"How do you know?"

"Listening to other peoples conversations does have it's advantages" Dougy said, trying to imitate a mysterious voice.

"You eavesdropped!" Sarah cried out, shocked at Dougy's own bravery.

"Na, I wouldn't say I eavesdropped as such, more over heard a conversation between Stephen and the major" Dougy explained.

"I didn't know Stephen and the major were on such intimate terms," Sarah observed.

"Neither did I. But Stephens trying to get his captaincy. So he is in a manner of speaking kissing the majors ass," Dougy explained.

"He's trying too hard. The major will only get annoyed with him and then he will never get his promotion" Sarah pointed out.

"Yeah, well that's his problem, isn't it? Now lets go and find out what's for lunch?" He said.

Sarah took Dougy's rifle and walked over to a grassy bank by the kitchens. She sat down beside another private whom she was on friendly terms with. They talked happily as Dougy got the food.

Ever since Sarah had returned to Sweden Dougy seemed to have taken it upon himself to become her own personal bodyguard. He seemed to think he had to look out for her. The reason for him doing this was maybe because he was the only one who knew what Stephen was really like to Sarah, uncaring and showing her no fatherly love what so ever. So he had clearly felt he should take it upon himself to look out for her and take care of her.

Two days later Stephen had received strict orders that he, Dougy and three other privates of his choice needed to clean the regiment's equipment, bit by bit. They had been at it for almost two hours when their peace was disturbed by Sarah running into the bunker, her face flushed with excitement and happiness.

"What's up with you?"Dougy asked he looked at her glowing face in confusion.

"I did it, I did it!" she cried out.

"Did what?" Stephen grumbled.

"I got promoted into this regiment, so I'm officially one of you lot, you bloody idiots," she practically yelled in her excitement.

"Oh, at last, congratulations!" Dougy exclaimed.

They all stood up and went over to hug her and congratulate her.

A lieutenant strode in and gave an amused smiled at the odd scene of happiness before him, it was so rare in these troubled times.

"The major is holding a meeting in ten minutes and the whole regiment has to attend. That does include you five," he said, pointing at the five privates.

They all nodded to show that they understood and the lieutenant walked back out of the bunker.

N0 10, Downing Street, London, England

CHAPTER FOUR

It was only early evening, but it was already pitch black outside. There was a strong wind howling past the windows, making everything harder to hear. It whistled noisily down the grand chimneys of Number 10, Downing Street.

The British Prime Minister, Stan Newman, Deputy Prime Minister, Robert Ford and the Foreign Secretary, Liam Woodworth sat in comfortable white coaches, in one of the front rooms facing Downing Street.

"This situation is just getting worse. The Nazis are now attempting to cross the English Channel. They now have complete control of half the countries in Europe. They may even attempt once again to try and enter Asian territory," Liam was explaining. There was a large-scale map laid out on the coffee table, showing a highly detailed map of Europe. There were red pins placed on the map, showing the exact location of where the main German armies were stationed at that point in time.

"There is very little we can do about it at the moment. We just don't have the manpower with which to tackle this situation. The German army is twice the size of ours and half our army is out of action through the outbreak of a serious strain of Rubella. Plus we are very low on supplies of injections for this Rubella epidemic. Frankly Prime Minister, our whole army is falling apart" Robert Ford argued critically.

"I am fully aware of our armies problems, Robert. But there is very little I can do about it. We just don't have the resources to rectify such problems. There are more important things we need to be spending the money on. We can't afford any more medical equipment for the army" Stan Newman said quietly.

"More important things to spend the money on! Oh and what is more important than hundreds of dieing soldiers, may I ask? What's so important it needs this money more than an army full of people infected with German measles?" Robert Ford asked, so angry he was almost yelling.

"Military equipment" Stan answered him simply.

"Military equipment! Military equipment is more important than the health of our troops? Bloody hell, this country is loosing its senses if it's spending more money on guns and tanks than on the very soldiers that are meant to protect it. Jesus Christ!" Robert exclaimed bitterly.

"If we don't have the Military equipment then even more people are going to die. I'm sorry but medication isn't our top priority at the moment" Stan said apologetically. He leaned forward and rubbed his hands over his weary face.

"Your sorry? Try saying that to the hundreds of dieing troops stuck on French soil with the German army bearing down on them!" Robert yelled. He stood up his face red with fury.

"I hate to disturb you gentlemen, but we do have more pressing issues to discuss" Liam interrupted them.

"I agree" Stan said. He was more than a little relieved to have the subject changed. Robert slowly sat back down again.

"Most importantly we need to discuss our situation with America" Liam said.

"I was completely unaware that we had any situation with America? They refuse to be drawn into this conflict. Especially after they have just come out of their huge economic crisis" Robert commented.

"Exactly, that's our problem. We need the American army; they refuse to give us any troops. We cannot win this war without them. We are in desperate need of more troops. If only we could get the Americans to join up with us, then our army would be more powerful than the entire German army put together. But we can only do it if the Americans agree to this."

"That's the problem. They don't want to draw themselves into this dispute. They say it's nothing to do with them," Robert pointed out.

"Neither did we. But we had no choice as we were once part of the EU."

"What do you think, Prime Minister?" Robert asked.

"Well we can't keep relying on negotiations. They are clearly not getting us anywhere. Is there any other possible way that we can draw America into this dispute?"

"No, Prime Minister, we tried everything possible."

"I get the feeling that Gavrian will somehow find his own way of drawing America into this conflict. He always manages to find a way of getting what he wants one way or another and this will be no different," Stan stated thoughtfully.

Liam nodded in agreement to what he had just said. There was a sudden loud knock on the door.

"Enter" Stan called.

A sergeant entered and saluted him. "Sorry to disturb you, Prime Minister, but we've received more information on Operation Le Havre," He said.

"Yes, go ahead, sergeant" Stan said. Robert and Liam leaned forward to listen to the sergeant.

"The German army is larger than we first anticipated, Prime Minister. We work out on average that they have a ratio of three troops to every one of ours, Prime Minister" the sergeant estimated.

"Oh my God!" Robert Ford exclaimed in shock and horror.

"Sergeant, are you quite positive about that estimate? Is there any way that you could possibly be wrong?" Stan asked.

"Quite positive, Prime Minister" the sergeant assured him.

"I can see this campaign turning into a complete disaster," Stan grumbled thoughtfully, again rubbing his hands over his tired aching face.

"We don't know that yet, Prime Minister. What the sergeant just told us are only estimates," Liam said pointedly.

"Sergeant, where exactly did these estimates take place?" Stan asked, looking at the sergeant.

"They took place at Le Havre itself, Prime Minister."

"Oh God. That's where we're sending our main army and it seems now that we are sending them to their deaths. If there are that many Nazis then we have a huge problem on our hands" Stan said.

"Then what do you suggest we do, Prime Minister?" Robert asked.

"I have no idea," Stan said, looking totally lost and bewildered.

"Thank you, sergeant. You may leave now," Liam told the waiting sergeant.

"Yes, sir, thank you, sir." The sergeant saluted them and left the room, leaving behind three confused and exhausted ministers.

"This is turning into a total mess and I think this is a war we cannot win" Stan stated. He leant back in the couch and ran his fingers shakily through his thinning hair.

"It could be possible to win this war if only we could get the Americans involved somehow" Robert said bitterly.

"But how can we if they are refusing to co-operate?" Liam said pointedly.

"I know; that's why I feel this is a war that we are only going to loose."

Everyone sat in silence, trying to think of some possible solution to a situation that looked like it could never be solved.

There was a sudden loud wailing noise. The sirens. People outside could be heard shouting and screaming. They could then hear the unmistakable sound of gunfire; then the cries of people dieing.

"What the bloody hell is going on out there?" Robert cried out angrily.

They all stood up as German soldiers burst in to the room. There were five of them, four privates and a very threatening looking sergeant. They were all aiming their weapons at the three helpless Ministers.

"What the fucking hell is going on around here?" Stan demanded angrily.

"I am sorry, Mister Prime Minister, but chancellor demand you under arrest" the sergeant said in broken English.

"He demands what?" Stan cried in total shock. "Do you know whom your talking to here?" he cried out furiously.

"Yes, Mister Prime Minister" the sergeant said sarcastically, he gave an evil smile.

Stan could only stare at him in dismay. Then he was led away by a private. He found himself being more or less dragged out of the room. Liam and Robert were right behind him. While all of this was happening the Sirens continued to wail out their warning and the hum of approaching aircraft grew louder as the Luftwaffe approached the Capital city ready to begin its nightly attack.

CHAPTER FIVE.

A strong sea wind blew into Sarah's face and she could taste the bitterness of sea salt in her mouth. She stared with a bored expression down at the murky waters of the English Channel. It was raining heavily, adding to that the seas were very rough and the waves were crashing powerfully against the ships side. The ship was rocking very dangerously from side to side. Half the men onboard were laid down with seasickness and even the strongest of sea dogs were starting to feel a bit creasy with the increasing roughness.

"God, I feel sick" Dougy commented next to her, looking at her with a pail face that was very unlike his normal cheerful expression.

"Ah, I'm sure you'll live" Sarah answered, staring thoughtfully out at sea. "You got any idea where we are, by the way?"

"Don't know, English Channel?" Dougy said.

Sarah just looked at him and he shrugged his shoulders helplessly.

She turned away from the railing she was holding onto and quickly headed down the back of the ship to find Stephen, who it appeared was definitely beginning to feel the full force of the sea.

As she climbed down the shaking, unstable stairs to the next level she saw some brave privates attempting to play chess. They were using chewing gum to hold the chess pieces in place. Sarah smiled at this leisurely scene. Then she headed of towards the cabin Stephen was sharing with another sergeant.

She ducked her head down as she entered the cabin through the tiny doorway. The cabin was small, dark and cold, it was in no way comfortable. The walls creaked noisily and every time the ship hit an exceptionally high and powerful wave the walls seemed to shudder as if in an earthquake.

"Hello, sergeant, how are you keeping?" Sarah asked, walking over to Stephens cabin bed and perching herself on the end of it.

"Could be better, Sarah," Stephen admitted, as he struggled to sit up in bed.

The sergeant that shared the cabin with Stephen came marching in. He nodded at Stephen as though he were Stephens's superior and acted as if Sarah didn't even exist. She was a private and was there fore of no concern to him. Sarah looked at Stephen and he shook his head with an amused smile.

"Sergeant, I hope you don't mind me asking, but where are we?" she asked, looking at the sergeant.

"We are just approaching French territory," he answered with his back facing her, rummaging through his backpack as he looked for something.

"How long before we reach Le Havre, sergeant?" Sarah asked.

"Don't know, another hour or so I should imagine," he answered. Then he strode out of the cabin. As he did so he bashed his head hard against the frame of the door. Sarah almost burst out laughing and Stephen sat there on his bunk bed, grinning broadly. The sergeant rubbed his sore head in annoyance and headed to the officers cabins, clearly angry and humiliated.

"Do you think it will take that long to reach land?" Sarah asked looking at Stephen in some trepidation.

"Yeah, most probably" Stephen said, staring of into the distance with a very preoccupied look in his eyes.

"Your nervous about this mission, aren't you?" Sarah asked. She looked at him with concern in her eyes.

"Well yeah, I'm fucking terrified actually. I don't think we have a hope in hell of winning this battle. Half of the soldiers on this damned ship are so poorly trained. A five year old playing cowboys and Indians could shoot better than them" Stephen commented.

"Am I like that?" Sarah asked curiously.

"You, no, you can shoot properly, you can. You have the gift of your father's incredible military abilities. You use them well and that's why you are so good," Stephen said.

"How could you possibly know that?" Sarah asked, Stephen had told her that he had never known a Marques Murray; after all they hadn't even been in armies fighting for the same country. She didn't resent him if he wanted to forget such a man though, Marques had not been the kind of person you could call a friend.

"Ah, well I may have not been entirely truthful with you there, I'm afraid. I did in fact meet him, when my regiment was sent to Germany on a mission. That was just before he had disappeared though, I probably know less about him than you do, Sarah."

"But you told me you knew nothing about Marques, that you had only heard rumours of his disappearance?" Sarah asked in bewilderment

"No, I did meet him just before he disappeared in such sinister circumstances. Didn't like him much though. He was a bit of a bastard; he was very arrogant, he was a good soldier though. I think you inherited that from him." The way with which Stephen uttered all of this sounded strange, but Sarah couldn't quite put her finger on it.

"So for god sake, Sarah don't ever turn out like him, will you? He was just so determined to become a captain that he had become obsessed by it and it consumed him. His problem was he was a good fighter, but useless at organising troops. But unlike him you are incredibly organised" Stephen commented. Then he grimaced as the ship gave a sudden lurch to the left.

"I think I take after my mother there," Sarah said. She was trying to keep the conversation going to keep Stephen's mind pre-occupied. "She was very good at organising things. She would have made a good soldier if she hadn't married Marques so young. Though she did take up a job teaching at the local Primary school. She was good at that."

Sarah looked sad and cast her eyes down to the floor.

"You miss her, don't you?" Stephen said, looking at her with sympathy.

"No, not really. I'm past that stage now. I don't even remember that much about her. All I remember is that she was really pretty with long curly blonde hair. That's why I hate looking at myself in the mirror. I look more like my dad, I fucking hate it." Sarah looked up at Stephen and he saw the pain and anger in her eyes.

"There's not much similarity there though, no one could tell you were Marques Murray's daughter" Stephen said, instantly regretting he had said that as the words left his mouth.

"I resent even looking like Marques in anyway though, because I don't want to turn out like him. I don't want people to go she's just like her father."

"You want to be more like your mother, April, don't you?" Stephen asked.

"How did you know her name?" Sarah asked confused.

"Well apart from you saying it a hundred odd times, I used to know your father a little bit don't forget. I never actually met her, but your father did talk about her. From what I heard she was a special person," Stephen explained.

There was a brisk clanging on the door. Stephen called for the person to enter. Dougy came in smiling and with a cheerful spring in his step.

"Sorry to disturb you, sergeant, but I've come to tell young Sarah that grubs up and if she don't get a move on she'll get nothing to eat."

"Go on then, Sarah, I'll see you later. Dismissed" Stephen said quietly and then promptly hid under the sheets to try and get some sleep.

Sarah and Dougy quietly exited the cabin and Sarah shut the door behind her.

They climbed the steps passing the chess players, heading for the dinning area and the prospect of something to eat.

There was a babble of friendly conversation as they entered the cabin assigned as the dinning area. The smell was anything but appetising though.

"We've got bloody stew again," Dougy grumbled in annoyance.

They each took a plate of rather unappetising stew and found two places in one of the long benches serving as tables.

As they quietly gulped down their stew trying to ignore its bitter salty taste, two other privates that they both knew well came to join them.

"Hello, Murray, Dougy, how you feeling?" the one who was called private Williams asked cheerfully. He bit happily into a mouldy looking apple. He was one of the few lucky people who never seemed to suffer from seasickness. He showed not a single sign of being affected by the harsh weather and rough seas that day. His companion, private Brown looked pale and tired and showed definite signs of having been violently sick.

"We're bearing up," Dougy said sardonically and smiled bleakly at them.

"Aye, well you'll feel much better once you get onto dry land" Williams said in encouraging.

"Oh, yeah, that's really going to make me feel better. Knowing that instead of throwing up I could get my head blown of" Dougy said, raising his voice slightly in annoyance and anger.

"It all depends on how many bastards there will be and how good they really are," Williams said pointedly.

"Well if their shootings anything like half the soldiers on this ship then good luck to them," Dougy said.

Williams didn't even bother to respond to that. He knew as well as Dougy how lazy and useless a lot of the privates were becoming, especially the younger privates who had only been in the army for more than a couple of months.

"I'm not like that, am I?" Sarah asked, who still felt very insecure about her capabilities on the battlefield.

"No love, your good, better than you think you are." Williams told her truthfully.

"Yeah, but will it be enough to stop me from getting killed on Le Havre beach?" Sarah asked.

No one even answered that question, because none could think of an appropriate answer. No body knew what was going to happen, anything could happen on that beach. How many people were going to die and whether they were going to succeed or not was anyone's guess. The three men

337

just sat there looking uncomfortably at one other, while Sarah looked at each of their faces in turn with a questionable expression upon her face.

"Hum, I just remembered I had to do something up on deck" Williams said, suddenly looking uncomfortable with the whole situation.

"Yeah okay, see you later" Dougy grumbled.

Williams and Brown stood up and strode calmly out of the cabin. Williams patted Sarah on the shoulder as he left. But Sarah made no response; she was now deep in thought.

CHAPTER SIX.

It was coming up to two o'clock in the morning. The ship was still stuck out at sea, they hadn't been given the all clear to approach Le Havre yet and now all they could do was wait for their next orders. The rough seas of the day before had subsided. The sea was now perfectly flat and calm. The only breaking of water was from the ships bow, which sliced through the water like a spoon cuts through a warm liquid. There were no clouds in the sky, just the endless stars. The moon that was only a half moon tonight offered very little light. The only other light there was came from the ship. Men could be heard laughing and cheering in the cabins as Williams had found a violin and was attempting to play some traditional Scottish tunes, while the other privates clapped and whistled and attempted to dance appallingly badly to the music.

Sarah was totally oblivious to all of this. Her small grey eyes darted over the horizon, trying to see if there was any sign of approaching allied ships, but there were none. It was as if the Nazis didn't even exist. Sarah only wished that were true.

She sat perched on the railings, her hands gripping onto their smooth, icy surface. The cold of the railings was a welcoming relief from the unbearable heat of the night. Even the strong wind that whipped past her hot, sweating body bought no real relief from the unbearable heat. There were also signs of a very bad fog in the morning. That was going to prove pretty disastrous because they would be launching their first major attack on the Nazis that morning. But the way events seemed to be proceeding things would go really badly tomorrow unless the British found a way to break through the German defences, with or without the fog.

"If your thinking of committing suicide by jumping over the railings don't bother, I'll just go in right after you," Dougy said loudly, walking up behind her.

"No, I wasn't thinking of committing suicide. It's just my turn to be the look out, that's all" Sarah explained, as she continued to stare out at the ocean that spread out before them.

"No, it's my turn actually. The serge says you need to get some sleep. I already had a couple of hours, which will do me. You can't fight properly if your going to fall to sleep on the job now, can you?" Dougy said, leaning against the rails.

"Okay, thanks for that. I'll see you later then" Sarah told him gratefully. She sluggishly made her way down the ship towards the stern, where she shared her cabin with the rest of the regiment.

Dougy climbed over the railings and sat down comfortably on them. He looked through his binoculars and scanned the horizon for any unwanted enemy. But like Sarah he found nothing. He hung his binoculars around his neck and took out a crumpled packet of cigarettes. A luxury hard to come by since rationing was introduced. He lit the match and covered the flame with his hand, partly to stop the flame going out, partly to stop any enemy from spotting the sudden spot of light. He lit the cigarette and threw the used match into the murky depths of the sea. He inhaled the cigarette deeply, enjoying the feeling of the nicotine flowing through his lunges. He instantly felt more relaxed. This might be the last cigarette he would ever smoke he suddenly thought on an impulse. But who would care anyway. Both his parents were dead, killed in an air raid, which was only too common these days. He had no brothers or sisters to speak of; he had been an only child. So he was alone in this big and scary world.

He stared down at his cigarette and was suddenly sickened by the sight of it. He threw the remainder of the cigarette into the sea. It was no good trying to fight when nicotine from your cigarette was clogging up your archeries and making it hard to breath. He watched the stub as it sizzled out and sank into the dreary depths of the channel.

Dougy looked over to the horizon and gave a heavy sigh. He then placed the faded gold packet, now almost empty back into his pocket.

Three hours later the sun was starting to rise in the east. Thankfully there had been no visible sign of the fog everyone had predicted would come. It was a clear morning that was going to lead to a very hot day.

Everyone was hastily running around the decks trying to get everything organised, including themselves. Some of the privates had already been sorted into their units and were starting to board the narrow tin boats that were to take them to shore. These were specially designed boats that were meant to be both bullet and bombproof. These boats could take up to a hundred men and were very deep to protect the soldier's vulnerable heads.

Sarah was standing patiently in line waiting to board the next boat with her rifle slung over her shoulder and fully loaded, her backpack sat snugly in its rightful place. Stephen stood in front of her with Dougy right behind her.

Stephen turned around to face her, with a very serious expression on his face. He looked her straight in the eye, so she would listen to every word he had to say.

"When we reach the beach I want you to stay very close to me and don't at any cost leave my side. If I get hit stay by Dougy. Don't worry about me. Do you understand me?" Stephen said. There was immense fear in his eyes and Sarah knew he was absolutely terrified of what would happen once they reached the beach. Nobody knew quite what they were up against and this showed on everybody's face. Sarah had even seen soldiers embracing each other, wishing each other goodbye and farewell.

"Yes, sergeant, I understand, sergeant," She said, trying to sound far calmer and more controlled than she felt. On the inside she was completely petrified, feeling the fear mount the longer that they had to wait.

Stephen then turned back around to face the front and yelled out the orders for the soldiers to board the waiting boat. As Sarah boarded the boat she felt a sudden pang of excitement and dread. This would be her very first proper land attack, something with which she had no experience in at all. She was absolutely terrified, but was at the same time telling herself to keep calm and focus on the operation ahead. If she didn't stay calm she would be killed, there was no easier way to put it.

The soldiers climbed into the boat single file, each one of them was showing a certain amount of fear in their eyes. They all felt the same amount of trepidation. Every one of them completely understood that the majority of them would probably not come out of this conflict alive. It was just a matter of fact to them; it was their job to die for king and country.

Sarah felt a cold, chilly shiver of fear as she sat on the icy metal seats of the boat. She could hear Dougy muttering frigidly, "this seats bloody freezing" as he sat down next to her. It was a welcome relief from the sweltering heat though.

Then when everyone had sat down and was protected by the rigid walls of the boat, they were given a shunt to start up their engines. The boats then moved quickly forward. They were now directly in the danger zone right in front of the German lines. As an older, more experienced private took control of the boats controls and forced the boat to speed up to it's maximum limit, bombs started to strike the water around them. Sprays of water drenched the waiting soldiers as the boat was steered towards Le Havre beach, now a scene of devastation, with the beach littered with bloodied bodies. There were huge craters in the delicate sand, where bombs had exploded. The few men who had escaped the Nazis powerful weaponry were crawling helplessly up the sand towards the stone barriers of the army base, trying to find some way of escaping. But there was no escape; above the walls of the base Nazis were positioned, specially trained to shoot from high vantage points. This was the Nazis strong hold in France and they weren't going to loose it without a fight.

The boat started to rock dangerously as a barrage of bombs continuously rained down on it. Sarah grabbed tightly onto the icy cold seat to try and prevent herself from falling of it. The boat-lurched forwards towards the shallow waters.

There was a loud clattering noise as a small object hit the boats floor. As Sarah glanced down, looking in the direction of the noise she realised with horror that it was a bomb. It was little more than a hand grenade, but it was still deadly.

The bomb started to roll uncontrollably around the floor of the boat. None of the privates would touch it. They were scared that the smallest touch would detonate the bomb.

A newly recruited private stared down at the fist-sized bomb as it rolled over to him and settled by his feet. He muttered something unintelligible and then screamed in agony as the bomb blew up in his face. He slouched forward, and then fell of his seat, landing on his front. The boat leaned dangerously over to the port side. The privates limp body rolled over onto his back, revealing a massive hole where his face had once been.

Sarah stared at the dead private in revulsion, thinking that could be her soon. Or maybe even worse.

They were now in view of the beach and the boat would soon be grounded and at that point they would be open to full frontal attack from the Nazis.

A short whistle blast gave the order for the soldiers to prepare themselves for the jump from the boat onto the beach to make the attempted attack on the Nazis across the beach. From this distance it all looked so vast, the Nazis so far away. Sarah didn't have any idea how they were ever going to get across the beach. What she now felt went far beyond fear.

The boat gave a shudder and there was a grinding sound as it scraped the seabed, signalling that they had by some miracle managed to reach the beach. Stephen yelled out the orders for them to get out of the boat and to 'shoot them bastards down like flies.' But as soon as the men got of the boat and tried to run up the beach to the stone defences the Nazis shot them down with great accuracy, slaughtering them like cattle. They were just far better trained than the British and there were so many more of them. Some of the bullets landed harmlessly in the sand, leaving tiny bullet holes where they struck. But most unfortunately reached they're intended target and hundreds of men were falling to the ground, screaming in agony. All around Sarah men were falling like dominoes, to die a cold, horrible death.

As she stepped out of the boat Sarah immediately looked for Dougy. He grabbed her shoulder, and dragged her down into the sea. Sarah could feel the back draft of the bullets going past her, she was just so glad Dougy was there.

They crawled on their bellies along the shoreline and the sand clung to their uniforms, making them uncomfortable.

They made slow and steady progress up the beach, using the dead bodies that lay all around them as a means of protection, as the bombs and bullets continued to rain down on the beach. They made loud thuds and bangs among the screams of dieing men, the noise was absolutely deafening.

Sarah felt a hand gently shaking her shoulder. She swiftly turned around in alarm. But clearly relaxed when she realised it was Stephen.

"Head west towards the western defences" he shouted loudly to Sarah and Dougy over the deafening sounds of gunfire. "That seems to be the least guarded. If we break through that part of the defence there is a good chance we can try and gain control of the place."

Dougy and Sarah nodded understandably and immediately followed Stephen west across the beach. A number of other soldiers were following behind them. They seemed to trust Stephens's judgement; they knew he was a good and reliable commanding officer.

Sarah stayed behind Dougy and every few minutes Dougy would glance around to make sure that she was still there.

For some inexplicable reason the Nazis didn't seem to be shooting at them at all. They seemed to be more concerned at killing the approaching regiments in the boats. They didn't even seem aware of the small band of soldiers proceeding up towards the western side of the defences.

"Sarah, you stay behind with Dougy and don't leave his side" Stephen shouted, as he crawled up behind her. She nodded vigorously to show that she understood. This type of warfare they were about to attempt was completely new to her and Stephen didn't want her to do anything that could cost Sarah her life.

They reached the wall of the fortress and yet still the Nazis seemed totally oblivious to the small band of soldiers trying to get around the fortress. The defences only held up to nine armed soldiers, none of which looked like they had their hearts in the job. They all looked far too young to be guarding a fortress of such significant importance. Even though Sarah still wasn't quite sure what the Nazis were trying to accomplish by this mission, other than to hold onto the ground that they had already gained. All she had been told was that the Nazis were trying to prevent the British from gaining control of the fortress. Then the Nazis had to keep the French at bay until more enforcement would arrive and drive the British back in to the sea again.

"How the bloody hell are we going to get in there?" Dougy asked breathlessly, as they all leaned against the crumbling stone of the fortress.

"I have no idea," Stephen admitted.

Another sergeant came up behind Stephen and they seemed to be discussing how to get up into the defences. Dougy gave Sarah a reassuring look, which she returned in response. The two sergeants finished their discussion and Stephen turned around to look at the patiently waiting soldiers. He beaconed them closer to him and they all crowded around him like primary school children about to go on their very first big outing.

"Alright, this is what is going to happen. I want Williams, Brown, Dougy, King and Patterson to lure the Nazis away from us in anyway possible.

You then try and keep them well occupied while us sergeants, Murray, Green, lance corporal Taylor and McBride try to enter the fortress. The rest of you will all stay out here and shoot any bastard that dares to cross your path. Understood?"

They all nodded in response and Stephen started to issue orders. The five nervous privates given orders to provide the distraction moved quickly to the front of the line. There they waited for the next orders. Stephen watched the barrier intently, waiting for just the right moment for when he should issue the orders. It was no good giving them at the wrong time; they would most certainly get shot down. The five privates watched his face carefully, waiting for the signal to move. He finally nodded his head and they leapt to their feet. They ran out into full daylight and the enemies firing range. There was a long arching curve in the barrier with a metal balcony jutting out of it. This was where the Nazis were standing guard.

Dougy started to instantly fire at the Nazis, who shot back in response. But they were nowhere near as experienced as Dougy, or as relentless. Dougy already had two of them down. The other privates didn't seem to be doing anything to help him. They just let him do the work. It was quite a sight, watching Dougy screaming his head of in fury and shooting as fast as he could at the enemy.

Stephen gave the other group a signal and pointed to a metal door fixed to the wall of the fortress. It seemed to be the only entrance into the fortress itself. Stephen stood up and made a dash around the corner of the wall. The other five soldiers were right behind him. The Nazis saw them immediately though and started to shoot at them. Sarah shot back in response and managed to hit one of the bastards straight in the chest. He gave an agonising scream and fell of the balcony onto the sandy beach below.

They ran swiftly along the beach, jumping over the hundreds of bodies that now covered the beach with care. Then they threw themselves against the wall and Stephen signalled for Sarah to come over to him. As she moved up beside him he pointed to the door.

"Murray, see if you can kick that door in," he said. A number of years ago Sarah had taken up kick boxing and gymnastics as a means of getting away from Janet for at least a couple of nights a week. It had been a while ago, but she had never forgotten any of it and she had possessed a certain gift for both activities.

Everyone gave her some space as she backed up and prepared to kick the door down. Then with a powerful surge of energy, she swung her leg at the door and kicked the rusted door with surprisingly violent force. It wobbled dangerously on its hinges, but didn't collapse. Sarah gave one more powerful kick. The door gave a loud grown and fell inward.

Sarah literally pounced into the building. She then realised she had entered a dingy corridor. She had her finger on the trigger of her gun, waiting to kill any unsuspected Nazi who passed in her wake.

The other soldiers followed close behind her, bearing their weapons.

"There's no one here, sergeant" Sarah informed Stephen, as he walked up beside her.

"Probably ran of in the other direction when they heard you breaking the door down" He said, patting her on the shoulder.

McBride walked up beside Sarah and smiled warmly at her. He had been transferred from a Scottish regiment to the British army after he had fallen in love with the female lieutenant of his regiment. As that was against all regulations he was transferred. He was a good couple of feet taller than most other soldiers, with scruffy black hair and chestnut brown eyes. But he did have a sort of handsome face, in a rough sort of way.

Stephen gave them a warning look to keep them quiet as they approached some, rusted metallic stairs. They came out of the narrow corridor and entered a large open area stretching across much of the building.

"Jesus, what is this place?" Taylor asked, his mouth gaping open.

"It looks like a prison" Stephen remarked.

The place in question was set out on three levels, with metal staircases leading up to the top most floors. The floors were made of metal meshing that allowed them to see right through to the bottom. They made a hollow clanging noise as the soldiers walked on them. The other floors above the ground level were little more than balconies and strong netting hung between these balconies. It may have been there to stop people jumping, but for one obvious thing, there didn't seem to be anyone there. The place was cold and eerie and had the feeling of somewhere that had been left derelict and unused. But the soldiers knew one thing; they weren't going to die there that day, at any cost.

"What's this place used for?" Sarah asked, in awe of the entire place. It definitely wasn't used as a prison that was only too clear, because there wasn't a single cell to be seen.

"I don't know" Stephen answered. Then he made some flapping motions with his arms, signalling for them to be silent.

He moved to the edge of the balcony and leaned cautiously over the railings. The others walked quietly over to him; they were completely confused at what he was supposed to be doing.

"Get down" Stephen hissed suddenly, as a Nazi marched across the ground floor. They swiftly knelt down on their knees and watched the Nazi tensely as he marched as stiff as a pole up the stairs. He was wearing a black uniform, informing them he was part of the SS army, Hitler's own private army; which for them was not good. The SS were lethal and a much more powerful breed of soldier.

"Ah, Jesus Christ, he's heading straight for us" Stephen hissed furiously. He got everyone's attention by waving his hands and then gestured to the staircase. Green, Taylor and McBride moved towards the stairs and Sarah made to follow them, but she felt a tense and nervous hand grip her shoulder. She looked around and stared straight into Stephens face. He shook his head, warning her not to follow them.

"You must stay with us to guard the other sergeant and myself, understood?" he whispered.

"Yes, sir" she answered quietly without protest. She felt a great tension suddenly going through her. Stephen smiled at her and gave her a reassuring pat on the shoulder and pointed at the SS soldier again, who was thankfully walking of back in the other direction again.

They quietly moved down the stairs after the other soldiers.

Two more Nazis entered the corridor on the ground level. The soldiers froze and by Stephen's directions they knelt down once again.

McBride started to fiddle nervously with his rifle, trying to reload it with bullets. But his hand was still cold and stiff from the seawater, so that he couldn't get a proper grip of the bullets. One bullet managed to slip out of his grip and it fell to the metal floor with a loud clatter that sounded ear piercing in the silence of the building. McBride and every one else stared at the bullet in complete horror, as they froze in terror.

The Nazis, who were deep in discussion, heard the noise at once. As soon as the bullet hit the ground they instantly stopped talking and stared straight up in the direction of the sound. One asked the other a question, but he just shrugged his shoulders in response. They looked at each other and then proceeded to draw revolvers out of their holsters. Then to everyone's horror they began to walk up the stairs, their boots clanging loudly against the cold hard metal.

"Well don't just stand there you stupid bastards. Shoot them!" Stephen hissed angrily.

Green came to life and pounced down the staircase towards the two startled Nazis. The others followed suit. The Nazis had reached the second floor and were trying to yield their weapons in a threatening sort of manner.

McBride swung his weapon around and hit one of the Nazis in the face with his full force. He knocked the Nazi against the railings almost lifting him up in the process, the Nazi screamed in agony as McBride's weapon broke his ribcage. The other Nazi bashed McBride around the nose with his fist.

McBride fell to the ground with a grunt, as the blood literally exploded out of his nose.

Green gave an angry cry and shot the Nazi in the chest. The Nazi who was turning around to face Green threw his arms up in surprise. Then the Nazis body gave a jerk as the bullet smashed into his chest. He collapsed against the railing. His whole body bent dangerously over the rails until there was a loud cracking sound as the Nazis spine snapped through the weight of his body. His body then finally gave way and slid slowly over the railings to the ground below. His body landed with a loud thud and blood started to trickle out of his wound. His arms lay limply by his face and his eyes were still wide open in a look of horror.

Everyone stood staring at the bloody body. Then the other Nazi turned to stare at Green. With an angry German curse of 'Du Morder' he raised his gun and pointed it directly at Greens heart.

Sarah who was standing by Stephen, following his orders to stay with him and the other sergeant, saw the shot coming. She yelled down at Green to watch out. The other soldiers had no bullets left in their weapons and would have to reload. But there wasn't enough time. They just wouldn't be fast enough to stop the Nazi. Sarah was the only one who could react quickly enough. With a heavy feeling of trepidation she leaned against the railing. She aimed the rifle towards the furious Nazi. She took a deep breath in and pulled the trigger back. She felt the gun push forcefully against her collarbone as the bullet was forced out of the barrel. Then she could only watch.

It all seemed to happen in slow motion. McBride grabbed the barrel of the Nazis revolver, while Taylor grabbed the Nazis head and attempted to slash his throat open with a knife. Then as if by a miracle Sarah's bullet went straight through the Nazis heart. The Nazi jerked violently through the force of the bullet. As Taylor let go of him he fell to the ground, where his body jerked a couple of times, then came to rest on the cold, metal floor. Blood started to trickle out of his body and dripped through the holes in the meshing.

The whole place suddenly went quiet again. Every body's eyes were on the body of the dead

Nazi. There was the same expression in each soldier's eyes of surprise and of confusion.

Sarah breathed a heavy sigh of relief and leaned against the rails. She gripped the hilt of the gun and rested the barrel of the rifle on the floor. She felt a great sense of triumph through the pure fact that she had achieved shooting someone from long range and on the first shot.

Green looked at her with a look of pure relief in his eyes. Stephen walked over to her and squeezed her shoulders. She looked up at him and gave him a meek smile.

"It's okay, it's over now. Well done, that was an incredible shot" Stephen praised, smiling proudly back down at her.

"Thank you, sergeant" she answered quietly.

"Come on, we've wasted enough time already" Stephen then said, as he turned his attention back to the matter at hand.

Stephen marched down the corridor and the other sergeant followed him down the stairs to the three patiently waiting privates. He patted Green on the shoulder. But Green didn't respond.

Sarah slung her rifle over her left shoulder and walked quickly after them down the stairs towards the busily chatting sergeants. Then suddenly the sergeants headed for the stairs again. The privates followed them obediently.

The ground floor had no rooms or doors to speak of. So what this buildings purpose could be was a complete mystery to the soldiers. There were just two arches at each end of the room, leading to other corridors and other parts of the building.

"Which way, sergeant?" Taylor asked.

"I have no idea," Stephen answered, shaking his head in confusion.

"Lets try this way," the other sergeant suggested, pointing to the right of them.

They walked quietly down the corridor. It was rather a large corridor, with powerful strong lighting and the walls were painted with a cheap emulsion. Sarah noticed that the ceiling was very high. Even if McBride, who was now sniffing loudly and trying to stop his nose bleeding, tried to touch the ceiling with his hand, his fingertips wouldn't even brush it.

The corridor led to another set of stairs leading up to a wooden door, white washed with a small pane of glass in the middle.

The other sergeant beckoned to them and they all pressed themselves against the walls out of the view of any people who may happen to glance through the window of the door.

"Right, when I give the signal I want all of you to run in there and shoot down every Nazi in that room, understood?" he whispered as he pointed to the door. They all nodded nervously.

The sergeant stared at the door for a few seconds, then glanced at the patiently waiting soldiers and nodded once, giving the signal to attack. Taylor ran up the stairs and turned the handle on the door, which was much to his relief open. Then the others followed him, running into the room with their weapons held in front of them. The room they entered so abruptly was just like any other control room, with a large window that showed an aerial view of the war torn Le Havre beach.

Surprised Nazis tried to grab their guns, but were shot down by an over enthusiastic McBride who was shooting every Nazi that came within his sight. He was screaming and swearing at the top of his voice, making the other soldiers cringe.

A Nazi came up behind Sarah, holding a huge axe aloft in his hands. Sarah was completely unaware of his presence behind her. She had a young soldier trapped in the corner of the room and he had nowhere else to go.

Green turned around to see if Sarah was ok. He saw the Nazi slowly lifting his axe up behind Sarah. He screamed something unintelligible at her. She turned around to face the Nazi. With her concentration somewhere else the Nazi behind her now had control. He bashed her around the back of her head with all the force of his gun. She screamed in pain and surprise and fell against one of the computers, making it fall with a crash to the floor. It shattered loudly making the two Nazis glance at it in alarm.

Green ran across the room, followed closely by Stephen. He grabbed the axe less Nazi by the neck and took his hat of. It revealed dark, greasy, lice ridden hair. Stephen threw Green his pistol and Green shot the Nazi in the head. Blood flew everywhere, hitting the screens of the computers and slowly running down them. Green then dropped the dead Nazi in disgust and shot the Nazi who had been yielding the axe in the throat. The Nazi automatically reached for his throat and the axe hit the floor with a loud clatter. The Nazi dropped to his knees as if praying; making loud wheezing noises, as he was now unable to breath. Then he finally collapsed onto his stomach, exhaling for the last time.

Whilst Green was busy with the now axe less Nazi, Stephen grabbed Sarah's arm and yanked her of the desktop. She had a nasty cut straight across her forehead where the Nazis rifle had made contact. She felt dizzy and her head was now screaming in pain. She knew she would have one hell of a headache later on that night.

All of the Nazis that had been present in the room were now either dead or dieing. Taylor marched over to the door and stood guard beside it as the other sergeant and McBride ran to where Green, Sarah and Stephen were.

"Is she badly hurt?" the other sergeant asked in concern, as Stephen tilted Sarah's chin back to get a better look at her cut. He gently prodded the cut with his finger and took out a bandage to wrap around the wound.

"No, she'll be fine. It's just a head injury that's all. She'll be as right as rain," Stephen explained, putting the unused bandages back in his pocket.

Stephen then removed his portable radio transmitter from his utility belt. He turned the frequency on and the only response that he got was loud static. He turned the knob with expert hands to try and get the right frequency. He eventually got some kind of a response. They could just hear the voice of corporal Adams over the loud explosions of bombs and the deafening bangs of guns going of.

"Hello, corporal, this is sergeant Collins. We have succeeded in breaking through the barriers and now have power over the control room. But we only have four privates and two sergeants here to guard the place. We need more back up if we want to maintain control of this room or the Nazis may try to attack us," Stephen explained. He glanced at

Sarah, who was trying to get shakily to her feet. But as soon as she got up she fell back down again.

"Yes, sergeant, we know all about your situation, because I'm standing next to private Douglas as we speak. He has explained about your little adventure, well done, sergeant. We will send up more troops when you have given us directions" the corporal congratulated them. They could hardly hear what he was saying.

"Certainly, corporal. You pass through the busted in metal door and turn right into the corridor" Stephen began.

"Wait a minute, sergeant. We will need to organise some troops first. I will just turn of frequency, and then as soon as we have some troops I will get in contact again, which is when you will give me the directions," the corporal explained.

Before Stephen had the chance to say anything else he was cut of. Loud static filled the room again. Stephen turned of the portable radio transmitter and placed it back on his belt.

"Now, let us see what this place is all about then, shall we?" he muttered quietly to himself. He wondered over to one of the computers left still working. His face was creased in concentration.

"Is there a problem, sergeant?" Sarah asked, as she slowly walked over to him and looked over his shoulder at the screen. But all the little numbers and digits made no sense to her. She had never been very good with computers.

"No, no, it's nothing. It's just all these numbers and figures. I can't make sense of them," Stephen told her, pointing to the digits on the screen.

"Why? What's wrong with them, sergeant?" Sarah asked.

"Well for a start these figures aren't for Le Havre, their for somewhere completely different" Stephen explained, sitting down in a chair.

"Well, what are they for then?" the other sergeant asked walking over to them. Sarah stepped aside to allow him to get through.

"That's the thing. I don't know. The only information the computer tells me is that its code name is 'Operation England.' But I have no idea how that is connected to this battle. The number of troops shown on this chart is enormous. Running into hundreds of thousands. Far too big a number for what was involved in this battle. There are also planes indicated on this chart. But there weren't any aircraft involved in the battle outside. What ever this chart is trying to explain it is one hell of a large campaign," Stephen explained, studying the chart carefully and pointing out figures to them.

"Well, where is it then?" the sergeant asked, sounding agitated.

"As far as I can tell, England" Stephen retorted.

"Well we know that, but where exactly in England?" the sergeant asked angrily.

"I don't know! Look, all that I know is that it's in England. Alright!" Stephen said angrily.

The other sergeant just raised his arms in protest and then walked of in the direction of Taylor and

Green. Green who was starting to get bored of standing around, walked over to the large window at the far end of the room. The window was so extensive it practically took over the entire wall. It gave an almost breath taking view of the beach itself, although the view was anything but breath taking. It most certainly didn't convey the typical view of a beach. The place was covered in dead bodies; there were so man bodies on the beach that the blood, which was slowly draining out of their bodies, was turning the sand to a dark pink colour. Even the sea was turning pink; it would take a very long time for the blood to be broken up by the tides after this conflict was over. The bodies would be buried long before the blood was washed away.

"The corporals coming up with some troops now, sir" Green suddenly bellowed across the room to Stephen making them all jump in surprise.

"About bloody time too," Stephen grumbled. He got up from the chair he had sat down on and walked across the room to the door.

Sarah walked over to Green and stood beside him. She stared in disbelief down at the carnage spread out before them.

"How's your head?" Green asked.

"It's okay, it's still bleeding a little. It's only a small cut on the head, Green, it isn't that bad. Honest, look." She lifted her helmet of her head and showed him a bloody mass of hair.

"Well, I don't think I want to know what your idea of a bad injury is then. But if you hadn't been so quick I would probably be dead now. So it's only fair to do you a good deed in return," Green explained.

Sarah didn't bother to respond. She turned around to face the window. Clouds were starting to build up out at sea. It would help to break up the blood, but it would be uncomfortable for those still alive but trapped under the dead bodies.

"Pathetic, isn't it?" Green asked, breaking the silence.

"What is?" Sarah asked looking at him.

"All this" Green said, gesturing at the beach. "All of this destruction just so one man can gain complete control of Europe. It just doesn't make any sense. So much death and all for one mans greed, its not right at all" Green said bitterly.

"Not everything in this world makes sense, Green. You just have to learn how to cope with it" Sarah said quietly.

"Well it's bloody wrong. Such a waist of lives. Think of all the families who lost loved one's out there today; all caused by one single mans beliefs" Green said.

"I'm just glad they didn't have to witness seeing how their loved ones died. It's hard to imagine ever witnessing such a scene, unless you see it with your own eyes, no one should ever have to look at such a sight," Sarah said thoughtfully.

"You would be right there," Green agreed.

Their conversation was cut abruptly short by the arrival of more troops. They came bursting into the room and the silence had been broken like a spell.

CHAPTER SEVEN

"This place has to be the most boring place I've ever seen," Dougy grumbled bitterly, yawning through boredom.

It was seven o'clock in the evening and Taylor, Green, Dougy, McBride and Sarah had been sent to search the surrounding countryside to find any Nazis that hadn't already fled the immediate area with their other comrades.

"You can't complain really though. At least you don't have to live here," Sarah said pointedly.

"If I had to live here I would stay in my Anderson shelter twenty four hours a day" Dougy announced.

"If I had to live here I would have moved already" Green said. He was feeling frustrated with being sent on a pointless search, when he could be doing much more important things.

"Alright, just keep your mouths shut for a minute. The noise you lot are making is enough to wake the dead," Taylor snapped at them grumpily.

"Yes, corporal" they all answered in unison. Taylor being the lance corporal and being of higher ranks he was left in charge of the other four.

They headed down the main street of a local village not far from the base. It was cobbled, very narrow and incredibly steep, a typical French village. There were small local bars dotted along the street, along with the usual array of shops and grocery stores. The bars were the key places the soldiers were going to concentrate their search on. Because if Nazis were anywhere they would be in a cheap bar, drinking as much alcohol as they could afford. Then they would normally go into a field and shoot themselves before the British could. That was the way it was, if they returned to their army they would get shot for deserting. If they strayed too close to the British army they would get shot because they were German and the enemy.

Sarah glanced through the window of one of the bars and spotted three Nazi privates sitting at one of the wooden benches. They had their legs slung over the table and they were smoking heavily.

"Corporal" she called gently to Taylor. He turned around to look at her with a questioning expression on his face. "There's some in here, corporal," she said, jerking her head towards the bars entrance.

He walked hastily over to her and glanced inside the bar.

"Right, I will go in and face them with McBride. Green you will watch the door in case they make a run for it. Dougy and Murray you come with me as back ups. Dougy you keep a watch on Murray. I gave sergeant Collins my word I would keep her safe," Taylor ordered. Sarah actually rolled her eyes at this comment in frustration.

They marched into the dingy bar. Green stood guard by the door, his rifle poised at the ready. The bar was only small, but it was completely packed out with people. These were mostly soldiers on leave from the army, or the usual array of old men.

The small group moved towards the Nazis. The Nazis seemed totally unaware that there were British soldiers present there.

Taylor strode casually up to the three of them, yet still the Nazis seemed unaware of their presence.

"Guten Tag" Taylor said, breaking the silence. The three Nazis glanced slowly up at them.

One of the Nazis, the nearest one to Taylor, took a drag of his cigarette and then blew the smoke in Taylor's face. Taylor didn't even flinch. The Nazi smiled coldly at him and mumbled "Guten tag." He then leaned back in his chair and giggled. It was obvious he was completely and utterly hammered.

"Do any of you speak English?" Taylor asked them in poor German, his voice was very hard and cold. He was making it clear that he was someone not to be messed with.

"Welche?" one of the Nazis asked. His voice was breaking up, slurred and hard to understand.

Taylor who was feeling very tired from the previous days battle had had enough with fucking about with these Nazis. He suddenly lurched forward and grabbed the Nazi by the collar. Taylor lifted the Nazi of his seat and practically dragged him across the table. All the glasses fell to the floor and shattered into millions of pieces.

"Listen to me, you German bastard, I know you can speak English. So don't take the fucking piss out on me. Now start speaking," he said, he was screaming so loudly that spit came flying out of his mouth. The Nazi flinched visibly away from his face. The Nazi fell back in his chair and slid slowly down it. His hand quivered with fear as he took a long drag of his cigarette. The other Nazis stared at Taylor in utter disbelief.

"Yes ve speak a little English," One of the Nazis told him, speaking very slowly in broken English.

Taylor glanced around the bar, aware for the first time that everyone was now staring at them. They weren't scared of the English; the English protected them and took care of them. But they were scared of the Nazis.

"Then explain to us what you are doing on land that is occupied by the English and belongs to the

French?" Taylor continued to question the Nazi, now trying to ignore the gazes of the French, they were all watching him eagerly now.

"Ve are on land that rightfully belong to the Germans. So ve have right to stay here," the Nazi told him. He appeared to be the only one able to speak English. The others were staring at the English in fear.

"No you don't. This is French soil you Nazi bastard and you have absolutely no right to be here. Now why don't you crawl back in to that rotten hell of a country where you belong?" Taylor asked him angrily.

"Ve have EVERY right to be here. So you cannot make us go. Ve vill take over your shit little island and vhen ve do, you vill die first. One day

Germany be most powerful country in Vorld. So ve vill stay." The Nazi took a long drag of his cigarette and crushed it out in the ashtray on the table in front of him.

He sat back in his chair and folded his arms. He gave Taylor a sly smile while cigarette smoke drifted out of his nose.

Everybody silently watched Taylor's reaction. His face was quickly turning bright red with anger. Then suddenly he lunged for the Nazi, yelling at the top of his lunges "I'll kill you, you bastard."

But McBride grabbed hold of Taylor and managed to with strain him with the help of Sarah and Dougy.

"No, don't, corporal" Sarah said more calmly than she felt. "It wouldn't look too good if people found out the British were beating up Germans for no good reason, would it, corporal? Things are already strained enough as it is."

Taylor stepped back and shook them of him angrily. They all stepped away from him and awaited his next orders.

The Nazi sat there calmly rolling up another cigarette.

"Oh, by the way, there was one more thing," Taylor said leaning over the table. The Nazi looked at him with a puzzled expression as he blew out more smoke.

"Pot is illegal in France. So I'd better put that out before you get caught," Taylor said grabbing the Nazis face and forcing him to look him straight in the eye. "So get the hell out of France before I shoot your brains out" Taylor whispered quietly. He let go of the Nazis face and spat in his eyes. He gave a little laugh and turned around.

"Come on, lets get out of here. The sight of Nazis is making me feel nauseous," Taylor grumbled. The Nazi was wiping his face and hastily putting the cigarette out. But the anger in this enemy's eyes was unmistakable.

They walked solemnly out of the bar. Taylor threw some money at the landlord to cover for the cost of damages. The Nazis were picking up their backpacks and made as if they were about to leave.

"What the fucking hell did you do that for, corporal? If they go and grass on us then we're in serious trouble" Dougy cried out angrily, as they walked very slowly down the main cobbled street.

"No, they won't tell on us. After all we could grass on them for smoking illegal substances. Even the German army has its rules and one of them is that their not allowed to deal with illegal drugs of any kind. So I doubt their going to say anything," Taylor explained to him, his voice full of confidence.

"Uh, corporal. They may not grass on us, but they might do something else" Sarah said, she had turned around and was now walking backwards as she looked back down towards the bar they had just left.

Taylor turned around to gaze in the direction that Sarah was looking and his eyes widened in horror and disbelief.

The Nazis were running as fast as they could towards them. They had their rifles in the air and they were aiming right at the British.

"Ah, Jesus bloody Christ!" Taylor yelled angrily.

"Start shooting, kill the sorry bastards," he ordered, screaming angrily at them.

The Nazis were already firing at them and they had to take cover in the nearest doorways.

Sarah tilted her rifle up a little further and watched as the Nazi who Taylor had taken such a liking to came right towards her. She lifted her gun to her shoulder and pulled back the trigger. She watched as the bullet hit straight for home and the Nazi collapsed onto the street. Taylor shot one of the other Nazis who fell to his knees, clutching his wounded chest. He slowly looked up his eyes bulging out of his face. He made as if he was going to try and shoot somebody. But all his strength had gone and the gun slipped out of his hand. The Nazi raised his face to the sky. Blood started to trickle out of his mouth. Then he finally collapsed onto the road, his face pressed into the ground.

The last standing German was still running bravely towards them, yelling at the top of his voice in some kind of strange German language.

Green who was getting rather fed up with this screaming foreign maniac just fired his gun at random and shot the Nazi straight in the leg. The Nazi screamed in pain and fell to the ground. He was clutching his bleeding leg and crying out in pure agony.

"Shall we go and put him out of his misery, corporal?" Green asked. Taylor nodded in response. Green walked over to the crying, whimpering Nazi. He shot the Nazi a couple of times in the head. The Nazi jerked a couple of times, then lay still.

They all came out of hiding and walked over to Green.

"Good work men" Taylor said. "Now we had better get back to the base. The Americans are supposed to be arriving tonight. They have apparently relented and have agreed to join in the war effort," Taylor informed them.

They marched back towards the army jeep, ignoring the large crowd of French that stood and watched them by the entrance to the bar that the Nazis had occupied mere moments before. They were staring at the soldiers as they marched silently past them.

The little army jeep was parked on a grass verge. Taylor took his place in the drivers seat. Green sat next to him, with Dougy and Sarah seated behind them. McBride sat perched on the back of the jeep, clinging on for dear life, with his gun safely slung over his shoulder.

Aircraft roared overhead. They were heading towards the main army base, now situated on Dunkirk beach. It was the fortress the British had managed to take control of a couple of days ago. The planes were clearly marked with the stars and stripes symbol and looked to be in a better condition than any RAF aircraft.

As the jeep approached the base there was a lot of people standing by a convoy of pristine vehicles.

They were lined up neatly on the bases sweeping driveway.

The jeep came to a stop by the small barrier gate. The private guarding the gate saluted Taylor, pressed a button and the tiny gate started to rise.

The jeep passed through and Taylor drove straight for the vehicle shed. The doors to the shed were wide open, so Taylor went straight through and parked neatly by a row of similar army jeeps.

The soldiers clambered out of the jeep and made their way out of the shed and towards the crowd of people gathered around the vehicles.

"There aren't many of them, are there?" Sarah commented, as they walked up to the large crowd of people.

"Are you joking, this isn't even a small percentage of them" Green told her.

Stephen stood with major Johnson and officer Taylor, who were talking to two Americans. The Americans were wearing brand new uniforms, with brand new helmets and shiny new black boots.

Sarah glanced down at her own filthy, neglected uniform. It still had sand in it, which was irritating and itchy. Compared to the Americans her uniform was well worn and her boots were a complete state. They were meant to be a shiny black, but actually appeared to be a dull brown instead. The sea and sand had wrecked them beyond repair.

There was a look of thankful relief on Stephen's face as he saw Sarah and Dougy approaching them.

"Ah and here comes one of our finest new privates" major Johnson announced, pointing proudly at Sarah. The Americans looked at her with amused looks on their faces. Sarah knew exactly what was going through their minds. Sarah was indeed quite small and must seem weak and insignificant to the American's.

The Americans seemed all right though; in fact they turned out to be quite nice. They looked at Sarah with respect; they obviously remembered how hard it was at the beginning of their careers in the army.

Sarah listened vaguely to the conversation, which was mostly an explanation of the events of the attack on Le Havre beach, which had taken place a couple of days ago now. Occasionally the Americans would ask for more details on certain things. The major was only too happy to oblige to their requests.

After half an hour Stephen asked if he and Sarah could be dismissed. The major just nodded in response. He was listening intently to one of the Americans explain the methods that they used when in battle.

Sarah followed Stephen as he walked across the make shift driveway towards an archway that led to the blood covered beach of Le Havre. As they passed under the archway Sarah noticed immediately that all the bodies had been removed from the beach. Of into the distance she could see the thick smoke of a fire. They were burning all the bodies of the Nazis. Even Nazis that were alive were thrown onto the fires and burnt alive. Whilst the bodies of the British and the French were buried respectably in graves. Each grave was then blessed and marked with a small wooden cross.

Stephen sat down on the blood stained sand and took of his hat to reveal greasy unkempt hair. He suddenly looked very tired and old. He looked up at Sarah with a strained look on his face.

She sat down next to him and took of her own hat. She then gave him a puzzled expression, as if asking him why he had bought her down here.

"Ah... I don't know how to say this to you. So I'm just going to come straight to the point" Stephen began. Then he stopped and swallowed hard, trying to collect his thoughts together.

"Tell me what, Stephen?" Sarah asked.

"Well um... yesterday Lund and Malmo were bombed by the Nazis. Both places sustained severe damage. They recon 5,000 people may have died in the initial attack" Stephen looked at Sarah with grief stricken eyes. They looked so tired and red.

"What. Um... what about Kira and Janet?" Sarah asked. She was already fearing the worst.

"Kira's okay, a few cuts and scratches and a broken ankle. But Janet wasn't so lucky. She di...died, a...a b...broken neck" Stephen stammered, tears filling his eyes. He stared out to sea where more ships could be seen in the distance approaching the French coast.

Sarah slipped a comforting arm through Stephens arm and leaned against him. "I'm sorry," she muttered.

"Janet was in the wrong place at the wrong time At least Kira survived it" Stephen said. He sounded like he was really struggling to hold it together.

"How is Kira?" Sarah asked.

"She's okay, she is coping some how. All she keeps saying is that she has a bad headache. She won't talk about Janet at all, I think she is more than likely still in too much shock to talk about it" Stephen explained.

"Can I ask how Janet died? Or would you prefer I minded my own business?" Sarah asked.

"No, you're her foster sister. You have a right to know" Stephen answered and then he swallowed with difficulty, as this was obviously still so painful for him.

"Kira said a bomb had loosened the foundations of the house and the house was quite ancient with wooden beams supporting the roof. The sirens didn't go of straight away and by the time they went of the planes were already overhead. They tried to get out quickly, but were slowed down by Janet. She had fallen down the stairs the day before and had twisted her ankle. She was taking a very long time to get down the stairs. When she finally reached the bottom a beam collapsed and fell right on top of her. The beam broke her neck instantly. Kira tried to drag her from under the beam, but it was already too late" Stephen explained. Tears slowly fell down his cheeks as he spoke; he didn't even seem aware that he was crying.

He put an arm around Sarah, wanting and needing her comfort. They both sat there for quite some time, just looking silently over the great ocean spread out before them. It looked so big and somehow so powerful and held so many secrets of its own. It was also now the watery grave of so many soldiers, all of which were too young to face such a terrible death.

"So, what's going to happen now?" Sarah asked, at last.

"Kira has decided it would be better if she moved back to England" Stephen explained. He wiped the tears shamefully from his face.

"Why? England's going to be no safer than Sweden. In fact it's worse. The Nazis are concentrating their main aerial attacks on England now. No way is it any safer than Sweden!" Sarah cried out, her face full of horror.

"Yeah, well it's her home country, isn't it? She said she will feel safer there. If she does die she said she would at least be where she belongs and not some foreign country, where no one knows her" Stephen said.

"So, what will happen after that?" Sarah asked quietly.

Stephen just shrugged his shoulders, and then shook his head to show that he didn't know.

"What's going to happen to us? Are we going back to Sweden to be with Kira?"

"No, we're not going back to Sweden. We're staying in France" Stephen explained.

"Why WE. Why am I being kept in France? Shouldn't I be going back to Sweden so that I can be with Kira?"

"Because you're a soldier now, Sarah. You have responsibilities towards your regiment and you're good. The army is desperate for soldiers like you right now. So you are going to stay here," Stephen said, giving her a stern look.

"But what about, Kira?" Sarah asked.

"Kira is a fully grown adult. She can take care of herself" Stephen insisted.

"Okay" Sarah agreed calmly, nodding her head placidly.

"Right, I have to go back to the captain now. You just hang around with Dougy and the others. Don't get involved with any of those American soldiers, all right? They're nothing but trouble," Stephen warned her.

"Yes, sergeant" Sarah answered with a grin that said, "I know."

"See you later" Stephen muttered, grabbing Sarah's hat and placing it on top of her head so it covered her face too. She gave an annoyed grunt and swatted at him playfully.

Stephen got up and walked back up the beach, the sand crunching loudly underneath his feet as he walked slowly away.

CHAPTER EIGHT

No one was quite sure how many Americans arrived over the next couple of days, but there seemed to be a hell of a lot of them. To the British there was too bloody many. They kept themselves to themselves and any form of contact on the part of the British was always rebuffed. It was an awkward situation made worse by the attitudes of some of the American officers. A surprising amount were very well of and thought the American army was the greatest army in the world. So anything that the British had was always inferior as that of the American army in the eyes of the American officers.

Then there was the problem with the French. For some reason they had come to believe that the Americans were National bloody heroes. The French started to offer them gifts of cheese, bread and wine to make up for the lack of food that was supplied by the army. The Americans took these gifts graciously and they never shared such fine food with the British.

Two months later and more Americans were shipped to France. Not a great number of them, maybe 50, 000 troops or so. But between that period and the time the first Americans had arrived in France everything was relatively quiet. In fact nothing was really happening at all. The German lines had retreated back as far as the Champagne region and they seemed to b waiting for something. They appeared to be waiting for the right time to gather up their troops and launch fresh attacks.

Everyone was becoming restless, especially the Americans. They had somehow gotten the impression that when they reached France they would face great battles and much glory, with plenty of blood and violence for them to sink their teeth into. But as it turned out that wasn't to be the case. A lot of the time was spent doing mostly unnecessary tasks and scanning the surrounding countryside for any unwanted guests.

It was also August now and most days were getting unbearably hot. The thermometers stayed almost permanently between 90 F and 100 F. The blood on the beach, which had not yet been broken up by the sea and washed away, had dried up on the surface of the sand. It now gave of an unbearable stench and had created a slippery crust over the surface of the sand; to cross over the beach now for the soldiers was like walking through hell.

But even though there was a peace about the place they could all feel the tension in the air. They had the sense that something was going to take place and happen soon. It was just a question of where and when.

Before she knew it Stephen and Sarah left for England. The funeral was to take place in the old church of the town where they used to live. Sarah hardly recognised the place though. It was completely destroyed; even the church had one wall blasted out. Sarah just praised God it was summer and not freezing cold. But the church was also the only building left standing. On reaching the place Sarah didn't recognise anyone. Every single one of her old friends had moved on ages ago, or they had been killed like Nicole. Sarah felt totally alone at the funeral. Kira was weeping in Stephens's arms as the coffin passed them. The funeral was a disaster. There wasn't many living relatives left, they had all died in the war. There was only the three of them and some Aunts and Uncles Sarah didn't even know and these relatives showed they definitely didn't want to know her, or Kira and Stephen for that matter.

Sarah was only too glad when they returned to France. She couldn't stop thinking of Janet's funeral though and couldn't help but think that it was such a horrible way to die and she only prayed that she didn't go the same way.

Unfortunately when they returned back to France it was to find a land of chaos and destruction. The Nazis had returned with vengeance on their minds. They wanted to get retaliate against those they believed had taken their land from them, so they were now attacking from all sides to get it back. They didn't give a damn about whom they killed or how they did it. They believed they were doing it for the greatness of Germany and their mighty leader. Of course it was Gavrian who was the one organising all of these attacks. He was making the attacks even larger and far more deadly than ever before and he didn't care if hundreds of his own soldiers were dieing, he wanted that land back. So the Nazis were doing what Gavrian was ordering them to do and if they didn't they would die either way. The Nazi troops knew what punishment they would suffer if they dared to disobey the orders of their leader and they would rather witness the deaths of their enemies than suffer their own fate.

The villages that surrounded Le Havre were completely destroyed. They were like ghost towns. There were other things very noticeable about the surrounding countryside as well. Like the heavy silence that only comes with the lack of bird song. It was summer and there should have been an abundance of sound and colour, but there was none. The place was so quiet and had such a scary atmosphere. The Americans who weren't used to this kind of a situation were running scared, claiming the land was possessed by the devil. It was only the British and French that were managing to keep the whole thing together.

But the worst was yet to come. Stephen was keeping a deadly secret from Sarah. If she ever found out about this information it could even have the potential to kill her. Stephen didn't know how or why, but at whatever cost Sarah must not find out about it. He just didn't know how to keep the secret without her getting suspicious though. He knew she already suspected something was going on, she was no fool.

One thing Sarah was sure about though was that she and everybody else absolutely hated nighttime battles. They were highly dangerous because of the lack of light and they couldn't see what was going on. None of them ever knew what direction the enemy was coming from and their chances of dieing were so much higher. It seemed the Germans didn't agree with this point of view though.

It was around two o'clock in the morning and pitch black, the moon wasn't even out tonight. Sarah, Williams, Green, McBride, Dougy, Stephen, Patterson and a large number of Americans were cautiously walking down what was left of the main street of Bolbec. The entire town was a complete mess; it was completely unrecognisable now. It was just a mass of twisted metal, rubble and dead bodies. There were just so many dead bodies, Sarah had even seen a young mother with a bullet through her head, clutching a new born baby The baby had died such a short time ago that it's tears on it's little pail blue cheeks were still wet. But nobody could be bothered to clear the bodies away. There were occasional loud explosions as unexploded bombs went of. But the place still seemed so quiet. The Americans kept glancing around them fearfully; convinced evil spirits possessed the place.

"God, this place seems to have no life at all, sergeant" Dougy suddenly commented to Stephen, making the Americans jump in fright. Stephen nodded in agreement; ignoring their reactions.

"Yeah the general's speeches have more life in them , sergeant" Williams remarked with a glint in his eyes. He was trying to keep up the spirits of the group by telling them jokes and rhymes. So far the rest of his regiment was finding it amusing. The Americans weren't appreciating it though. They didn't seem to understand the British sense of humour.

His comrades laughed gently, all except the Americans, who remained sour faced and bored.

Somewhere close by the group there was a sudden shout in German.

"Quick everyone, take cover! If they find us our fucking heads will get blown of," Stephen hissed angrily at them.

They all crouched behind the remains of a wall and anxiously peered over the top for a sighting of the Nazi who had shouted.

Stephen gave Sarah a gentle tap on the shoulder and pointed to a pile of rubble close by. A Nazi was sitting on a large boulder with his rifle left carelessly by his feet. He was leaning back and casually smoking a cigarette. He didn't seem to care if any of the enemy noticed the faint glow that the cigarette produced. Nor did he notice the fact that there were a dozen or so British and American troops watching every little movement that he made. In fact if they launched an attack on him now he would be dead in a matter of seconds. But that was far too risky for the sake of just one Nazi. The best thing to do was to lie low and see what happened next.

Stephen tapped Sarah on the shoulder again and beaconed for her to follow him. He scrambled as quietly as possible over some rubble, while Sarah just jumped over it after him. Dougy followed behind them when Stephen gave him the signal to do so.

Stephen leaned against a rock and carefully aimed his rifle at the Nazi. He waited as the Nazi dropped his cigarette butt on the ground and crushed it with his foot. Then in a matter of seconds Stephen had pulled back the trigger and the bullet had made contact with the Nazi. The bullet went through the Nazis neck and the Nazi seemed to give a heavy sigh. His body slowly fell forwards of the rock. The cigarette he had just lit fell out of his hand and slowly burned out.

"Well, that's one down, sergeant" Dougy said cheerfully, trying to break the heavy tension that hung over them now.

"Yeah, but God knows how many more are out there" Stephen retorted, stating the rather obvious.

"Right, lets get a move on" he called to the other soldiers, who were patiently waiting behind the brick wall. "We will continue down the Main Street and then head northwest. Is that understood?"

"Yes, sergeant" everyone mumbled quietly. Sarah slowly scanned their faces for any kind of reaction. There was none. They were all stern faced and ready for action. They had to work as a team, but out on the battlefield they had to look after themselves as well. They had to be very strong because in the end they were all alone. Looking around Sarah realised this was what real fighting was about. The occasional Nazi wasn't much of a threat, it was when there could be thousands of Nazis everywhere you turn that the situation gets dangerous. They could be anywhere; there was no telling where they could be. They could be hiding in a ditch, behind some rubble and a crumpled wall. You just had to go on the knowledge that you had to get them or they would get you.

The small group of soldiers marched quietly down the street. There were regular flashes of orange light as yet more unexploded bombs went of in the distance. The occasional French soldier who had become separated from their regiment ran past them, not seeming to even know they were there. They were often so scared their faces were as white as paper.

On reaching the end of the street Stephen turned northwest up a tiny and completely dark alleyway. His regiment followed closely behind him.

Above their heads was a loud crumbling sound and a load of loose tiles fell down from the roof of one of buildings. Williams promptly stepped aside, pulling Sarah with him. They both barely missed being crushed under the falling debris. The tiles crashed down onto the road and broke up. A heavy cloud of dust rose from the rubble. It momentarily obscured their view so they couldn't see anything.

They squinted through the dust cloud and as it slowly cleared it became apparent to them all that they were no longer alone. They could all feel a sense of fear and panic rush through them. As the more the dust cloud cleared the more they realised that they were in serious trouble. Life threatening trouble.

As the last remnant of dust was blown away by a small gust of wind a large group of Nazis stood in neat rows at the other end of the alley, watching them. There was something oddly strange about these Nazis. Their uniforms were noticeably different for one and they just seemed far more threatening than any other Nazi that the British had encountered before.

Stephen squinted to get his vision back. When he realised who was watching them he opened his eyes wide in a look of complete horror. His eyes were so wide open you could see the whites around them and Sarah had the impression of Stephen's eyes popping out of his head. She had never seen him looking so scared in her whole life and such fear was spreading.

The Nazi soldiers started to approach them in a straight line. At a second glance Sarah saw there were a lot more Nazis than there first appeared. The British were now out numbered three to one. Things were starting to look ever more serious with every passing second.

Stephen took a deep breath in and muttered something unintelligible under his breath. He looked at Sarah deep in thought. Sarah knew what he was thinking. Should they run and escape from a battle they were unlikely to win and look like cowards? Or should he make them face the Nazis and then maybe loose all his troops, including the Americans and kill good men for nothing?

He took another deep breath in and seemed to make up his mind as everyone looked at him in panic. He opened his mouth, paused for a second and then he yelled at the top of his voice, "run!"

They turned around and fled as fast as they could up the alleyway, towards safety, open roads and away from the Nazis.

"Split up when we reach the end of the road. Try to break them bastards up, confuse them a bit. Murray, you stay with me," Stephen ordered, just loudly enough for them to hear him. The Nazis were in close pursuit, their boots were echoing loudly on the concrete and then crunching even more loudly on the rubble. The Nazis were relentless and would stop at nothing to kill their targets.

As the British and Americans reached the end of the road, they came to a junction. Stephen grabbed Sarah by the hand and pulled her with him, as he turned right. The others followed them, as the Americans turned left.

"Sergeant, if you don't mind me asking, where are we going?" Sarah asked , running along easily beside Stephen, as he panted heavily, short of breath.

"We're heading for the square. Somewhere where we will be safe and can see the bastards coming" Stephen explained, gasping heavily.

"But what if there are more Nazis waiting for us when we reach the square, sergeant?" Sarah asked pointedly.

"Ah shit, I hadn't thought of that," Stephen said angrily, slowing down slightly.

"The best thing I think we should do is get into pairs and kill them one by one," He muttered thoughtfully to himself.

"I get the feeling this is going to be one hell of a bloody long night" Williams commented quietly to Green, who nodded in agreement.

Dougy suddenly grabbed Sarah's arm, making her jump. Then he said quietly to her " stay wi' me love. Collins trusts me better than that lot."

"Alright" Sarah agreed quietly.

They all split up at Stephens's orders. Sarah followed Dougy like he had said. Stephen let her; it didn't even bother him that she was going with another private. He seemed to trust her enough to know that she would make the right decisions.

They ran down another alleyway that was dark and murky. Some large dogs jumped up at them making them jump in alarm, the dogs were trying to get over a wire fence at the vulnerable British soldiers and they were loosing the battle.

As they left the alleyway and ran onto the street that led to the main square, there was another loud shout in that odd German language that they kept hearing. Sarah faltered for a moment to see who had shouted. But she continued to run when Dougy yelled for her to keep following him and not to look back.

A large bright searchlight wondered over the street out of nowhere, following in the direction of Dougy's shout.

Dougy stopped suddenly, staring up at an old, bomb damaged church steeple. Sarah ran up beside him and glanced at him. Then she squinted through the dark, trying to see what the hell it was that had caught his attention.

"What's the matter, Dougy?" she asked, looking at him.

"Have you noticed however far and fast we seem to run the Nazis always manage to catch up with us?" Dougy asked her. He was still staring at the church steeple.

"Yeah, so?" Sarah asked impatiently.

"Well that steeple is just about high enough to get a good view of the entire town. That steeple probably once contained bells. But if those bells were to be removed then a very good look out platform would be left in its place. So that the Nazis would have an advantage over us and could force us to go wherever they want us to go" Dougy explained as he carefully studied the steeple.

"Jesus Christ!" Sarah muttered under her breath, as she looked up intently at the church steeple as well.

They both looked at each other at the same time. They were thinking of the same thing at exactly the same moment.

Together they ran towards the church, which was practically falling down it was so bomb damaged. The entrance doors seemed as high as a two-story building. Even though the actual building itself had sustained a lot of heavy bombing, the entrance doors didn't even seem to have received a scratch on their less than shiny surface. Usually when a building suffers bomb damage it was the doors that went first.

Dougy took a small pocketknife from out of his pocket and he slid the razor sharp blade into the lock. He fiddled around with his knife until they both heard a satisfactory click as the door relented. Dougy pushed the large door open with all his strength and the door gave a low moan of protest as it opened inwards. Then Dougy gestured for Sarah to enter the building. He quickly glanced around to make sure that they hadn't been seen, and then he walked into the church and shut the door firmly behind him.

Inside the church it was pitch black. All except the meagre light that was seeping through the massive pane glass windows at the head of the church just behind the alter. But neither of them would dare to put their torches on for fear some one would see the beam of light.

Dougy touched Sarah's shoulder and gestured over to the right of them. He was pointing to a set of spiral stairs. The one's leading to the top of the bell tower.

They soundlessly moved across to the back of the church. There were holes in the ancient floor of the church where the Nazis had removed the large slabs, marking some ones grave. The dead bodies had been dug up and left on the church floor for all to see. It was thought of as an insult by the locals to do something so disrespectful, which was exactly why the Germans were doing it; they wanted to leave the locals with lasting memories of their invasion. Most bodies that were buried in the churches were important people who were respected by the locals, so the Nazis did it to anger and infuriate them. They were looking at a history of that town, which had now been destroyed by the

Germans. These bodies were a part of France that Gavrian himself wanted to be rid of.

"They've gone and bloody well ransacked the place," Dougy whispered to Sarah, as he scanned the church. Anything that might have been of value was now gone, even the bibles and wooden benches.

"Yeah, well the Nazis have no respect for anything, do they?" Sarah retorted bluntly.

They ducked under the small archway that led to the spiral stairs. By the steps there was a small pane glass window showing an image of Jesus dressed in white, surrounded by hundreds of angels. There was something about that particular image of Jesus that Sarah didn't like. It was the way the image was looking at her. But she wasn't sure what exactly she didn't like about it. Then it dawned on her what it was, it was the eyes. They had a spooky, hypnotic affect to them that made Sarah go cold inside with fear. But yet they seemed to be trying to warn her about something. Something that was dangerous and would possibly kill her. They seemed to follow her as she and Dougy went up the spiral steps. However much she tried she just couldn't take her eyes away from that strange image of Jesus as they slowly walked up the steps towards the top of the tower.

The stairs were dark and dingy. Because the roof was now gone the stairs were treacherously slippery and soaking wet. They had a layer of green moss on top of them, which had caused them to become unsafe. Both the soldiers were gripping onto the railings for dear life. But Sarah's thoughts kept drifting to that image of Jesus. There was just something about that image that was making her so scared. She couldn't seem to think of anything else.

Before they reached the top of the stairs, Dougy grabbed hold of Sarah and leaned towards her to whisper something into her ear.

"When we go into that room shoot every Nazi in sight. Don't think about it, just do it. Then we must get out of there as fast as possible and head straight for the main square. We should hopefully meet sergeant Collins there," he explained to her. His whispers seemed to echo of the walls. They sounded dangerously loud to Sarah.

She nodded to Dougy to say she understood. Dougy pointed to the door and then at his gun. He was telling her to get ready with her weapon because he was about to bust the door down.

She took hold of her gun and gripped it tightly in her hands. She glanced at Dougy and nodded to say that she was ready. Bloody terrified, but ready.

Dougy slowly counted down from three, counting down with his fingers. When he had reached zero he took a deep breath in and cried harshly "now!"

In a sudden rush of energy they barged through the tiny oak door and entered the room. They swung their weapons in every direction, preparing to shoot anything that so much as moved.

But there was no sign of life in the place. It was completely deserted. It had obviously been where the churches bell had once lived. But now it was hardly recognisable. There was no evidence what so ever there had ever been a bell there at all. There wasn't even ropes that were pulled to chime the bells. The hole in the floor that allowed the bells to chime freely was now boarded up with planks of wood nailed to the floor. In place of the bells were monitors and scanners set on desks. They were showing the positions of every German soldier in the village.

"Bloody hell, it's a control room" Sarah gasped, her eyes opening in wonder.

"That's how the bastards knew which direction we were heading in. They could fucking monitor us" Dougy remarked thoughtfully.

"Don't you think we should get in touch with sergeant Collins and tell him about this place" Sarah suggested, glancing over at him.

Dougy just stood there looking thoughtfully at the boarded up hole. He seemed to be totally unaware that Sarah was there at all..

There was a shrill cry behind them, then a very loud shout in German. Sarah turned around just in time to see three Nazis appearing at the tiny doorway. All three were privates. Their uniforms hadn't even been worn in yet. But all three looked like tough little buggers. They all stared in astonishment at the two British soldiers, as if they had never seen such a sight before.

Then they looked carefully at the two intruders, seeming to weigh out what their strengths and weaknesses were. All three seemed very interested in Sarah. Probably because she was smaller than Dougy and she was also a girl. Sarah gripped her gun tightly, her finger hovering over the trigger.

Sarah looked up at Dougy as if to say, "What do we do now?"

"I wouldn't worry. They look like thick bastards. We can talk as much as we like as well, because none of them look like they speak a word of English" Dougy said.

"But there are three of them and only two of us. We're a bit out numbered, don't you think?" Sarah whispered to him, the fear was showing in her eyes.

"Not necessarily, Sarah. It all depends on how good they are," Dougy told her. He seemed to be trying to reassure himself as much as he was Sarah.

Sarah licked her lips nervously and didn't once take her eyes of the Nazis. But what were they waiting for? Why didn't they just attack? Sarah could feel the fear building up inside of her, oddly mixed with a feeling of impatience and anger. But she tried not to show this on her face. One of the first things she had learnt in basic training was to never let your opponent see that you are scared.

Then suddenly as if he was given an order that no one else could hear, one of the Nazis gave a loud German curse and all three of them leapt towards Sarah and Dougy. Two of them were holding some weird looking weapons Sarah had never seen before. The other was aiming his gun straight at Sarah.

Before she even had time to think of what she was doing, Sarah lifted up her rifle and shot the nearest Nazi to her. The first bullet smashed in to his upper arm, spraying his blood everywhere. He dropped his weapon and clutched his bleeding ligament furiously. Sarah took more careful aim this time and the bullet smashed in to his unprotected chest. The Nazi gasped as his heart collapsed, then blood bubbled out of his mouth and his eyes bulged out. He collapsed like a puppet on to the boarded up hole, making a hollow thudding sound.

Then Sarah heard Dougy screaming to her for help. The two other Nazis were pinning him to the ground and were attacking him with the strange weapons Sarah had seen them holding. These weapons appeared to be some sort of sword. They were very thin and unlike anything Sarah had ever seen before. Dougy had slashes all over him, which were bleeding quite profusely.

Sarah took careful aim towards the two Nazis. At the same time being careful not to aim too close to Dougy. One false judgement and she could hit him directly in the head. Then she took a breath in and squeezed on the trigger. She felt the gentle push and heard the reassuring noise as the bullet was forced out of the gun.

The older of the two Nazis turned to face away from Sarah as her bullet smashed into the hardened flesh of his thigh. As the cold hard shell tore through his muscular flesh he gave a scream of agony and rolled over onto his back, clutching his damaged leg as the blood soaked through his trouser leg. There was only one more Nazi left who could still pose a threat to them now.

The other Nazi, who had his strange looking sword in midair, ready to swing it down on Dougy's neck, glanced over at his wounded companion. He would quickly learn this was a very fatal mistake to make.

Dougy glanced nervously at the Nazi, saw his opportunity and grabbed the Nazi by his neck, making him drop his weapon in shock. Then with phenomenal speed Dougy somehow managed to pull his pocketknife out.

Then he stabbed the knife right through the Nazis neck. The Nazi jerked once when the knife made contact with his flesh. Then his whole body flopped like a dead fish, leaning against Dougy. Dougy threw him viciously to the floor, a look of pure disgust upon his face.

Sarah walked over to Dougy to see if he was all right, not realising her own fatal mistake. The Nazi who had been shot in the thigh was crying through the agony, but had somehow managed to drag himself into a sitting position. He glanced at the ground next to him and saw a rifle lying there. He reached down for it and with what little strength he had left lifted it up shakily into the air and aimed it as accurately as he could at Sarah.

Before Dougy had time to figure out what was going on and could move Sarah safely out of range, the Nazi had already squeezed on the trigger. It was a touch sensitive gun and fired instantly, the bullet hitting Sarah straight in the arm.

She cried out in shock as the excruciating pain tore through her body. Then her whole world seemed to go blank and empty, everything went vague and distant. In a blur of confusion and pain she could just hear Dougy calling out her name. Then there was the familiar bang of a gun. She could vaguely see the Nazis face and wondered if the red stuff covering it was blood. She then lost complete control of her body and fell to the floor. She lay on her back slipping in and out of consciousness. She just wasn't used to getting shot, though in time she would become stronger against these attacks and overcome the agonising pain. But she didn't even make a sound. Unlike the bastard Nazi who Dougy had just shot, who had only just stopped screaming. Sarah was only just barely aware of Dougy tenderly taking hold of her wounded arm and covering the wound with a tight bandage to slow the flow of blood down.

"Come on girl, get up" Dougy said in encouragement. "You've got to get up, so as we can get out of here and back to the square. Then sergeant Collins can look at your damaged arm properly."

With his help, Sarah was able to sit up, her damaged arm now hanging uselessly at her side. Dougy took hold of her good arm and hauled her back onto her feet.

She stood still, swaying on the spot. Everything she saw seemed so unfocused and confusing. It was like being in a dream. Then she viciously shook her head until her eyesight started to focus properly. Already her arm seemed to hurt less, but she could also no longer feel that arm.

"Do you think you'll be strong enough to make it back to the square?" Dougy asked in concern. Sarah glanced at him and nodded slowly. She was trying to reassure herself as much as anyone else.

Dougy bent down and picked up his rifle, lying next to the rifle was one of the strange swords the Nazis had been fighting with. He looked at it with amused interest. Then he bent down and picked the blade up. It was incredibly light for such a long weapon. It was a strange object unlike anything

Dougy had ever seen before. It was sharp and incredibly strong, probably almost impossible to break. Yet it appeared to be set up into individual sections, as if the weapon could be dismantled.

As Sarah watched him, Dougy saw two individual buttons in the metal handle. He gave one of them a small unsure push and with a scraping sound the weapon seemed to almost disappear in on itself. It did so in the blink of an eye, so that all Dougy was left holding was the large metal hilt of the weapon.

"Jesus Christ almighty!" he exclaimed loudly, almost dropping the weapon in his shock. He had only just realised what this weapon was and he was deeply honoured to be holding such a rare and important object, very few soldiers in his position would ever be able to do what he had just succeeded in doing.

"Dougy, we really need to get out of here right now. We'll be completely defenceless from any further attacks" Sarah said, looking curiously at the strange contraption in his hand. She barely had enough strength to do this though; she was stumbling all over the place.

"Huh? Yeah right, just coming" he answered. He swung his rifle over his shoulder and secured his hat back on his head. Then he slipped the strange sword into his pocket. He would show this weapon to the general when he returned back to base, the general would be very interested to see this. He quickly followed Sarah out of the room.

As they closed the door behind them a shadow moved in one of the dark corners. Then quietly a fourth Nazi emerged from the murky shadows of the bell room. He looked down at the three dead Nazis on the floor and tutted sadly. He strode over to one of the computers and sat down in front of it. He quickly tapped something down on the keypad and sat back to wait for a reply. Then he leaned forward to speak through a little microphone attached to the computer. "They are heading for the square, mien Herr," he said in German through the mini microphone. He tapped something else down on the keypad. He leaned back in the chair again and the chair gave a groan of protest. The Nazi rested his hands behind his head and grinned broadly as he awaited his next order.

Meanwhile Sarah and Dougy were staggering down the staircase, Dougy was now taking the full support of Sarah. She was loosing a lot of blood and having such little experience with such injuries she was taking it quite badly.

"It's alright lass, we'll get there soon enough. Then we can get you out of here and you can get treatment back at base" Dougy reassured her.

"Dougy, is it always as bad as this the first time you get shot?" Sarah asked, through a fog of pain and blood.

"I wouldn't know, I haven't been shot yet", Dougy answered. Sarah chose not to answer.

In the distance the sun was rising. There would be a greater risk than ever that they would get caught in daylight than at night. They had to get out of there as swiftly as possible before they were all dead.

Berlin, Germany CHAPTER NINE

The place was dark and it held an oppressive atmosphere. It was also very cold, bone chillingly cold. The condensation was so heavy it was dripping down the walls. Outside a bored looking officer was standing to attention. A rifle was slung over his shoulder and there was a strange looking weapon hanging of his utility belt. He stood right outside their cell as if they would try to escape or something, not that any of them could possibly even think of attempting it. They could see him through the rusty iron door with it's assortment of scratched messages in every language known to man. What little light that actually managed to get through the tiny barred window gave them just enough light to see each other's figures in the tiny cramped cell.

Stan Newman, who had been British Prime Minister for over two years, sat on the only bed in the entire cell. It was as old as time and squeaked with the smallest of movements. He groaned quietly in agony and pain caused by an agonising headache and starvation. He hadn't had a decent meal in so long. The migraine was caused through a lack of sleep and utter stress. The only comfort he could think of were his family, who were probably worried sick for his safety.

Sitting close by was Liam Woodworth. He had been Foreign Secretary for a year and a half, when a Nazi had shot the other Foreign Secretary in the back before war had broken out and things had started to become really unsettled. Of course the German government had denied it completely when this incident had taken place. He lay on a dirty blanket on the cold, wet floor, dozing lightly. He seemed capable of sleep through anything.

Lying next to the Prime Minister was Robert Ford, the Deputy Prime Minister. He cradled his left wrist, which had been brutally broken. Gavrian couldn't get some certain information out of him so in his anger he had made a soldier to carry out this horrific deed. Through his tears he had still refused to give him the information, but he was suffering badly for it. Now he sat in misery on the bed with all three ministers ties were being used as a make shift sling to give it some support. But if he didn't get medical treatment soon the injury could become infected and he might die.

"How long are those bastards going to keep us locked up for? I'm bloody starving and none of us have had a wash in days" Liam grumbled furiously.

From the moment he had become a minister, Liam had shown a short fuse, with an often-violent temper. His temper had almost cost him his job many a time, but the thing was he was good at what he did, so every time he had gotten away with it. That temper of his seemed to gradually worsen the longer they were being kept in that cell. Stan wasn't even sure any more how long they had been locked up. Each day seemed to merge into the next, it no longer mattered. He didn't have a watch anymore. They had been stripped of any valuables by the Nazis when they had been captured.

"I don't know. Now be quiet, you need to conserve your energy. If you don't it will be so much easier for the Nazis to get the information they want out of you. So try to get some sleep" Stan told him.

"I've conserved enough energy already" Liam complained angrily, standing up and stretching until his bones cracked.

Down the other end of the corridor they could hear the terrified shriek of someone. He was probably being dragged out of his cell to be taken outside where he would most certainly meet a painful death.

"Sweet Jesus, that could be us" Robert Ford murmured in pained tones, as he struggled with all his strength to sit up. He gave a heavy moan as he leaned against the wet, cold brick wall. This wall was poorly constructed and uneven bricks were sticking into his back.

Then the petrified screams of the prisoner suddenly stopped and everything went quiet again,

Newman dreaded to even think what torture was being inflicted on that poor defenceless man.

"Tell me again, why it is they are keeping us hostage here?" Robert asked in a thin raspy voice, looking at Newman.

"It's so that they can obtain vital information on our main armies next movements, so that they can find an easier way of defeating the British" Newman explained.

"Well their doing a bloody good job of it, aren't they?" Woodworth said angrily. Newman had the sudden urge to go over to Woodworth and hit him in the face. If anything just to have a bit of peace. Woodworth was the only one out of the three of them who had given up hope of ever getting out. He seemed to have lost faith in his country and their own people, but the other two knew better.

Newman and Ford had faith they would do everything within their power to get their PM back on home soil. But Woodworth didn't believe it, he had simply given up and because of that he was getting everybody else down as well.

There came the echo of army boots marching up the corridor. All three ministers looked up at the door with the same feelings of fear and trepidation. Every time the footsteps sounded like that they had been dragged out for more interrogation by Gavrian. There was a loud clanging of keys then an audible grating noise as the key was pushed into the lock. A loud clicking followed this and the door was unlocked, then it was shoved brutally open.

The three ministers blinked painfully in the sudden bright light that filled the tiny room. It was now apparent what a state the room was in.

Everything was dirty and there was a hole dug in the middle of the cell that served as their toilet. This gave the place an unbearable stench that no living animal should put up with, let alone the British Prime Minister himself. When their vision had fully returned they saw quite a number of men standing just outside their cell. The bright light from the door illuminated their bodies, giving the ministers the impression that these men were Gods, which they clearly thought they were. There were five of them, four privates and a high-ranking officer that none of the ministers had ever seen before.

"We very sorry disturb you, but mien Fuhrer wish to speak to you. Follow me this way please," one of the privates said slowly. He could speak English, which was unusual for a Nazi. They believed that German was the divine language and no other should be spoken. But this soldier still spoke pretty poor English that was broken and he clearly felt uncomfortable speaking it.

The three ministers stood up slowly. Newman helped Ford to his feet and they reluctantly followed the four privates and the stranger out into the corridor. One private placed himself in front of them; two placed them selves on either side of them and the last behind them, so that they were trapped in like caged animals unable to escape. They felt so helpless, as if they had done something wrong and were being punished accordingly

Newman studied the new and unfamiliar soldier curiously. He was by the markings that were sewn to his arms a marshal. Also by the way he was talking to the privates about Gavrian, he was

Gavrian's right hand man. He was incredibly tall and menacing, about six foot five. Newman was six foot tall and this soldier seemed to tower over him. The soldier was in his mid forties with hair long since gone grey and it was starting to recede very badly. His cold blue eyes darted from cell to cell as they walked quickly down the long, dark corridor. He continuously clenched and unclenched his hands, which Ford noticed were bloody massive and the huge muscular fingers could do a great deal of damage. The new soldier seemed to be totally unafraid of the fact he was about to stand in the presence of one of the most feared men of their time. The privates that were circling the ministers looked completely terrified; their faces were waxy white with fear. Even though Gavrian was a very small person he had a presence about him that would put the fear of god into any man. He was incredibly strong and powerful for someone of his height. Once when Gavrian was questioning them they saw him throw a soldier twice his height out of a window. When he looked at you, you knew he was dangerous. He somehow seemed to possess the devil. But the marshal showed no fear what so ever. He acted as if he was going to see an old friend, who he had known since they were tiny children. Newman just couldn't imagine Gavrian as a young and innocent child.

At the end of the corridor was a very large steel door that appeared to have no lock. But from what he had seen Newman knew the world of the Nazis could be very deceptive. True to form on one side of the door was a code panel, which was used to gain access to the room beyond. There were a further two soldiers standing on each side of the door. As the enormous marshal approached them they snapped to attention and saluted him with great fear on their faces. The marshal seemed to almost sneer at them and gave them a salute that was little more than a small flick of his wrist.

Then one of the privates by the door moved to face the panel. He made sure that he completely blocked it from view as he hastily punched the code number in. A low buzzing sound was emitted from the door, and then a loud click as it was unlocked. The other soldier stepped forward and gave the door a hard push so that it swung inwards. Both soldiers hastily moved back to their original positions as the small group passed through the door. They entered a huge room with precious furniture in it at all. There was just a very large statue of Adolf Hitler in the centre of the room. The only furniture was a large marble desk and the most expensive desk chair Newman had ever seen. On the desk was a single file with Private written in large gold lettering. On either side of this file were the German flag and the Nazi flag, the Swastika. Apart from that the room was bare.

Newman glanced quickly around the large room. It was enormous, far too big to be an office. It was like a massive conference room. Newman remembered only one other room as big as this. It was when he went to the conference room at the EU summit, forcing Germany out of the EU just before war broke out. The room had a roof that was triangular and was more like a massive skylight than a roof. Right behind the desk were two huge windows that gave a breathtaking aerial view over Berlin itself.

The huge marshal barked out orders in German. The privates came to an abrupt halt in front of the desk. The one that stood in front of the ministers took a step aside and saluted Gavrian, who sat impatiently behind the desk. Gavrian chose to ignore him and didn't salute back. Then Gavrian stood up wearily, leaning against the desk. The marshal stood next to him, standing at ease with his hands clasped behind his back. Everything went quiet as everybody in the room waited for Gavrian to speak. But for a long while he didn't say anything, he was making them wait, the fear building up inside of them.

"Now Mr. Prime Minister" he said finally. "I grow tired of trying to obtain information from you on the next movements of your army, when whatever I do you refuse to co-operate. So I am prepared to make a small deal with you. But there are certain rules that have to be taken into consideration" Gavrian said. He looked from one minister to the next, to see what their reactions would be. Newman felt a cold shiver go down his spine and yet again he had the great urge to slap Gavrian across the face as hard as he could. But to take such a risk he would almost certainly die.

"What kind of agreement?" he asked cautiously. He didn't trust this man at all. He was just like his great uncle had been, ruthless and cunning. Any kind of generous offer he may give was never to be trusted.

"You give us the information we require on the next movements of your pitiful army and in return we will offer your Deputy Prime Minister what ever first aid that he may require" Gavrian said. Not once did he take his eyes of Newman.

Newman looked at Ford, raising his eyebrows in question. But Ford shook his head viciously in response, his look saying that what ever they were about to face, under no circumstances were they to give Gavrian such information.

"I thank you for your kind generosity, Chancellor" Newman said, looking back at Gavrian. "But how ever much you threaten us and torture us we would never even consider giving you such vital information. Because we would never place our army in such danger. So we will thank you for your generous offer, but I'm afraid we will have to sadly decline."

Gavrian made no response to what Newman had just said. He just stood there quietly, taking a deep breath in. Then he impatiently snapped his fingers once to get the attention of the marshal. The marshal moved forward and stood next to Gavrian. Gavrian spoke something angrily in a strange language to the marshal, it sounded like German and yet it was so different. The marshal glanced over to Ford, who shuffled nervously on his feet. The marshal nodded and then said something to Gavrian who nodded. The marshal approached Ford.

Suddenly with no warning at all, the marshal grabbed hold of Ford's broken wrist. He twisted the wrist so hard that they could all clearly hear the broken bones crunching and snapping.

Ford gave a loud scream of pain that seemed to tear right through Newman. Newman shut his eyes tightly and Gavrian smiled with pleasure. Then Ford clenched his teeth together until they could see the muscles bunching up at the sides and blood trickling down his mouth as he bit into his tongue. Tears of pain trickled down his cheeks and mingled with the blood.

"Okay, that's enough, I'll tell you!" Newman screamed out. He could no longer bear to see Ford go through any more pain.

"Please go ahead, Mr. Prime Minister" Gavrian ordered.

Newman took in a sharp intake of breath, cursing him self for being so foolish, but he now had no choice. Then he finally said, "Rouen, they are heading towards Rouen."

"Ah, so they are heading towards the Capital. Much as I had suspected," Gavrian said quietly to himself. Then he looked slowly up at Newman.

"I thank you for that useful piece of information, Gentlemen. We had to use unnecessary force though I'm afraid. But we did get there in the end. However because you refused to co-operate in the first place I am afraid we cannot offer the Deputy Prime Minister any medical attention. Be warned the next time that this happens we shall not be so lenient with you" Gavrian said.

"Hang on a minute. We had an agreement. You would give the Deputy Prime Minister the required first aid in exchange for the information that you wanted from us. Now we gave you that information, we expect you to keep your side of the bargain!" Newman cried out furiously.

"That agreement fell through when you refused to give me the adequate information when I asked for it. So I don't keep my side of the so called bargain," Gavrian said, sitting down at his desk with a satisfied smile on his face.

"But we still gave you the information that you wanted and yet you refuse us the first aid that we need?" Newman asked angrily.

"Not when I asked for it, you did not. I am sorry, but if you don't give us what we want at the required time then there is no deal. I am sorry, Gentlemen, but those were my terms" Gavrian explained. He was acting as if he were talking to ordinary civilians instead of fellow ministers.

"We had a deal, Chancellor" Newman hissed angrily, his face was contorted with anger and fury as he stared at the Chancellor

"No, Prime Minister, we had a deal before you decided that you would recklessly ignore it. Do not forget I am a much more powerful leader than you will ever be. At least I have the full respect of my people. Whose respect do you have? I never understood British Politics, always fighting and squabbling over the most trivial of things. They are like spoilt little children. I believe that way I am a much more powerful leader than you are, everyone listens to me. They don't argue and disagree, they certainly don't interrupt me. One day I will be the greatest leader ever. I will be even greater than the President of the United States. I already control most of Europe. It will not be long before I will control the whole of this continent. One day I will be the most powerful leader the world has ever known. It is just a matter of time" Gavrian said with a look of longing in his eyes. He was describing to them in his minds eye, his plans for the future. The disturbing thing about all this was that his ambitions were becoming a devastating reality. If something wasn't done to stop him he could take over the world.

"You will never take control of my parliament and my country. Not while I am Prime Minister" Newman said, his body shaking with anger.

"You are forgetting, Prime Minister that you are my prisoner now and that I have complete control over you. I can do what ever I wish with you. That I'm afraid also includes the fact that I have full control of your pathetic country and your Parliament."

"That will never happen. The UN would never allow such a thing!" Woodworth cried out suddenly, his face a picture of pure anger.

"May I remind you, my country is no longer part of the UN, or the EU. So they can do nothing to prevent me from taking over any country that I desire" Gavrian said, clasping his hands together. His face looked so calm and void of emotion that it was very unnerving and made the Prime Minister even more angry than ever.

"You may no longer belong to the EU, but they can still prevent you taking over the UK. You can't keep doing what ever pleases you, it doesn't work like that" Woodworth pointed out angrily. Stan looked at Woodworth furiously, angry that Woodworth could never keep his mouth shut.

"Germany is no longer part of the EU, so we are our own country and can do what ever we see fit to do. We do not have to follow petty rules that the EU decides we should obey. We can make our own rules and do just as we wish. That includes, I am very much afraid to say, being able to invade Great Britain" Gavrian said, a small smirk on his face. He knew that it would be fairly easy to take control of Britain with the main army abroad, fighting in Europe. Look how easy it was to capture the Prime Minister for example. That's what was worrying Newman, Gavrian was getting too ambitious. But this could also be his undoing.

"But that doesn't mean that you will find it easy to gain control of the UK, Chancellor. There are many countries that are perfectly willing to help the UK stop your petty armies from even reaching our shores," Newman informed him quietly. He could see these talks were getting them nowhere. Gavrian had the information he required, so why did he not send them back to their cell?

"You forget Germany also has a lot of countries supporting it, Prime Minister. They are also perfectly willing to help us invade the UK. Do not under estimate my powers, Prime Minister. I am far more powerful than even you realise" Gavrian said in a threatening voice.

"And who would possibly want to help you invade the UK? No country is that stupid" Woodworth asked.

"Many countries in Asia are more than happy to help me, for the good of their own countries. I am perfectly aware Asia is a great distance from Europe. But they are large countries, with an unlimited supply of soldiers. Which all works in my favour" Gavrian explained.

"Just because you have a large army, does not mean they are capable of fighting a fully trained army such as the British. Do not under estimate my army, Chancellor" Newman said threateningly.

"Even so, there is nothing you can do about it. You are prisoners, what possible use could you be to the British army now? Our army is more than perfectly capable of fighting yours. Now guards take them away. I have wasted enough time with these prisoners. Take them back to their cells until such time as I wish to enjoy their company again" Gavrian declared, standing up and gesturing to the marshal, who had resumed his place at his side.

The marshal saluted and gestured for the guards to have the ministers removed from the room.

"You'll never get away with this!" Woodworth screamed at Gavrian, struggling against the guards. Then he was forcefully removed from the room.

"I think I already have" Gavrian muttered to himself in German and sat down at his desk again.

CHAPTER TEN

The sun beat down strongly on the hot land, as the temperatures soared and water supplies were becoming dangerously low.

Sarah lay down beside Dougy, with Williams and Patterson on her other side. They had lain like this for ages, awaiting their next orders. They were lying flat on their stomachs in crumbling trenches, where even the smallest breeze blew suffocating dust in their faces, obscuring their vision. Even though all the soldiers had been given bits of material to wrap around their faces to prevent dust from getting into their mouths, it didn't stop it from blowing into their eyes.

"Quiet, wait for the order" a sergeant bellowed furiously, as some of the privates began to grow restless.

Stephen came up behind Sarah and patted her on her back, making her jump out of her skin. She glanced up at him and he smiled down reassuringly at her.

Then he leaned down towards her and said, "when the officers give the order to go over the top I want you to stay close to Dougy at all times, what ever happens. Make sure you follow Dougy's orders and no one else's. Is that understood?"

"Yes, sergeant" Sarah answered. Then she looked back nervously out towards the fields. Between them and the Nazis was a huge arable field, which appeared to have not been used since the beginning of the war. It seemed a very long distance to run from where she was lying.

Williams gave Sarah a gentle nudge and pointed over to the Nazi trenches. A young lance corporal was wondering around aimlessly on the field just by the Nazi trenches. He kept glancing at the American trenches. The Americans refused to fight unless the trenches were declared theirs. They completely ignored the fact that three quarters of the men in those trenches were actually British. Above Sarah's head was the biggest Stars and Stripes flag she had ever seen. It completely drowned out the Union flag fluttering right behind it. Major Johnson had tried to persuade them not to hoist the huge flag at full mast, but the Americans refused to take the flag down. They said if the flag went, they went. They said it was a matter of national pride.

"He can't be very important if their letting him wonder as he pleases above the trenches. His right in the line of fire" Patterson commented, talking about the wondering corporal.

"Go on girl, shoot the bastard" Stephen whispered, patting her on the shoulder to get her attention.

"Yes, sergeant" Sarah said, smiling happily as she aimed carefully at the lance corporal. Her gun rubbed on her bandages that covered the injury she had received in the bell room. She flinched and then completely ignored her discomfort. The lance corporal now appeared to be saying something to soldiers below in the trenches. Sarah squeezed gently on the trigger and felt the small push as the bullet was forced out of the barrel.

The bullet hit the lance corporal squarely in the chest and he grabbed his chest screaming. Then he staggered backwards and fell into the trench.

Then with no warning hundreds of Nazis came like a flood over the top of the trenches and headed at incredible speed towards the American trenches. The Americans started to panic and against orders some started to jump over the top, getting instantly shot by the Nazis in the process.

"He was a fucking decoy", major Johnson cried out in despair. "Right men, over the top" he bellowed and blew loudly on his whistle.

All the men leapt to their feet and jumped over the top of the trenches. Dougy touched Sarah's arm and she leapt up enthusiastically, jumping over the top and onto open ground. They quickly ran across the field towards the freshly dug trenches of the Germans.

Hundreds of Nazis ran towards them, they uttered screams of fury and challenge. They seemed to think this was some kind of tribal battle and not a war between countries.

"Get down, you stupid bastards!" major Johnson screamed across the field as loudly as he could be heard.

Without a moments thought they all threw themselves to the ground. The Americans kept running though. The British prepared their guns and waited for their next order.

"Aim, fire!" major Johnson screamed.

There was a chorus of loud bangs as the British shot at the Nazis. A large number of Nazis fell, slowing the ones behind them down, but a great deal more kept coming. Running towards the now unprotected trenches of the British. The Americans were supposed to be the one's who were protecting the trenches.

"Fire!" the major screamed again. There was another chorus of loud bangs. More Nazis fell, but they still kept coming.

"Okay men, charge!" major Johnson yelled loudly.

The soldiers jumped up again and continued to run across the open field towards the Nazi trenches, which were a lot better protected than the British one's were.

Sarah could feel the adrenaline pumping through her veins. They were so close to enemy lines now she could make out the sides of the trenches. Sarah felt a pang of fear going through her. She could see the Nazis aiming their guns at her and the other soldiers around her. She could smell the grass underneath her feet and it was rubbing against her ankles. Sarah quickly glanced to the left of her and spotted faithful Dougy running calmly at her side. True to the promise he had made to Stephen he was sticking close beside Sarah and not letting her out of his sight. It didn't matter what happened to him, he didn't care if he died as long as Sarah was safe.

Dougy suddenly touched her on the shoulder and pointed directly ahead of them. Two high-ranking officers were running directly for them.

They had a mad look of death in their eyes and were screaming out cries of challenge and fury.

"Go on, shoot the bastards. Their worth more than every private on this fucking field" he called out to her, as they came ever closer to the Nazi trenches. Acrid smoke filled the fields as bombs flew past the running British soldiers. The sound of death was all around and a smell of soil and blood filled Sarah's every sense, blotting out her vision, making it harder to fight and a lot more confusing.

Without a second thought Sarah dropped to one knee and aimed her rifle up in the direction of the rapidly approaching officer. Looking back she couldn't even remember if or when she had squeezed the trigger. But the next thing she knew the officers limp body had fallen to the ground, his head was a mass of blood and tissues.

She continued to sprint across the field, spotting Dougy shooting down the other officer with pinpoint accuracy. Then he immediately followed her to the enemy trenches. Everywhere there were the sounds of guns firing and the agonising screams of dieing men. There were loud explosions and the ground shook as bombs were falling all around the British and Americans. Even more screamed their last dieing breath as the bombs hit home.

They were so close to the trenches now that Sarah could actually see to the bottom, which was very much like their trenches, filled with dust and infested by rats.

"Right men, stand back!" Stephen bellowed at them as he ran past them. Sarah and Dougy stared at him in utter bewilderment. He was pulling something out of his pocket and slinging his rifle over his shoulder as he continued to run for the practically deserted trenches of the Nazis.

"What in Gods name is he doing?" Sarah shouted at Dougy, as she watched Stephen. Dougy didn't seem in the least bit puzzled about what was going on though.

"He's going to blow up the officers bunker!" he answered, watching his sergeant jump boldly into the trench and disappear from sight.

"Where's the officers bunker?" Sarah asked, squinting to see if she could make out a metal door in the muddy wall of the trench. The reason they placed metal doors on the officers bunker was to prevent the place being blown up. Of course it didn't help if there was no one there to protect it.

"Right in front of you, you bloody idiot" Dougy answered. Then Sarah caught the glint of something metal and saw the faint outline of a metal door through thick layers of mud. Then she realised that the door was wide open.

Stephen lobbed the bomb through the open metal door and jumped out of the trench as fast as he possibly could, then threw himself to the ground as a loud explosion seemed to shake the earth beneath him. The metal door was blown of its hinges and flew several feet into the air. A wall of flames then swept through the officers bunker. Agonising screams could be heard as the officers; helpless to save themselves were burnt to death. Out of the dingy darkness a young officer suddenly appeared, his whole body engulfed in flames. He ran almost blindly up the metal ladder and onto the field. He screamed out in help, his arms waving in the air as the flames burnt through his clothes and started to penetrate his skin.

Sarah aimed her weapon at the screaming, burning mass of flesh. She fired and flames arched out from his body as the bullet hit home. The officer screamed continuously through so much pain. He fell to the ground and died slowly as the fire burned his body away into ashes. Sarah doubted there would be anything left when the fire burnt out.

"You should have just let the bastard burn," Dougy said.

Sarah didn't answer.

Dougy stood up and ran over to Stephen. He helped Stephen up and Stephen brushed himself down. Then they both glanced into the trench.

Stephen led Dougy, Sarah, Patterson, Williams and a number of British that Sarah didn't recognise down into the trench.

Her boots squelched deeply in the thick, sticky mud that covered the floor of the trench. A pungent smell of rotting flesh and wild rats filled her nostrils as Stephen lead them towards the officers newly burnt out bunker.

A Nazi came running around the corner. He stopped just in front of them. Then his eyes widened as he saw they were British. He started to shout at the top of his voice in German. But not more than a couple of words passed his lips. Because Patterson gave a heavy sigh and shot him in the chest. He fell backwards and his body started to sink into the mud.

They all glanced into the officer's bunker, which was completely burnt out now. Large black objects lay on the ground, thick black smoke rising from them. They looked like human beings, but what ever they were they were now no more than charcoal.

"What do we do now, sergeant?" Sarah asked. They all looked at Stephen as he stood shifting his feet nervously.

He took in a sharp intake of breath and glanced into the burnt out bunker again .He looked at each individual officer in turn. Then he glanced up at the burnt, blackened beams that kept the whole thing up. Earth and mud started to fall down from them.

"Okay every one get the hell out of here! The whole bunkers going to collapse at any moment" he cried out, pushing the soldiers forcefully away from the door.

True to his words the roof gave a loud groan and the beams gave way as the whole ceiling collapsed. A cloud of dust rose from the door, causing the soldiers to choke harshly.

"Alright, we definitely need to get out of here. Head down the right of us until we should hopefully reach their idea of a main control room. Then we kill as many of the bastards as possible, until we have complete control of this hell hole," he explained. "Is every one clear on what I just said?"

They all nodded, but some still looked a bit apprehensive.

"Alright, lets get moving then. Come on you lazy bastards, they won't be waiting for us, you know" Stephen ordered, urging them on.

They followed Stephen at a slow jog; it was far too risky running in the ankle high mud, one wrong move and they would be sliding right over. They headed down the trench, jumping over the dead bodies that now covered the bottom. Their boots sank and slid in the mud. There were hundreds of dead bodies covering the ground, some British and American and even more Germans. Some of the Germans may have even drowned in the muddy rainwater. Fallen asleep and just sunk into the thick mud where they lay.

They turned around a corner and came face to face with about a dozen Nazis, all covered in mud, all looked close to madness. At first they seemed confused, confronted by British who had some how gotten through their defences. Then without a single warning they began to shoot at the small group of British. Several Nazis drew out more of those strange new weapons that Sarah was now seeing more frequently. Only certain types of soldiers seemed to have these weapons, which to her seemed very peculiar indeed.

One of them leapt towards Patterson, swinging his sword in a threatening manner above his head. In response Patterson smacked him hard in the face with the butt of his gun. The Nazi was knocked unconscious and fell over backwards. Another Nazi in trying to catch his comrade dropped his own sword. He caught the unconscious Nazi, but in doing so lost balance and fell over himself. He fell onto his weapon and it went straight through him and his companion. They lay on the ground, the sword piercing through them like a large metal spike.

One Nazi slashed through Sarah's sleeve and into her arm. She tried to ignore the stinging pain and the blood that was seeping into her clothes. She responded by shooting him directly in the chest.

The small group of soldiers ran quickly past the Nazis and continued on their way down the trenches, towards what they all hoped was the main control room.

Now there were no Nazis in the trenches at all, they were either fighting on the field against the onslaught of British, or they had already surrendered to the British, but this scenario seemed very unlikely though.

As they turned the final corner that led directly to the main control room they came face to face with a small regiment of Americans. The Americans looked at them with surprised expressions on their faces. Stephen responded with a stern expression, while the others stood panting heavily behind him.

"The captain has sent out orders for all soldiers to return to the American trenches. The Nazis have surrendered" one of the lieutenants informed him. He gave them all a cold hard stare and a look of complete dislike.

"We have not been informed of this, are you sure your facts are correct, lieutenant?" Stephen asked, not trusting this arrogant American.

"Their quite clear. Do you see any Nazis in these trenches? They have all moved onto the field in an act of surrender. I wouldn't lie about something like this" the lieutenant insisted.

"Okay, thank you for informing me, lieutenant" Stephen said graciously. He gave the lieutenant the same cold stare the lieutenant was giving his men.

The lieutenant saluted him and he returned the salute. Then the lieutenant led his men past them and the small group of Americans headed down the way Stephens men had just come.

"Oh, by the way, lieutenant" Stephen called out suddenly. The Americans stopped and turned to face him. "We might be from different countries, but that doesn't mean you treat your superiors any differently. Next time address me as sergeant and don't forget your manners. You may live to regret it" Stephen warned him. Then Stephen turned around and climbed up one of the ladders attached to the side of the trenches.

When Stephen's back was turned the lieutenant spat on the floor in his direction. Patterson responded by pointing his rifle at him. The lieutenant held his hands up in the air as a sign of piece, and then he continued down the trenches, the other Americans following him obediently like dogs following their master.

Sarah then quickly followed McBride up the ladder and he hoisted her the rest of the way onto the blood soaked field when he had clambered back onto the field.

"Well would you look at that? Now that's a sight for sore eyes, isn't it, lass?" McBride commented, as they stood looking over the field.

Sarah made no answer. She stared at the field wordlessly taking in the full horror of it all. In only a few short hours a lush green field had turned into a kind of living nightmare.

"Right men. Let's get back to the trenches. We don't want them to have all the fun without us do we now?" Stephen said a lot more cheerfully than he felt.

As they approached the safety of their own trenches they saw a large number of Nazi soldiers already tied to make shift wooden poles. They were blindfolded and were mumbling prayers frantically. They knew exactly what was about to happen to them and they knew there was no way out of this situation; no one would be saving them now.

"Do you really think we should let the lass watch this, sergeant? She's only been in the army a short while; do you think she is really ready to witness this sort of thing?" McBride asked.

"I think now is as good a time as any, private. She will witness such events with time. She needs to learn about these things, McBride, we can't keep protecting her from such terrible events, you know" Stephen answered.

"Protect me from what?" Sarah asked McBride.

"You will soon find out lass, just be patient and you will see" McBride answered. But he refused to tell her anymore than that.

The small group of British soldiers stood a fair distance away from the large group of mainly American soldiers that were crowded eagerly around the terrified Nazis, they clearly knew something was about to happen.

Even though officers were shouting out orders for the soldiers to be quiet it did little to calm the situation. The soldiers were yelling insults at the

Nazis and throwing anything they could lay their hands on at the still praying enemy.

"What's going to happen to them?" Sarah asked Dougy.

"You'll see. Just wait and all will become clear to you" Dougy told her.

All of a sudden everything went absolutely silent. The cheering soldiers went quiet and stopped throwing things at the Nazis as they stopped praying.

Sarah strained her head to look over the heads of those in front of her and caught a glimpse of a neat line of soldiers marching towards the Nazis, forcing their way through the crowds. The crowds followed them as they stepped up to the make shift poles and lined up to face the enemy. Nobody said a word as an officer walked up to the line of soldiers and stood in front of them.

"For the crimes you have committed and the deaths that you have caused" the officer began, speaking loudly and clearly in German. "We see no fit punishment other than to sentence you to death."

All the Nazis began to protest. They started to scream out loudly and pulled desperately on the ropes that were keeping them tied to the poles. But one Nazi seemed unaffected by what the officer had just said. Then suddenly he spoke up, speaking loudly and clearly in perfect English.

"You may kill us, but that does not mean you will have victory. The more you kill us the more we will just keep coming. You cannot win this war. We have too many on our side and we are too strong a nation. The Chancellor will hear of this atrocity caused by his enemies and he will become angry. Don't test our Chancellor, for it is more than your life's worth. He will hunt you down and kill you in cold blood. He is a very powerful man and you will learn this, in time you will learn this."

"Okay, kill him" the officer said to the soldier next to him. The soldier aimed his gun at the Nazi and shot him in the head.

"You wait, he will find you!" the Nazi screamed as he slowly died.

Sarah gasped in horror and looked at Dougy.

"So, that's what they're going to do. That's why McBride didn't want me to see this? All those Nazis are going to be shot to death!" she said understanding.

"Yeah, that pretty much sums it up " Dougy said rather coldly.

They continued to watch while the officer screamed out orders and the British soldiers loaded their weapons. The Nazis heard the clicks as the bullets were loaded and some of them even started crying.

McBride who was standing next to her turned around and shut his eyes. He couldn't bear to watch any more of it.

"Aim, fire!" the officer screamed.

There was a chorus of loud bangs and ear piercing screams as most of the bullets hit home. Some bullets strayed of course though, causing the Nazis even more pain than. Sarah could only stare in horror.

There was a loud rumble of thunder in the distance. While their attention had been diverted rain clouds had developed in the sky. They were now very thick and dark. It would be a welcome relief from the months of drought, but the rain hadn't come at exactly the right moment.

"Come on lass, let's get out of this rain. I think you've seen enough for today," McBride said. Every one started to head towards the shelter of the trenches as the firing squad completed its task and the heavens opened.

CHAPTER ELEVEN

Rain fell down in heavy sheets turning the dry, dusty roads into thick slippery mud. The rain made loud banging noises on the canvas of the officer's tents. Outside there were continuous claps of thunder and flashes of lightening. This continued all day, as did the bombs of the enemy. But no one was concerned about such far off explosions; as long as they didn't get any closer they were posing no threats to the soldiers.

Soldiers sat calmly enjoying what little rest they could get and they waited for their next orders. Some were sitting on food crates, playing with cards or cleaning their weapons. Others sat on the cold, muddy floor, using their jackets to sit on. It had rained continuously for four days now, not stopping once. But even though the weather was dismal the general spirit of the regiments was high. They were all cheerfully larking about and teasing each other. The only soldiers that weren't cheerful were the Americans. They had ignored orders to stay by the trenches to keep guard over them and were well and truly paying for their lack of obedience. Many of them were also becoming badly homesick having been away from home for such a long period of time. Many of them weren't used to being in the countryside. They were accustomed to the hustle and bustle of city life. They had never experienced the calm serenity of the endless rolling hills and acres of woodland.

Even though almost every one had a cheerful temperament, there was still a feeling of nervous tension in the air. Even though they may have won the battle that took place a couple of days ago, it was still only a minor victory. Hardly significant to the importance of the war. Over on the border between France and Germany larger scale battles were being fought and the British were loosing. The Nazis seemed to be getting more powerful and were gaining more land as each day passed. Every day Gavrian Hitler seemed to be inching ever closer to the British Channel. The situation was getting closer to desperation and what made it all worse was that every one knew the Nazis were actually winning the war. What ever the British and Americans did to stop them the Nazis just crashed straight through their barriers and went on to win yet another pointless victory, while laughing in Britain's face.

All that could be done now was that the soldiers just kept going; they had no other choice. The armies had to be kept organised, because if they didn't then the whole world might as well surrender to Gavrian Hitler. Then he would have won the war and completed the campaign that had theoretically started so long ago.

While the rest of their regiment sat close by, playing cards, Dougy and Sarah were sitting on their jackets under a make shift tent. They were all waiting for Stephen to return. He had been summoned to the office's tent over an hour ago. They were all anxious to hear what the general had to say to him.

As Dougy walked out of the protective cover of the tent Williams strolled in and sat down beside Sarah. She glanced at him, and then tied her ammunition bag tightly and safely to her backpack.

"You sorted everything out yet?" he asked, putting his backpack on the floor and starting to go through its contents.

"Almost" she answered, as she started the pain staking process of cleaning her rifle.

"There's a rumour going around at the moment that we won't have enough ammunition to last us through the next battle. Apparently the Germans found out what ships are delivering our military weapons to us and they blew them to kingdom come. Things just get better don't they?" Williams said sarcastically, getting out his pocketknife and sharpening it against another knife.

"Jesus, what all of it? Can't they ship anymore over?" Sarah asked, looking at Williams in shock.

"Not at the moment, it's far too risky. The Germans seem to know exactly every move that we make. No one can figure out how, but they know too much. Maybe someone leaked out the information to them? But no one knows who that could be. It doesn't seem to be anyone in this army. And there haven't been many deserters of late" Williams explained to her.

"Really? I thought there would have been loads," Sarah said. She flinched as she felt a fresh stab of pain going through her arm. The injury she had received only a couple of days ago had only just stopped bleeding and was beginning to heal very slowly. What ever those weapons were they were razor sharp and left very deep cuts. She had cleaned the wound with anti-septic and wrapped a bandage around it to slow the flow of blood. However it was still bleeding and stung like hell. But there was a very short supply of painkillers only used in extreme cases, so she had to put up with the pain.

"No, for some reason they're just not deserting. I mean have you seen the way the other side have to live? It makes us look like we live a life of luxury. Most of them are starving to death, they are all sleep deprived and some have been known to fall asleep while marching" Williams explained to her with a look of disgust.

"Thank god I was never on the other side. Anyway I doubt they would have allowed me to join the German army. They live in a different era, where women are treated like second-class citizens" Sarah commented.

Williams smiled at this and said "that's true lass, them lot are stuck in the past. It does make you wonder how they're even winning the war."

Then the conversation died a bit as Williams continued to scrape his knives together. Sarah was meticulously cleaning every part of her gun with an old oily rag. Outside the rain continued to pour, never seeming to relent. It drummed constantly on the tent making large puddles of water outside the tent that went up to your ankles.

The peace and quiet of the tent was abruptly cut short by the appearance of Stephen. He seemed to be in a fowl mood, his face more thunderous than the weather. He walked angrily over to them and sat down with a heavy sigh next to Sarah. She glanced at Williams, who shrugged his shoulders in response. Then she looked at Stephen again.

"What's the matter, serge?" she asked wearily.

"What's the matter? I'll tell you what the fucking matter is!" Stephen suddenly burst out in fury. Then he suddenly stood up again and started to pace around the tent. "The army in their ever generous nature have decided to send me and my regiment, meaning you lot, on a mission to Berlin. I mean Berlin, the capital of fucking Germany! Why don't they just shoot us all or something, it's a much quicker way to die? It's certainly faster than sending us into the middle of enemy territory."

"Yeah, but what's the mission, sergeant?" Sarah asked. She cringed again at the fresh pain shooting through her arm.

"The mission is a very complicated one. We have to go and rescue the British Prime Minister and some other vitally important ministers from the Nazis, who are currently holding them hostage", Stephen proclaimed. He stopped walking around the tent and stood in front of the two privates. He watched the reactions on their faces as it slowly dawned on them what he had just said.

"But how the bloody hell did they get through the security to get to the Prime Minister in the first place? Surely he was far too well protected for them to even get close to him?" Sarah said, totally shocked.

"Apparently there wasn't nearly enough protection. There were too many Nazis; they were simply over whelmed. Now the Nazis are demanding pacific information for the safe return of our Prime Minister."

"What kind of information, sergeant?" Williams asked.

"Military information. Mostly about the movements the British army will take in the next few months. But they also want to know about certain soldiers and what equipment we actually have. That sort of information."

"And if we don't give them this information?" Sarah asked.

"They will either kill the Prime Minister, or get the information out of him anyway they can" He explained.

"But they can't possibly get all the information out of the Prime Minister" Williams said. "He doesn't know every single movement the army makes."

"Yeah, but you see that's the problem. They are also holding the Deputy Prime Minister and the Foreign Secretary hostage," Stephen explained.

"Why are they holding the Deputy Prime Minister hostage as well, sergeant? He won't know anymore than the Prime Minister himself" Williams asked.

"So that he can't run the country in the Prime Ministers absence. The Nazis want to try and make it as hard as possible for the English, to allow for maximum confusion and that way their attacks will have a far greater impact."

"Sergeant, where do we come into all this?" Sarah asked. Then she openly cringed at the pain in her arm. A trickle of blood escaped her bandage and ran down her arm. Her hand started to visibly shake.

Stephen and Williams glanced down at her arm in concern.

"Look, Sarah, let me have a look at that injury. I don't want it going septic. That could cause permanent damage" Stephen insisted. Before Sarah had time to protest he sat down next to her and took hold of her arm, gripping it tightly. He pulled her sleeve up and proceeded to unravel her bandage. It revealed a sticky mass of blood and flesh. The cut was still oozing and it was so deep that it almost reached to the bone. Stephen took a bottle of antiseptic out of his rucksack and wet a clean scrap of material with it. Then he gently patted the wound on Sarah's arm with it.

"This is a pretty nasty wound girl. It may take quite a while to heal. You should really see someone, it might need stitches," Stephen said, studying the wound as he cleaned it thoroughly.

"Oh well, as long as its still serviceable I'll be fine" Sarah said, ignoring what Stephen had just said.

"Well if you see any signs of the wound going septic at all I want you to go straight to a doctor. Now that's an order," Stephen said sternly.

"Yes, sergeant" Sarah said.

"Where we come into all of this, Williams" Stephen said, returning to their former subject. "Is that we have been chosen as the poor buggers who are going to rescue the Prime Minister from these bastards. And guess what! They have only given us a deadline to do it in. Three days, I mean what do they think we are? Bloody miracle workers. The only good thing to come out of this campaign is that we are guaranteed a weeks leave to allow us to return home" Stephen explained to them. The more he explained it all to them the angrier he became and the harder he rubbed on Sarah's wound with the scrap of material. Then suddenly Sarah flinched away as he put too much pressure on it. Stephen patted her arm and she reluctantly let him hold it again. He gently gripped it and continued to clean the wound.

"Do you think the regiment is capable of completing such a complicated mission in the time given, safely?" Williams asked.

"No, I don't think the regiment is capable of even reaching Berlin in the time permitted. Not on foot or by transport. It's far too risky. We wouldn't be able to get through the German barriers."

"We can't refuse this mission though. The army would force us into doing it even if we wanted to or not" Sarah said pointedly, as Stephen gave her arm a final pat and threw the blood soaked rag into the dieing embers of a fire near by. Sarah examined her arm carefully and when he was satisfied with it Stephen wrapped a clean bandage around the wound.

"Murray's right, sergeant. We have no choice on the matter. We have to do it whatever," Williams said pointedly

"Yes, I am fully aware of that, Williams. But what I don't understand is why they chose my regiment. I would have thought they would have chosen a much larger regiment, one more capable of completing such a deadly mission. We're not even a proper regiment, just ten men and they still expect us to fight against the entire German army in bloody Berlin."

"Then why did they choose us, sergeant?" Sarah asked.

"I have absolutely no idea what so ever," Stephen admitted. There was something in his eyes that made Sarah suspect that he was lying though.

"Maybe it's just because no one else was stupid enough to take such a mission on? Or maybe we were they're last resort, sergeant? Maybe there was no one else" Williams suggested.

"Thank you for sharing that thought with us, Williams. But I fear it's a lot more complicated than that. There's something else behind all this. Something they aren't telling us, especially you, Sarah" Stephen said.

"Me, what would they be hiding from me?" Sarah asked.

"I don't know, but I intend to find out" Stephen promised her.

He leaned over to a can of something that was cooking over the dieing fire. He picked up the can and looked into it with disgust.

"What the hell is this stuff?" he asked, scraping the stuff around the can with his metal spoon. What ever this was it stank to high heaven.

"It's meant to be vegetable soup," Williams told him.

"Where are the vegetables?" Stephen asked.

Suddenly Dougy burst into the tent, panting painfully. "You will not believe this. They have run out of ammunition. Something to do with the Nazis blowing up a certain ship" he announced in disgust.

All the others looked up at him for a second. Then Stephen shook his head in disbelief and put the can back on the rack over the fire. Williams looked at Dougy and cocked an eyebrow in amusement. Sarah continued to clean her gun.

The next morning they all stood outside the officers tents, fully equipped and ready for anything the Germans had to throw at them. At least that was the plan.

Major Johnson walked briskly out of the tent, holding a piece of paper in one hand and a cigar in the other. He walked up to Stephen and handed him the piece of paper, which Stephen took saluting smartly.

"Excuse me, sir. But what is this?" Stephen asked him, looking at the paper with a puzzled expression.

"That, sergeant" major Johnson said. "Is your instructions on how to reach Berlin. You will see written inside is a message explaining that you will have transport taking you as far as Hanover. There you will be given German uniforms as a disguise and you will continue on foot to Berlin" major Johnson told him.

"But I can't speak German very well, sir. None of the lads can, the Nazis are going to suspect something straight away, sir" Stephen said.

"Then let Murray speak, sergeant. She speaks German fluently and if the Nazis become suspicious then just kill them" the major said.

"Yes, sir" Stephen said. Then he suddenly said, "Sir, why are we only being dropped of at Hanover, why not Berlin?"

"Because, sergeant it wastes fuel. It's too expensive to get you any closer to Berlin than Hanover. I am sorry sergeant, but that's the way it is" the major told him; his temper was beginning to wear thin by now.

"Yes, sir" Stephen said quietly. He saluted major Johnson, who returned the salute, and then walked back into his tent without another word.

Stephen marched angrily to the vehicle tent, his company following obediently behind him.

When they had reached their appointed vehicle they all stared at it in shock and disbelief. The vehicle in question looked like something that had been built during the last century. It was a very old army truck that had no cover of any sort over it for camouflage. There were just metal bars for the people sitting in the back to hold onto. There were no seats in the back of the truck, just wooden crates containing ammunition in case the truck came under attack from the Germans. But in all manner of speaking the truck was a complete mess. It didn't even look like it could reach the German border, let alone Hanover.

The driver, who was an ex-officer, stood patiently by the truck. He was leaning up against it with his arms and legs crossed.

"Where the bloody hell did they drag this old heap out of?" Stephen asked in disgust, as they approached the rusted heap of metal.

"In its defence this vehicle is one of the best trucks in the army" the driver said proudly as he stood up straight. It was obvious that he loved the ugly old mess next to him.

"How old is it?" Stephen asked suspiciously.

"They were using this truck to shift troops around with equipment when the gulf war was on" the driver told them proudly, tapping the bonnet of the truck.

"When was the gulf war?" Sarah asked, looking at Stephen.

"A very long time before any of us were born, Murray. It was a war that took place out in the Middle East during the 1980's" Stephen explained.

Sarah looked at him in bewilderment.

"Right men, I know it's not exactly first class, but it'll have to do. So we'll get on in an orderly fashion, starting with the youngest" Stephen said, gesturing to the truck.

McBride and Green hoisted Sarah onto the back of the truck. The last to get into the truck was King. Stephen then banged loudly on the side of the truck and jumped into the passenger seat as the driver steered the truck out into the muddy road. The engine sounded like it was in a very bad condition and kept making loud grinding noises.

The driver, who was no driving expert suddenly jarred the truck into first gear, then sped of down the road. He drove straight through a regiment of Americans, causing them to scatter across the road in order to get out of the way. Then the truck sped away from the safety of the camp, leaving a trail of dust and fumes in its wake.

"Sweet Jesus Christ. This truck is so old it's running on diesel" McBride exclaimed out loud, as he leaned over the back of the truck and stared in wonder at the exhaust pipe as it shook and blew out great billows of black smoke.

"What's that?" Sarah asked, shouting over the sound of the engine.

"It's a type of oil that was once used for cars. They stopped using it some years ago when they ran almost completely out of the stuff. It came out of the ground as crude oil. The stuff used to bloody stink" Dougy explained to her

"Why did they use it in the first place then?" Sarah asked.

"Because it was the only good thing they could use in those days. You see in those days they weren't quite so intelligent," Dougy told her. At the last remark he smiled then laughed heartily.

As the day drew on and it grew hotter they stopped at a river to fill their water bottles with fresh cold water. They sat by the river to have a rest. As they gazed across the beautiful French landscape McBride commented on how good the harvest was looking that year, but that lead to wondering how long that was going to last before the Nazis destroyed the crops.

The further into France they went the clearer the extent of the war became to them. Not one single house seemed to be left standing. Compared to France England had only suffered a light bombardment from the Germans. But for many months now rumours had been circulating through the British army that the Nazis were planning a huge campaign to do a mass attack on England. London was now terrified that there could be another repeat of the bombing they had already endured, or even worse.

At two o'clock in the afternoon Sarah had her first ever glimpse of the Nazis notorious biker regiments. A regiment of up to fifty soldiers on large black bikes that were incredibly fast. The motorbikes could travel up to a maximum of two hundred miles an hour over flat ground. They were a fast and dangerous regiment and mass murderers on the battlefields.

When a battle commenced the biking regiments were often the first on the battlefield. They split up whole armies, mesmerising the soldiers into blind terror. They could kill literally hundreds of men in a single battle. The British had their own biking regiments so as to make sure as many Nazis died as British. But they were nowhere near as notorious as the Germans biking regiment. The French called them, "killers on wheels." They wore the classic German uniform, black camouflage with Swastikas on the top right arm sleeve. But wherever they went they were always on bikes. The British joked that their trousers were sewn to the seat of the bike and how they would love to pull them of their bikes to see if their trousers tore of. But really the biking regiments were no laughing matter

Stephen figured out it would take them another half a day to reach the German border. Then they would have to make the rest of the journey by foot and travel by night to reach Berlin.

That night they continued travelling nearer and nearer to Germany. They travelled until midnight where they stopped at a tiny and very old bridge. The river that should be flowing under it was bone dry, even after the torrential rain that had fallen. So they slept under the bridge, taking it in turns to keep watch while their companions slept. They set of at the crack of dawn, planning to reach the German border by the afternoon. Then they would reach Hannover at nightfall, so they could reach Berlin in the relative safety of darkness.

Sarah had noticed lately Stephen had been acting weirdly. He only answered anyone in short sentences. Eventually out of curiosity Sarah asked him what the matter was.

He pulled her away from the others. He led her out of earshot and made her sit down on a broken wall that surrounded an orchard. Stephen took a swig of very weak tea from a Billycan. Then he looked at Sarah and sighed deeply.

"You remember your father, don't you?" he asked.

"Well, yes, why?" Sarah asked confused, wondering why Stephen was bringing up the subject of her father at such an inappropriate time.

"You remember he went missing and a couple of days later they found a burnt body in a ditch they thought was his? Everyone assumed that he had been murdered," Stephen asked.

"Why? Do you know who may have killed him?" Sarah asked eagerly, she leaned nearer to him in excitement.

"No, I'm afraid it's nothing like that, Sarah" he said, looking very sombre. Sarah's face fell and it broke his heart to see her like that.

"Then what is it?" she asked, her voice suddenly full of concern.

"There's no easy way to say this, so I'm just going to come straight out with it. Your father's not dead."

Everything went completely quiet, as Sarah's face slowly went from concern to utter confusion. It took her some time to digest exactly what Stephen had said to her and even then she couldn't really comprehend what he was trying to tell her.

"What?" she asked finally. "What do you mean he's not dead? He has to be dead. I mean they found his burnt body lying in a ditch. He has to be dead, Stephen. It doesn't make any sense. If he was alive he would be looking for me, I'm his daughter."

"Well if that had been his body and that seems very unlikely, he must have had a twin brother that no one knew existed. You remember how burnt that body was, Sarah? It couldn't be identified, it had no physical features at all" Stephen said.

"Sorry, not following you?"

"Lately I have been noticing a certain person whom seems very close to Gavrian Hitler, closer than anyone else in fact. I hadn't noticed it until lately because I've been too fucking blind. But that man looks exactly like the man in the pictures of your parents, Sarah. Your father is still very much alive and now he is fighting for the other side."

"No, it's not true. I don't believe you!" Sarah insisted, refusing to believe him. "I know he was a bastard and everything. But he hated the Nazis and everything they stood for, he would never join them. He would rather die."

"Sarah, you said he was German and worked in the German Government whilst he was in the German army?" Stephen said quietly.

"Yeah?"

"Well if the German army ever visited England Gavrian could use that as a means to gain access to the British army long before he had ever posed a threat to us. Therefore he could easily gain access to the British Government without anyone noticing something was wrong. I'm sorry, Sarah, but it appears Marques was never on the side of the British to begin with. Everything that he did for the British army seems to have been to aid Gavrian's eventual plans."

"No, that can't be true. Marques absolutely hated the Nazis. He would never ever betray England like that; he loved the country. I don't believe you, Stephen, I'm sorry but I don't. What's more I won't believe it. You're lying. He is dead and there is nothing more to say" Sarah said angrily. She stood up from the wall and quickly saluted Stephen. Then without another word she walked back towards the bridge.

"No, Sarah, wait…!" Stephen called out to her helplessly. But his voice trailed of as he realised that she was no longer listening.

In the distance the flash of exploding bombs could be seen as the Nazis continued their persistent night campaigns on the French countryside. But nothing else seemed to stir in the night's sky. Not even the stars and moon would show that night. It was just as if the Nazis had killed of life itself and it honestly felt like it.

They continued on their journey just before dawn broke. There was a definite chill in the air as cold as the atmosphere surrounding the soldiers. As the sun rose dark clouds appeared in the distance.

Sarah was unusually quiet that day and she refused to speak to a living sole. She seemed to be in a constant daze, as if someone had hypnotised her and forgotten to wake her up. When Dougy nudged her and tried to get a conversation going she would only answer by grunting. In the end he gave up and turned to talk to McBride and Green instead.

The day was long and very hot; around lunchtime they eventually came into view of the German border. But they had to enter the border where they would go unnoticed by any Nazis. Attracting attention to themselves would only get them killed before they had even crossed into enemy territory. So the driver turned left onto a small dirt track before the Nazis guarding the perimeter of the German border could spot them. But they wouldn't have probably even noticed them if they had driven straight through the gates. Both of the Nazis were short and stocky in build and in no fit state to go running after enemy trucks. They both sat there reading newspapers and smoking cigarettes.

The truck continued it's slow progress up the dirt track. The truck was bumping into potholes the size of craters in the road. Occasionally the silence was broken by someone swearing as he hit his head on the metal bars that they were hanging onto.

Eventually they came to a stop by a wooded area. The only boundary there was some electric wire attached to very insecure looking poles. This was far easier for all of them than the thick barbwire that no man could climb over, which protected most of the German borders.

"I'm sorry but I ain't going any further than this. It's too risky and I'm too old to do that sort of thing any more. I'll just bid good luck to you and get out of here as fast as I can" the driver told Stephen, handing him a box containing German uniforms. Stephen didn't look too impressed.

"Right men, get out of the truck. We will go into the woodland next to us and change into these uniforms. Then you will proceed back to this exact point and wait for my next instructions. Is every one clear on that?"

"Yes, sergeant" they all answered. Then one by one they jumped out of the truck and were given their uniforms by Stephen. Then the driver drove of waving a cheerful goodbye.

Within a matter of minutes they were changed into German uniforms and were standing in a neat line by the roadside awaiting their next instructions.

"Hmm, very nice. You lot could almost pass as Nazis" Stephen commented, as he walked up and down the line checking the uniforms.

"Almost, sergeant, if any of us could actually speak German" Green said loudly.

"Ah, you see, that's where Murray comes in," Stephen said, looking at Sarah. "Murray, if we get stopped by any Nazis I want you to do all the talking so hopefully they won't get suspicious."

"Yes, sergeant" Sarah said quietly.

"Right men, we now have a change of plan. We will either have to travel to Berlin without stopping, no rests. Or we find alternative transport. But the first thing we have to do is get under this fencing without setting any alarms of' Stephen said. Then he turned his attention to the fencing that lay before him.

"Now the best thing to do is crawl under the wire, one at a time. But remove your backpacks and throw them over the fencing first. I want nothing to make contact with it." He looked at the soldiers, and then continued.

"Green, you will go first, Murray, you will go last" he said. "Does everyone understand what we are doing?" he asked. Every one nodded and said, "Yes, sergeant."

Then one by one they proceeded to crawl under the wire. They all took great care in not touching the wiring, because even though they were unsure that it was alarmed they were positive that the fencing was electric. They could hear the constant little clicks as insects hit the electric wires.

As Sarah crawled under the wire and was dragged up by Dougy and Green she felt a cold shiver of fear pass through her body. It ran up her spine and filled her heart as her feet touched German soil. Yet it wasn't even that cold, in fact the weather had now turned bloody boiling. Most of them had stripped down to their t-shirts. It was just the thought of them no longer being in the safety of France that scared her. This was her first big mission that she was involved in where she had the protection of her regiment and her regiment alone and she was absolutely petrified. What made it scarier was the fact that they hadn't been spotted by any Nazis yet. The border should be far more protected than this. It felt like they were walking straight into a trap.

Taylor and McBride dragged Stephen up on to his feet and he picked his bag up of the ground. They had made it through the barriers without even getting noticed. They were standing on German soil. They had made it into Germany and were standing in the land of the enemy. But they were also now totally on their own and would have no back up to call upon. The mission had well and truly begun.